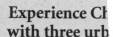

Experience Ch_____
with three urb_____

USA TODAY **bestselling author**
SUSAN WIGGS

"Wiggs proves she's a master of both historical
and contemporary romance...."
—*Library Journal*

"Wiggs' writing shimmers...."
—*BookPage*

USA TODAY **bestselling author**
NANCY WARREN

"Sexy and wonderfully witty."
—*USA TODAY* bestselling author Lori Foster

"Nancy Warren puts passion in high gear...."
—*Barnes & Noble Review*

and bestselling author
JULE McBRIDE

"McBride spills onto the pages languid feverish
phrases that keep devoted fans up nights reading."
—*Charleston Daily Mail*

"McBride has a gift for creating characters
who are both humorous and deep...."
—*Romantic Times*

"Your storytelling fills in the little holes in my soul," wrote a reader of **Susan Wiggs,** and this comment perfectly captures what the author hopes to achieve with her writing. Noted for their scenes of emotional truth, evoking both tears and laughter, her novels regularly appear on national bestseller lists. Wiggs lives with her family on an island in the Pacific Northwest, where she is working on her next book. Readers can visit her Web site at www.susanwiggs.com.

Nancy Warren got her big break when she won Harlequin's 2000 Blaze Contest. Since then her novels have appeared on several bestseller lists and won numerous awards; still, for Nancy nothing beats the thrill of hearing from readers. She lives in the Pacific Northwest, where she spends her days sensibly employed inventing men who combine amazing sexual prowess with sensitivity to a woman's needs, and women who aren't afraid to fight for their dreams. Readers can visit her Web site at www.nancywarren.net.

Jule McBride's dream to write romances came true in the nineties with the publication of her debut novel, *Wild Card Wedding.* It received the *Romantic Times* Reviewer's Choice Award for Best First Series Romance. Since then, the author has been nominated for multiple awards, including three lifetime achievement awards. Having written for Harlequin Intrigue, Harlequin American Romance and Harlequin Duets, Jule currently makes her happy home at Harlequin Temptation and Harlequin Blaze. A prolific writer, she has over forty titles to her credit to date.

SUSAN WIGGS

NANCY WARREN
JULE McBRIDE

IT HAPPENED ONE CHRISTMAS

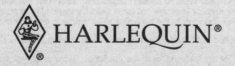

HARLEQUIN®

TORONTO • NEW YORK • LONDON
AMSTERDAM • PARIS • SYDNEY • HAMBURG
STOCKHOLM • ATHENS • TOKYO • MILAN • MADRID
PRAGUE • WARSAW • BUDAPEST • AUCKLAND

ISBN 0-373-83581-7

IT HAPPENED ONE CHRISTMAS

Copyright © 2003 by Harlequin Books S.A.

The publisher acknowledges the copyright holders of the individual works as follows:

THE ST. JAMES AFFAIR
Copyright © 2003 by Susan Wiggs

A CATERED AFFAIR
Copyright © 2003 by Nancy Warren

A PHILADELPHIA AFFAIR
Copyright © 2003 by Jule McBride

This edition published by arrangement with Harlequin Books S.A.

® and TM are trademarks of the publisher. Trademarks indicated with ® are registered in the United States Patent and Trademark Office, the Canadian Trade Marks Office and in other countries.

Visit us at www.eHarlequin.com

Printed in U.S.A.

CONTENTS

THE ST. JAMES AFFAIR

Susan Wiggs

CHAPTER ONE

ELAINE ST. JAMES hurried along Fifth Avenue, trying to outrun Christmas, but it was gaining on her. She was only a few steps ahead of a troop of apple-cheeked carolers belting out "Hark the Herald Angels Sing" and collecting donations from shoppers and tourists. She dodged to avoid a Santa reeling in the crosswalk, his breath smelling of too much holiday cheer too early in the day.

Although she had a cell phone glued to her ear, Elaine could barely hear Byron, her boyfriend. Still, she'd heard enough to know the news was not good.

"A bra model?" she yelled into the tiny daisy-decorated phone.

His response was a garbled remark ending in "Huh?"

And so she yelled even louder, "You're dumping me for a bra model?"

Too late, she realized the heralds had stopped harking, and the stoplight had brought traffic to a halt. Everyone within half a city block had heard her.

Caught in the glare of dozens of curious looks, Elaine dropped her hand to her side and hitched her purse strap up on her shoulder. Byron's mosquito-voiced reply squawked faintly from the receiver, but she didn't want to hear another word. Belying the flames of humiliated color in her cheeks, she held her head high and said to no one in particular, "Whatever."

Then she clicked off her Star-Tac, turned on her kitten-heeled boot and headed up the street. Behind her, traffic started up as the light changed. The carolers struck up "Silver Bells," and the city sidewalks became busy sidewalks again.

Okay, so it's Christmas, Elaine told herself, appalled to feel a sudden sting of tears in her eyes. *Tears.* Not for Byron, she realized. But for yet another dream gone, just like that. It was hard to say goodbye to a dream, hard to close the door on hope.

Elaine squared her shoulders and soldiered on down the avenue. The fact was, she had enormous reserves of self-discipline. She'd been raised to do what was expected of her, and she was extremely good at it. She just had to get through the day. How hard could that be?

She tried to get into the spirit of children laughing, people passing. She saw smile after smile and even made a valiant attempt at smiling herself, but it felt more like gritting her teeth.

Why was Christmas so easy for some people, but so impossible for Elaine? Where had she been when they were passing out Christmas spirit?

She knew where she'd been—in the chill confines of the right boarding school, the right summer camp, the right college. She'd been so busy training herself to do what was expected of her that she'd forgotten to ask herself what the point of all her efforts was.

At the next crosswalk, a woman laden with glossy bags and beribboned parcels shoved herself in Elaine's way like a barge pushing into port. Elaine bit her lip to keep from making some smart remark, but she couldn't help scowling. She was later than ever for her lunch, and in no mood. Given her current situation, a slight edge of crankiness was justifiable.

There had been a time, long ago, when the bustle and noise of the season had filled her with a sense of magic. She missed her former self, but had no idea how to revive that breathless, boundless feeling. Clearly Byron was not the answer. Of course, she should have known that from the start, but in spite of all the ways life had disappointed her, deep down, she still had this secret, frisky inner self that wanted to believe in magic.

Someone had a set of real silver bells. She heard them chiming like a windup alarm clock.

A moment later, she found herself confronted by

an elf holding out a collection jar with a picture of a grinning orphan. Clenching her teeth, she merely stared straight ahead, pretending she hadn't seen him. If she didn't make eye contact, she might be able to shake him off. Elaine was pretty successful at avoiding contact. It had kept her safe for years.

These street singers for charity were bogus, she reminded herself, thinking of the reeling Santa. The donations went into the collectors' pockets, to be spent later at the pool hall or package store. Falling for that game merely encouraged more panhandlers.

"Soon it will beeee Christmas day," sang the elf.

Duh, thought Elaine, eyeing the swags of plastic greenery and twinkling lights that had infested the city since the day after Halloween. The season seemed to descend earlier every year. Yet every year, Elaine couldn't help feeling a little secret jolt of excitement. And hope. *Maybe this year will be different,* she always thought. But nothing ever changed, and she grew more cynical and brittle as time went on.

"Come on, lady, gimme a break. Bestow a trifle." The elf rattled the collection jar at her. He had a sing-along songbook and a stick-on name tag that said, "Hi! My Name Is Larry." He wore a bright red muffler and an unjustifiably cheerful grin.

The light changed and she joined the surge of

pedestrians in the crosswalk, but the persistent caroler kept stalking her.

"Just a little something for Westside Children's Charities." He flashed an official-looking permit.

It was probably forged, Elaine thought.

"Do it for the kids, lady." Jingle bells bobbed from his pointy cap.

She scowled at him. "Go away."

He gave her a puppy-dog look.

Be strong, she told herself. If she gave in to this one, another would take his place, and the next thing she knew, half the city would be wanting something from her. Pointing her face into the icy wind, she strode on.

"Away in a Manger" swept through the marauding carolers. The elf bobbed along at her side. "Look," he said, "it's not my fault the guy dumped you for some bimbo. Don't take it out on the kids."

Finally she could hold her tongue no longer. "This is not endearing you to me."

"Think of the kids, then. There's magic in giving, don't you know that?"

"I don't believe in magic." There. Saying so aloud made it as real as the pitted, frozen sidewalk beneath her fashionably clad feet.

"That won't keep it from happening. But you have to make a donation. Come on. What's five bucks to someone wearing thousand-dollar Manolo boots?''

An elf who knew footwear. This was getting stranger by the moment.

"Five bucks, and the magic starts happening," he said. "Guaranteed."

"What, I pay you, and you disappear?"

He winked, and sent her a gladsome look. "Trust me, you won't be sorry. Help us out, and the world will start helping you."

"What makes you think I need help?"

"You can't keep edging your way along the crowded paths of life, warning all human sympathy to keep its distance," he pointed out.

Great. Not only did he know shoes, he quoted Dickens. *I live in a world of fools,* thought Elaine.

"Make it a ten, and I'll throw in a miracle," Larry offered.

"Oh, for Pete's sake." As the last threads of her patience unraveled, she reached into her purse, then shoved a twenty at him.

"Merry Christmas, Elaine," he called cheerfully.

"Whatever."

Then it struck her that he'd called her by name. She stopped, causing a businessman to slam into her from behind, then walk around her with only the gruffest of apologies. She searched the bustling crowd, but Larry the elf was nowhere in sight. How had he known her name? A lucky guess? No, he'd probably seen something with her name on it when she'd whipped out the twenty.

Dismissing the incident with a shrug, she continued up the avenue. The herd of carolers brayed, "We Wish You a Merry Christmas."

Christmas didn't mean merriment of any sort to Elaine. It hadn't for a long time. These days, the holiday meant more meetings to schedule, more events to plan, more clients demanding her time.

Without Byron, it meant one less gift to buy this afternoon. The only discomfort his defection would create was a pained and awkward explanation to her parents, who had given Byron the St. James stamp of approval. The only fallout would be invisible to the world and felt only by Elaine. And she was getting awfully good at covering up her pain.

She ducked down a side street, mercifully uncongested except for a panhandler in an army surplus jacket and his scruffy dog. They watched her from a stoop next to Fezzywig's Bar and Grill.

In her haste, she dropped her handbag and half the contents spilled across the dirty, rock-salted sidewalk. Gritting her teeth in irritation, she squatted down and scooped up the spillage—her cell phone, a tin of breath mints, her Coach leather agenda, a lipstick and assorted other gear—and stood up.

"Miss, you forgot something." The panhandler

held out a cluster of keys, strung on a ring attached to a silver skate.

''Thanks.'' She grabbed the keys, stuffed them in her bag. She started to walk away, then hesitated and fished a bill from her wallet. Elaine was no pushover when it came to money, but she expected to pay for services rendered. Besides, the panhandler had given her back her silver skate key ring and for that he deserved a reward.

That key ring had a special purpose for Elaine. She kept it as a reminder of the price of giving her heart.

CHAPTER TWO

ELAINE HURRIED under the awning leading to Fez-zywig's, a supertrendy spot that had recently become the hottest in the city. Thanks to Elaine's publicity firm, the upscale place was currently the favorite midday rendezvous of the twenty-somethings whose names graced the society pages and celebrity columns.

She dashed inside, and was immediately enveloped by the sleek, dimly lit decor of chrome and leather, the cheerful clink of glassware, and—mercifully—no piped-in Christmas Muzak. Instead, sinuous strains of vintage Coltrane provided a tasteful sound track for the ultrachic crowd. Gratefully, she shrugged out of coat, hat and gloves and handed them to the coat-check girl.

She ducked into the ladies' room. Her ivory cashmere slacks and sweater looked fine—particularly with the buttery-soft Manolos, she thought—but her hair and makeup were a disaster. Yet another thing she hated about Christmas—the rough winds, not to mention the brutal cold and the icy streets.

She fluffed her hair back into a shining blond bob, then took out her compact and went to work, restoring order to her face with practiced strokes. Her mind worked furiously as she performed the damage control.

So Byron had dumped her. She had to decide the best way to play it. On the one hand, she could assume the role of the wounded party, fragile and in desperate need of support. That would allow her to bask in her friends' soothing platitudes about how the jerk didn't deserve her, how he'd never been good enough for her in the first place, how he'd grow old and bitterly regretful, thinking of the opportunity he'd passed up with her.

Leaning toward the mirror, she used an eyelash comb to de-clump her mascara. On the other hand, she could mask her humiliation and disappointment behind sarcasm, turning Byron Witherspoon into the joke of the day among their crowd. In throwing her over for a grade-A bimbo, he'd certainly given her adequate material.

Okay, she thought, holstering her lip-gloss wand and pasting on a smile. It's Christmas Eve. The perfect time for amusement. She'd breeze through this, pretending the loss of her boyfriend was nothing.

Except she didn't have to pretend. Her brow puckering a little, she studied her image in the mirror. Not bad, with that tousle-haired, cashmere-sweater, gold-earring thing going on. She hardly looked like a woman scorned.

Searching her feelings, she discovered she'd suffered no emotional breakdown over this. The only twinge of regret she felt was that losing Byron now meant showing up at her parents' party dateless tonight. How terribly inconvenient. She'd never hear the end of it.

She was actually a little disappointed in herself. Where were the pain, the trauma, the weeping and the wailing? The wallowing? Wasn't this supposed to be a personal train wreck rather than the emotional equivalent of a broken nail? At least if she wept and carried on, even for a few minutes, it would mean that she hadn't wasted the past six months dating a guy she didn't care about. But she had no urge to cry and carry on. She felt like getting some work done.

Although it was still early, a good crowd had gathered to fuel themselves for the last day of shopping and tonight's round of parties. Elaine greeted, waved and air-kissed her way across the room, her practiced smile untroubled by Byron's betrayal. She loved this crowd of socialites and actors and trendsetters, and they loved her. She was in her element here, in the spotlight as she made her way to meet with her partners, who also happened to be her best friends.

Yet Elaine had a problem. And it had nothing to do with her recent, very public conversation with Byron.

She wasn't sure why it happened, but sometimes, at the least convenient of moments, she felt something a person in her position wasn't ever supposed to feel. Loneliness.

It was absurd, given the full, busy life she led, but she couldn't help it. No matter how much she tried to deny the truth, she often found herself gripped by a sense of futility and the bone-deep ache of emptiness.

That emptiness was the enemy. She battled it with direct action. Land that account, grab that media spot, get out there in the glitzy world of fashion and entertainment and make a name for yourself. A willful, determined nature had compelled her to turn herself, in just a few short years, into one of the busiest, most influential publicists in the city.

Bolstering herself with the thought, she strode across the bar to the high-backed booth where her friends waited, nursing Seven-and-Skyy cocktails and chattering at warp speed.

"There you are, Elaine." Melanie paddled her hand in the air. "You're late."

"Sorry." Elaine slid into the horseshoe-shaped booth next to Bobbi, who was not just her best friend, but her very best friend. "I had a lot of calls to make from the office.'' She felt mildly annoyed at her partners. Just because it was Christmas, they thought they could take time off and neglect important business. They were supposed to know better. Public relations opportunities didn't disappear just because the calendar declared a holiday. In fact, that was even more reason to get busy.

Larry the elf was dead wrong. The magic of the season wasn't the spirit of giving. It was that Christmas added an extra media hook to their press releases.

Since it was past noon, she ordered a kir royale, slipped her purse strap off her shoulder and made a conscious effort to smile. Jenny P (her last name was Pinkwater but she'd dropped it long ago) looked perfect and polished in Kajal lipstick, black merino and knee-high suede boots. Melanie Benz, affectionately known as Bitchcakes by her adoring clients, laid out her Day Timer and Palm Pilot on the table. She was chopstick-thin. Her white-blond hair was spiked, her eyebrows pared into arches of perpetual surprise. Bobbi, graced with the looks of a supermodel, was a walking billboard for their clients in a T. Gallagher sweater and leather skirt, Chez Moi makeup and a hairstyle by Iago.

Elaine had handpicked Bobbi, a nobody from a North Carolina mill town looking to break into show business or modeling. Elaine and her partners had other plans. Through the magic of their power over the press, they turned Bobbi into the city's latest girl-about-town. They gave her the right look, posed her with the right stars and socialites, dropped her name in the right ears. And it had worked. She appeared in all the magazines that mattered—*W, Vogue* and *Quest.* Within days, the phone had begun to ring, invitations rolled in. Within weeks, *Cosmo* was calling to get her take on the best spot-reducing exercise for summer. Bobbi's launch was a ringing success.

There was an unexpected bonus in Elaine's project to create a media darling. As bubbly and refreshing as a split of Moët, Bobbi had become her best friend and confidant, the sister she'd never had. She was someone to share secrets and dreams with, someone to whom Elaine might even dare to admit that breaking up with Byron didn't actually hurt, but had frightened her by making her doubt her ability to sustain any sort of relationship.

No. She wouldn't go that far. Even her soul sister would not be privy to that fact.

Tonight Bobbi would play a key part in moving their firm up the food chain. It was going to be her job to beguile the mysterious and ambitious Axel, a hip Swiss parfumier they were trying to lure as a client. Everything important rode on landing this account. Axel would be proof at last to her parents that she was capable of doing something that mattered, of making a life for herself and standing on her own two feet. They'd always believed she was dabbling, their Upper East Side princess, playing at being a publicist to pass the time until she settled down and married someone with the right credentials, someone like Byron Witherspoon.

Now Elaine needed Axel more than ever. Acquiring the business of the Swiss billionaire would lessen the humiliation and soften the betrayal of losing Byron.

"If we manage to sign him, he'll open the door to major accounts in Europe," Elaine said as they went over the final details of tonight's event, known for decades in the society pages as the St. James affair. Each year, as her grandparents had before them, her parents invited everyone who was anyone to their annual Christmas Eve bash. Unlike past years, however, this time they'd allowed Elaine's firm to handle the planning. She didn't want to screw up.

"What's he like?" asked Bobbi. "I'm ninety-seven-percent sure I've never done it with a billionaire."

"He's perfect."

"What, you've done it with him?" asked Mel.

"Of course not. But Axel and I go way back. Boarding school days, actually. Looks that good should be banned from boarding school. You'll see.'' Elaine felt a surge of ambition. Playing the power matching game and teaching someone else the ropes were what she did best. She never stopped playing or thinking of the next move. It was what kept her going, how she made sense of the world.

Melanie and Jenny put their heads together like a couple of battle commanders, mapping out a seating strategy for the party.

''I guess I'll find out tonight.'' Bobbi lowered her voice. ''Um, Elaine…do you think I could get a teeny weeny advance on my check? I'm a little strapped.''

Elaine gritted her teeth. ''Your advances are already taking you into the summer,'' she said.

''I know, but it's so expensive to keep up this lifestyle. Everything just piles up. My credit cards are totally maxed out. Tomorrow's Christmas, Elaine. What do you say, honey?''

She forced her jaw to relax. Honestly, some people had no self-control or work ethic. ''Stop by the office in the morning and I'll write you a check.''

''Actually, I wasn't planning on coming in tomorrow.''

''It's our busiest time of year, Bobbi.''

''It's Christmas.''

''I rest my case. Busy.'' Elaine took a gulp of her drink.

"It's only once a year." Bobbi's tone wheedled. "I was hoping to fly home to see my family. My sister Jimmi just had another baby. Oh, Elaine. What could be sweeter than a baby at Christmas?"

"A contract with a Swiss billionaire," Jenny said.

Melanie ran a shiny-tipped finger down a list in her planner. "By the way, Elaine, your mom's a peach to work with."

Elaine forced a smile over the rim of her glass. "Isn't she just?" In fact, Freddie St. James had given only the most grudging approval to Elaine's list of suggestions. Despite her skepticism of the edgy menu items and trendy guest list, her appreciation of Elaine's handling of the press had persuaded her.

To Freddie, the only thing more important than putting on a successful affair was having the papers report that she'd put on a successful affair. Perversely, having this goal in common had brought Elaine closer to her mother than she'd ever been. Now they were merely oceans apart instead of galaxies.

"You look nervous," Jenny commented, tilting her head to one side to study Elaine. "You're never nervous. What's up with that?"

"It's my parents' party, for heaven's sake."

"So? We do parties all the time. We're the best in town. People are still talking about the Helpline

Foundation fundraiser we did last Thanksgiving in Bridgehampton. What's really eating you?''

Elaine took a deep breath. She might as well spill. ''I hate Christmas. I hate my life. Byron dumped me for a bra model.''

The announcement fell into a collective, stunned silence.

''But you were supposed to marry him,'' Jenny said after a horrified pause. ''His father practically owns a broadcasting empire. You two were going to be the ultimate media power couple.''

Bobbi leaned in close to give her a hug. Her forgiving nature made Elaine feel small. ''Oh, honey,'' Bobbi said in her delightful Southern accent, ''We're so sorry.''

''Don't be. I'm more annoyed by his timing than anything else.''

''It's not too late to find another plus-one for tonight.'' Mel started a search on her Palm. ''It's Christmas. You can't be dateless.''

Elaine bit her tongue. The truth was, she didn't want a date. Or even Christmas, for that matter. She just wanted to make it through the holiday rush and get back to work.

''Tonight will be perfect,'' Jenny declared, raising her glass. ''Your parents will be blown away, we'll have Axel eating out of our hands and everyone will live happily ever after.''

Elaine's smile felt stiff as she lifted her champagne flute to her friends' highball glasses. "To happily ever after."

The bright sound of clinking glasses penetrated the din of piped-in music and high-octane conversation. She would get past this, Elaine told herself. Loneliness and yearning were for losers. Tonight would be perfect.

She watched the bubbles in her champagne cocktail. Through the half-empty glass, she spied something—someone—that made her freeze. She forgot to breathe, to move, to think.

Everything receded into a blur of color and sound, everything except him. He came into sharp focus, each detail about him familiar despite the passage of—she counted quickly in her head—seven years. Seven years this very day, in fact.

She felt trapped, yet at the same time helplessly enchanted, as though she were drowning in honey. All the intensity of first love came roaring back at her, possessing her, waking up feelings she had thought long dead.

It was, she discovered, physically impossible to tear her gaze from that broad-shouldered stance and easy smile, that air of assurance and electric sex appeal. Time had only deepened and sharpened the attributes that still sometimes haunted her dreams.

A classic Bob Marley tune filled the air.

"Elaine, what's the matter?" asked Jenny. "You look as though you've seen a ghost."

Ducking her head to hide the flush in her cheeks, she set down her glass. "The ghost of Christmas past."

CHAPTER THREE

"WHOSE PAST?" Jenny demanded.

"My past." Shaken, Elaine propped her chin in her hand and continued to gaze across the room at the tall, unforgettable silhouette, outlined by frosty winter light streaming in through the wide window.

Memories flooded her, of a brief time when Christmas had meant more to her than juggling a social schedule with a business plan. Against her will, she remembered those nostalgic days when the softest, most vulnerable part of her had felt safe with an unexpected stranger.

They never should have met in the first place. She belonged to a social class governed by strict but invisible rules. One of those rules prohibited her from fraternizing with guys like Tony Fiore. He came from a different world entirely, and that world had rules of its own. He'd been raised in a large Italian-American family in Brooklyn that believed, as much as the St. Jameses did, in sticking to its own kind.

At eighteen, she was only just discovering the

world outside her privileged, insulated life. He was definitely a major discovery.

Now an older, possibly even more interesting, Tony Fiore stopped at a crowded table across the room. He started talking to the well-dressed patrons there. Every face at the table turned toward him as he spoke.

Elaine's friends followed the direction of her rapt stare. "Holy mistletoe," Mel said. "That guy?"

"Who is he?" asked Jen.

Bobbi patted Elaine's arm. "Whoever he is, he'll make Byron seem like a bad dream."

"His name's Tony Fiore. We met a long time ago, when we were in college." Their lives had intersected for the first time at the ice rink at Rockefeller Center during Christmas break. Tony was attending Notre Dame on a hockey scholarship. She'd never forget her first glimpse of him. Crowds of tourists and regulars had jammed the ice, yet Tony Fiore had glided effortlessly between couples and children and daredevil teenagers. His imposing profile and swift athletic strokes across the ice had caught her attention.

"Fiore." Jenny studied him, her expression that of a jeweler inspecting a flawless gem. Elaine followed her gaze. Pale daylight flickered on his thick indigo hair, which lay in glossy, unruly waves that defied a conservative haircut. "I've never heard of him," Jen continued. "How can that be?"

Elaine struggled to act blasé. She reminded herself of the way things had ended between them—or failed to end, depending on how you looked at it. They'd been Romeo and Juliet without the messy final act.

Hardening her heart, she said, "You wouldn't have. He's nobody." Even as she said the words, her throat went tight. Nobody but the only guy who had ever convinced her that magic was real. Nobody but the guy who, on the night she'd gone to offer her heart to him, had stood her up.

"He looks like somebody to me," Melanie said. "I can't quite place him."

"Maybe he's a movie star," Bobbi suggested, reaching across the table to snatch the cherry from Mel's drink.

"If he was a star, we'd know who he is."

"What's he doing?" asked Bobbi.

Holding a clipboard with a pen attached, Tony Fiore moved to another table and greeted the people seated there. Again, everyone turned to him, and their faces lit up as though he'd flipped a switch.

"Maybe collecting pledges or donations," said Jenny. "Who cares? Look at him."

He set down the clipboard, bracing his hands on the table and bending slightly to lend someone a pen. They could now see the reflective lettering on the back of his bulky parka.

"Well, how about that," said Melanie. "He's a cop."

Elaine stared at him. A cop? He was supposed to be a hockey star. That was the only way she'd made sense of what had happened to them. She'd assumed he'd realized he wouldn't be able to juggle a professional athlete's career with falling in love. Now she was forced to consider the idea that he'd thrown her over for the dubious glories of being a cop.

Bobbi shifted in the booth and fussed with the pashmina bunching in her lap. "He's coming this way, isn't he?"

Before anyone could reply, he approached their table.

Oh, that smile, Elaine thought, suppressing a groan. Those eyes, the color of melted chocolate. This man, she realized, had a face she couldn't seem to stop dreaming about no matter how many Christmases had passed.

"Afternoon, ladies," he said. That voice was another haunting memory that wouldn't leave her alone. It was deep and self-assured, faintly brushed with the real-world tones of his native Brooklyn.

Elaine fixed a smile on her face, though everything from the neck down froze in panic. "Tony Fiore. It's been a long time." She wondered if he realized that tonight was the anniversary of their doom.

"Six years tonight," he said, staring down at her with appreciation.

Well, thank God, she thought. If he'd failed to remember her, she would have died, right in the middle of Fezzywig's. But the warmth in his eyes, the extra layer of color in his face, confirmed that he had not forgotten her.

She wondered if he recalled the feeling of holding hands, gliding across the ice, if he could never listen to Christmas music without thinking of her, if he lay awake nights and wondered what his life would be like if only he had dared...

"Seven," she corrected him, not at all surprised he'd gotten it wrong. "But who's counting?"

He smiled, his generous, sensual lips forming a dangerous curve. Yet, like the young, unpretentious man she'd known, he appeared to be completely unconscious of his devastating effect on women. There was nothing so sexy as a guy who didn't realize he was sexy. His gaze frisked her from head to toe. "You look good, Elaine."

"You, too." She glanced questioningly at his clipboard. What she was really doing was looking for the expected wedding band. Surely a guy like this had a plump, happy wife and a couple of bambinos. Long ago, he'd told her he wanted exactly that, along with his NHL career. But to Elaine's surprise, she saw no ring. ''What's up with that?'' she asked.

''Fund drive,'' he said unapologetically, nodding to greet her companions.

Aha, she thought. He was just like Larry the elf. Only taller. Darker. Handsomer.

Then he did the grinning thing she remembered so well. His eyes, with their thick, criminally long lashes, took possession of everyone around the table. Elaine's friends opened to him like budding flowers to warm sunshine.

She had never been able to figure out how he did it, but he had a mesmerizing effect on people. Maybe it was the way he leaned forward a little, the warmth in his expression reaching out to everyone. It was like…magic. She flashed on another memory of the elf, promising her miracles.

Even Melanie, who was so cool she made ice cubes shiver, sighed audibly.

Elaine felt curiously exposed, running into Tony again like this. The past was behind her for a reason—so she wouldn't have to look at it. Straightening her shoulders, she was determined to hide her vulnerability and brazen it out.

She made the introductions in the smooth, polished way she had perfected over the years, and with a little laugh that completely covered everything she was feeling, she said, "This is Tony Fiore, who broke my heart back when we were in college."

"Yeah?" Jenny aimed a blatant invitation at him. "He's breaking mine now."

"I broke your heart?" He grinned, incredulous. "Very funny, Elaine. I did you a favor."

She gulped down the rest of her drink. Could he really believe that?

"So spill," Mel said. "You two were an item?"

"We dated like…three times," Elaine said blithely.

Jenny gave a low whistle. "For most guys, that's a long-term relationship."

"So what are you collecting for?" asked Bobbi, squirming in her seat.

"Kids' hockcy league," Tony said. "It's a pet project of my division. We fund coaching and ice time in all five boroughs."

Elaine wasn't surprised. Hockey used to be his life. It was supposed to be his future, his career. She couldn't help wondering about him as she studied this new, different Tony who hadn't changed a bit, who still set her heart on fire. What was his life now? Expired licences and shoplifters?

"What can we do for you?" Melanie asked.

That entrancing smile never wavered. "Anything you can spare. It's Christmas Eve," he reminded them needlessly.

"That's great that you're helping out inner-city kids," Jen said.

"It's an outstanding idea," Elaine announced.

"Thanks. I'm sorry to say, funds are low this year. We're going to need a miracle to keep the league going."

"You ought to have a gala." Jenny beamed at him. "Trust me, we know about this stuff. We're publicists."

He looked blank.

"We are responsible for getting our clients' faces in front of the press, or getting their products mentioned in magazines as the hot new must-have. That sort of thing," Elaine said. "I've never heard of your organization. You should do some PR for exposure. It would increase your contributions tremendously. Trust me, I know the benefits of PR."

"Yeah? What do you charge?" When she didn't answer, he grinned. "I can't afford you. Anyway, the time I put in is just as important."

Everyone went for their bags. It struck Elaine that she hadn't always hated Christmas. Sure, her self-disciplined approach to life had never allowed her to indulge too freely in the frivolities of the season. But, now that she thought about it, she once loved the warmth and joy of the season, the sentimental music and the spirit of generosity that took over even the most miserly of individuals. When had that hardened into annoyance and exasperation?

Watching Tony, she knew precisely when. It began the night he'd let her down. Right then had begun a slow erosion of the spirit. Hope had deflated, giving way to bleak reality. She'd begun to view the world through the eyes of a cynic. In the most holy of seasons, she saw greed instead of generosity, phoniness instead of sincerity. She'd learned to expect the worst of people and she was never disappointed.

Hiding her troubled thoughts, she rummaged deep in her handbag, sifting through gear she toted everywhere but the shower.

No wallet.

She frowned and rummaged some more, searching for the smooth leather case stuffed with plastic cards and folded bills.

No wallet.

"Something's wrong here," she muttered. She dumped the contents of her purse on the table, then put them back one by one. She felt Tony watching, and realized he had focused on her key chain, the one with the silver skate. It had been a gift from him, years ago, the only thing he'd ever given her. So what? she thought. Let him make what he would of it. She knew why she carried it.

As she sifted through the clutter on the table, a sinking feeling plummeted through her. "Somebody stole my wallet."

CHAPTER FOUR

"You're in luck," Melanie said, gesturing at Tony. "We got a professional right here."

"It was the elf, or maybe the panhandler," Elaine said, jumping up.

"You were with an elf and a panhandler?" asked Jenny. "Honey, you really do need to take some time off."

"I dropped everything right in front of him and he must have grabbed it." Elaine headed for the door.

A hand on her shoulder stopped her. "Don't be in such a hurry." Tony's voice was the same slow, intimate murmur that used to melt her knees.

"What do you mean?"

"Your friend's got it." He nodded in Bobbi's direction.

"Bobbi?" Confused, Elaine turned back to the table.

Bobbi's face hardened, and suddenly she looked like a stranger, not the sister Elaine had brought into her heart. "I don't know what you're talking about," Bobbi said.

"That spare wallet you're holding," said Tony.

"You've got to be kidding." Melanie grabbed Bobbi's pashmina, which had pooled in her lap, and there lay Elaine's red leather wallet.

"What is this, a joke?" asked Jenny.

"Harsh," Melanie muttered under her breath.

"I was only kidding," Bobbi said, her voice a nervous octave higher than normal.

Elaine felt as though she had been punched. This was Bobbi, whom she'd rescued from sandwich-cart-girl obscurity; Bobbi, who was her best friend in the world. "How could you?"

Bobbi shot to her feet. "How could I what? Wear your stupid clothes and go to your stupid parties in places I can't afford? Kiss up to your stupid clients?"

"I thought we were friends," Elaine said, her senses growing numb from shock—but not numb enough.

"Just because you put me in a pair of Pradas and gave me a cell phone doesn't make me your friend. What gives you the idea that any of us are friends? My salary barely covers the rent on my crummy downtown walkup. For that I should be grateful? Ha. For that, I should go drown myself in the East River."

"Well, that'd save you on the rent," Jenny pointed out.

"Hush up. You just want to marry someone important, and Melanie snorts everything she earns up her nose." As her voice rose, the genteel Southern accent turned twangy and raucous. She turned on Elaine. "They only keep you around because you grew up on the Upper East Side and you have connections. Don't ever mistake that for liking you. They're using you every bit as much as they're using me."

"Don't listen to her, Elaine," Melanie said. "She's obviously a nutcake."

"No, maybe I've finally had enough," Bobbi snapped. "You think this has been a picnic for me?"

"Actually, yes," said Elaine, thinking of yesterday's shopping excursion to BCBG.

"You would," Bobbi said, dramatically tossing her pashmina over her head and around her shoulders, Mary-in-the-manger style. "I wish I were dead."

"Be careful what you wish for," said Jenny, but Bobbi was already walking away, leaving a wreckage of hurt and confusion in her wake.

"She's toast," Melanie sputtered. "She'll never work in this business again."

"She'll never get so much as a dinner reservation

again,'' Jenny swore. "She'd better go back to Bubba Mills, Carolina, or wherever she came from.''

"I have no idea what came over her,'' Elaine said. "I told her I'd give her an advance tomorrow.'' But she wanted to fly home tonight, she reminded herself.

Tony still stood there, watching impassively. As a cop, he probably witnessed meltdowns and exploding relationships all the time.

"Forget her. Forget what she said.'' Melanie handed over the purloined wallet. "She has no class.''

Elaine forced herself to seem calm as she extracted a bill from her wallet and pushed it across the table toward Tony. "For your cause. And thanks for…getting my wallet back.''

He recorded the donations on the clipboard while the Marley tune wailed from the speakers.

Elaine withered inside. How had her life turned out this way? How had she wound up getting dropped by her so-called boyfriend on Christmas Eve, and getting stolen from by her best friend? Not to mention the Christmas Eve Tony had stood her up. Truly, this night was her own personal Bermuda triangle.

Could this sort of lousy luck somehow be her fault? Elaine forced herself to consider it. Bobbi was trash. She was disloyal, and yet Bobbi's tirade lingered in Elaine's mind like a morning-after hangover. To Elaine's horror, her ex-friend's words held an eerie ring of truth. Were Jenny and Melanie her friends, or did they just act that way because they needed Elaine for them to get ahead in business?

Her hand shook a little as she tucked the wallet away.

''Sorry about your friend,'' Tony said with genuine sympathy. Those brown eyes, so sincere, penetrated all the sturdy barriers she'd constructed around her heart. With just one look, he could remind her that life didn't have to be this way. ''Really, I'm sorry. I saw her lift the wallet from across the room.''

So he'd seen her first. He'd been watching her. Elaine tried to figure out how she felt about that. ''Um, thanks again,'' she said. Suddenly she found herself terrified of him walking away. But he would, of course. That's what everyone had been doing all her life. There had been a time when she'd thought he was different, but that had only been wishful thinking. Oh, she wanted him to stay. She wanted him to sit down and tell her that her life wasn't as awful as it seemed, that she'd just hit a speed bump. She wanted him to explain why he'd filled her head with dreams, then disappeared.

He stepped back as though to move on to the next

table, but Elaine put out her hand to stop him. "Hey, not so fast." She scooted over in the booth. "Join us, Tony. We're not letting you leave."

"Thanks," he said. "I'm about ready to turn in my numbers at the ice rink for the day, anyway. Thanks to you ladies, I'm looking fine. I'm just sorry your friend's not so fine."

"Yeah. Are you okay?" Melanie asked Elaine. "I know you thought the world of Bobbi."

Elaine burned with self-loathing over her foolishness. She was supposed to know better than to give her heart. Hadn't she learned that lesson? "I guess I should associate with a better class of people." She could hear echoes of her mother in the statement and cringed inwardly.

"Don't beat yourself up," Melanie said. "She had us all fooled, every one of us. What a day you're having, Elaine. First Byron, now this." She turned to Tony. "We usually have a sense of humor about these things. With a clientele like ours, we need it."

He leaned toward Elaine with genuine interest. Just as he had years ago, he managed to make her feel as though she mattered. "So she was a client?"

"No, we invented her," Jenny said. "It was Elaine's idea."

"She started out as a transplant from a mill town in the South," Elaine explained, "selling sand-

wiches from a cart in our office building while trying to get an agent. We fixed her up, and before you
knew it, she was clubbing with the Fixtures and
Jade, wearing stuff from boutiques no ordinary human can afford, featured in magazines, that sort of
thing. Everyone wanted her. She was the new cover
girl on the block.''

Melanie whirled a candy-cane swizzle stick in her
drink. ''It was a pure display of power.''

''Just call us the three Dr. Frankensteins,'' Elaine
said.

''Scary,'' said Tony.

Elaine tried to figure out why her career seemed
so trivial as she explained it to him. Maybe it was
because she'd had such big dreams back when she
had known him. She'd wanted to travel the world,
report on matters of international importance, make
a difference in people's lives. Yet now her world
consisted of high-end power shopping, over-the-top
event planning and puff-piece press releases. Making a difference meant changing the color of her
manicure.

''So anyway, we were counting on her tonight,''
Melanie was explaining to Tony. ''We needed her
to land a big account.''

''On Christmas Eve?''

''That's what's so great about this job. Work is
as much fun as play,'' Elaine said with forced

brightness. But her comment rang hollow as apprehension clutched at her stomach.

"I have a brilliant idea." Jenny covered Tony's hand with hers. "You have to come tonight. It's a fabulous event put on by Elaine's family. The—"

"St. James affair," Tony finished for her, then grinned at her surprised expression. "I live in Brooklyn, not in a cave." As he slowly and charmingly removed his hand, the message was clear. He would not be condescended to.

"I'm sure Tony has plans," Elaine felt obligated to say. And why wouldn't he? Just because he didn't wear a ring didn't mean he wasn't married. She arranged her mouth into a lighthearted smile. "I bet you have some sweet Italian girl waiting for you at home. Toys to put together for your kids."

He lifted the corner of his mouth in a half grin. "Hey, if I had that, I wouldn't be out in the cold today."

"I always figured you'd marry young and have a big family," she said. Even if he was still single, he was definitely a family man. She'd always known that about him.

"I'm not so old, and I still plan to have kids. You know how much family means to the Fiores."

She still remembered the warmth in his voice when he'd told her about his family. They were a loud, unwieldy Italian bunch that had lived in the same brownstone neighborhood for generations. She'd never met them, of course, but in her mind she carried a picture of Mama Fiore in a ruffled apron, stirring a kettle of puttanesca sauce on an old-fashioned kitchen range. She was definitely not the sort of woman who would leave her youngest son unaccounted for on Christmas Eve.

"So what do you say, Officer Friendly?" Jenny prodded.

Say yes, Elaine caught herself silently urging. How strange that she could still believe, even after all that had happened, that there was something special about Christmas Eve.

"I guess I could stop by for a while," he said.

Her heart took a leap before she could remind herself not to let it matter. But the fact was, it mattered a lot. She had the absurd feeling that he was rescuing her. She'd never liked her parents' annual affair. Overdressed people eating tiny hors d'oeuvres and talking about nothing while jockeying for position in front of the society column photographers.

This year, the event would improve somewhat, given the infusion of youthful energy and imagination of her partners. But to Elaine, it would always be excruciating. Having Tony present could not possibly make the night any worse. In fact, he might just make it better.

CHAPTER FIVE

ELAINE BEGAN to doubt her naive sense of hope a short time later, when she stood on the curb, nearly turning into a Popsicle while trying to flag a taxi. At the same time she talked on her cell phone, trying to fill the void left by Bobbi. Axel liked supermodels, but, so far, all the SMs she knew were busy tonight. Maybe he'd bring his own, she thought, stabbing another number into the keypad.

The marauding carolers had migrated to the other side of the street, but she could still hear happy strains of "Joy to the World" above the throaty sound of traffic and the distant chimes of an old-fashioned church. Larry the elf was a liar. He'd promised magic and miracles, but things had only gone from bad to worse. And into the middle of everything had walked Tony Fiore, stirring up emotions she'd worked years to bury.

The number was busy. Exasperated, she hung up and scanned the avenue. Through a thickening curtain of snowfall, not a single available cab appeared.

Christmas was for the birds, she thought, scowling at a moon-eyed young couple walking arm in arm past glowing shop windows. Christmas was nothing but a commercialized excuse for people to knock off work early and overeat. Who needed that?

Spying a taxi half a block away, she made a desperate bid for it. Relief flooded her when it pulled alongside the curb. She pulled open the door, welcoming a waft of heat from the interior of the car.

Then, seemingly out of nowhere, a woman and a boy on crutches appeared. Some unthinking impulse nearly made her ignore them and get in. At the last second, she realized what that would make her and backed off.

The boy glanced in her direction, his sweet round face lit with a smile, before carefully folding himself and his crutches into the taxi.

''Thanks,'' said his mother, a harried woman in a plain cloth coat. She carried one of those humiliating clear plastic purses the retailers made clerks carry in order to control employee theft.

Elaine called herself a pushover as she handed the driver a bill to cover the fare.

''Thank you,'' the woman called. ''Merry Christmas, and God bless.''

Elaine gave a nod, then stepped from the curb and scanned the roadway for another taxi. There was none in sight. She envisioned herself standing here, freezing to death, while everyone else hurried away to celebrations and family gatherings and chestnuts roasting on an open fire. Who would miss her? she wondered forlornly. Who would even notice she wasn't around anymore, that she had turned into a curbside ice sculpture for the pigeons to land on?

Irritated, she tried to get Zora on the phone. Zora was the hardest-working modeling agent in town, but her voice mail picked up. What was wrong with everyone? You'd think a national holiday had been declared.

A black sedan pulled alongside the curb and the tinted window slid down. "Need a lift?" asked Tony Fiore.

Her heart did it again—sped up with excitement even though she cautioned herself to get a grip. "Thanks," she said, hurrying to open the passenger-side door. The car smelled of baby-powder-scented air freshener. The console was covered in electronic gear she couldn't fathom. It felt strangely intimate to ride with him, giving her a glimpse into his life. There was an official ID card and a bank of permits affixed to the console, a pad of sticky notes with a scrawled reminder: Pick up Nona's ham, buy duct tape, WD-40.

He pulled into the logjam of traffic. The wind-shield wipers slapped at the thick, soft flakes. The snow turned the bustling city into a sparkling world of color and light. Tony glanced over at her. She felt that glance as though they'd parted only yesterday. No man had ever looked at her the way he did, with so much interest and caring and frank desire.

"So. Where to?" he asked.

"You guessed right when you headed north."

"The upper East Side."

"You've got it."

"Didn't fall far from the tree, eh, Elaine?"

The remark was friendly but pointed, marking off the boundaries between them. They'd never really had a chance, thanks to their different backgrounds. People liked to say such things didn't matter in this day and age, but, the fact was, it absolutely did. Especially to Elaine, whose parents' approval meant everything. And to Tony, whose sense of duty to his family dominated all his choices.

She felt unaccountably defensive, as though it was all her fault she'd grown up in the rarefied world of the Gold Coast. The proper address was everything to the St. Jameses. Her parents had a park-view apartment, and a summer house on the Sound in the Hamptons. They'd sent her to Marymount and Bennington, and she now lived in a perfect, elegantly restored pre-war luxury building in the east nineties. She led, from all perspectives, a charmed existence. On paper, everything looked peachy. In truth, she rarely had time to sit back and think about the things that were missing from her life.

"How about you?" she asked, mildly annoyed.

"I didn't fall far, either. I got a place in Park Slope."

She didn't know much about the neighborhood, except that it was in Brooklyn. And she didn't know much about Brooklyn, except that it was the destination of the creaky, local F train she would never take.

He drove the next few blocks in silence, and she thought about how weird it was to be with him after all this time. Her phone chirped, and she hurried to answer it, but it was only Jenny saying they were still scouting for arm candy for Axel.

As though he felt her stare, he turned and glanced at her. "It's good to see you, Elaine. You look great."

"Thanks. So do you." Elaine was usually good at small talk. It was her stock-in-trade, a power tool in her arsenal. Yet the customary name-dropping and light witticisms would not work in this situation, with this man. He didn't want to be impressed by her or entertained by her. As he had so many years before, he simply wanted to know her.

And what she feared was that he could already see all there was to know, that she was all surface. Peeled away, there was nothing of substance inside.

Unanswered questions and old business hung in the air between them. He reached down and flicked on the radio, and Christmas music eased through the car. He hummed along with chestnuts roasting.

"I meant what I said earlier. I'm sorry about your friend," he remarked.

She had to think for a moment about which friend he meant. They were all sorry in different ways. "Oh, Bobbi. I don't know what to say. It's a little embarrassing."

"Unfortunately, one of the things I've learned in my line of work is that people are betrayed all the time by people they trust."

"That's a cheerful thought for Christmas Eve." She concentrated on the view through the windshield. Throngs of pedestrians, hurrying and hunched against the thickening snowfall, streamed past brightly lit windows of busy shops. Twinkling fairy lights held every available tree in a choke hold.

Again, the silent questions hovered. Where were you that night? Why didn't you keep your promise? How come we didn't fall in love and live happily ever after?

"So who's Byron?" Tony asked, seemingly out of the blue.

She'd been hoping he wouldn't mention her ex, but no such luck. He must have developed a cop's instincts.

"Some guy I was dating." She downplayed it, of course. Byron was really supposed to be the one. His credentials were perfect. He came from the right family, had gone to the right schools, lived at the right address. Her parents adored him, and his parents admired her. Freddie St. James was already picking out china patterns. Elaine had almost convinced herself that he was going to be her first husband.

In reality he was a single woman's nightmare. He was self-centered, irresponsible and sometimes even faintly, subtly cruel.

"*Was* dating." Tony navigated the traffic with infinite patience.

She nodded. "He threw me over just before lunch today."

"Yeah? Tough break."

"For a bra model."

"Even tougher."

"I announced it to everyone on Fifth Avenue." She explained about the phone call and the carolers, and turned sideways on the seat to watch him. He had such a great face, saved from being too pretty by a slightly crooked nose caused by an old hockey injury. His mouth was the sort you kept staring at, helplessly, as though it were a Godiva chocolate truffle.

"You'd better not be laughing," she warned him.

"I would never do that. Why would I laugh about something that's hurting you?"

She shifted her gaze forward and concentrated on counting the evergreen swags strung from the street-light poles. This was a particular talent of his—saying something sweet and sincere just when she needed it.

"So, did you love him?" Tony asked.

"I've never been in love," she blurted out, then covered her honesty with a laugh. "Look, I'm all right. Byron wasn't that…special. I suppose I tried to make him seem that way, but the two of us simply didn't have it." She despised the way that made her sound. Superficial. Shallow. Heartless.

Honestly, what must he think of her? Dumped on Christmas Eve, robbed by her latest best friend, and here she was behaving as though she had missed a hair appointment. The fact was, she had put such thick layers of insulation around her emotions that nothing could penetrate anymore. Not the hurt—but not the joy, either.

"You don't have to downplay this, Elaine," he said. "You're entitled to feel like crap, at least for a while."

"That's a total waste of energy, and it's not going to fix anything."

He draped his wrist over the arch of the steering wheel. "How much of a hurry are you in?"

She glanced at her Gucci watch, a little token of appreciation from a client. Then she glared at the silent phone. Well, here was a choice. She could spend the afternoon fretting about the St. James affair. Or she could surrender control for once in her life. She felt a glimmer of…something. Possibility?

"Actually, none. Everything is under control for tonight. Thanks to Byron, I have no last-minute gifts to buy. Why do you ask?"

"I need to make a stop." He swung into a spot marked Official Vehicles Only and came around to the passenger side. He held the door open for her as she stepped out, batting her eyelashes against snow flurries. The giant, gaudy Prometheus sculpture, aglow in floodlights and drowning in the blare of Christmas carols, marked the entrance to the ice rink at Rockefeller Center.

"What is this?" she asked with a laugh that sounded phony even to her own ears. "A trip down memory lane?"

"You got a problem with that?"

She forced herself to look him square in the eye. "Not if you don't."

CHAPTER SIX

"GOOD. I need to drop off this stuff." Holding the clipboard and a flat, zippered bag, Tony led the way across the jammed concrete labyrinth.

The chill in the air, the echoing music and the unanticipated breathlessness Elaine felt stirred recollections of their first meeting. Every detail still lived in her heart, though no one knew that about her. She kept her most cherished memories a secret, like a delicious dream that would be ruined by the telling. Even the painful aftermath of her encounter with Tony Fiore did not dim the power of the memories. Instead, it turned them brittle and delicate, brushed with the bittersweet shadows of what might have been.

Elaine had never been the shy type. The first time she'd seen Tony on that fateful Christmas Eve, she hadn't hesitated to make her interest known. A privileged upbringing had given her an unearned sense of self-confidence and the conviction that she would never be rejected. Eighteen years old and unafraid, she'd approached him and said, "Hi. I'm Elaine. I've been watching you skate."

His cocky grin had melted her bones, at the same time assuring her that bashfulness was not an issue with him, either. "Tony. I've been watching you, too."

It wasn't exactly a date, but an encounter like a chemical reaction—brief and unexpected, leaving them both forever changed. At the end of the evening, they'd gone their separate ways, he to his family's traditional celebration followed by midnight mass, she to her parents' gala affair. The day after Christmas, he'd left for Indiana to resume the hockey season, and she'd gone skiing in St. Moritz. She'd thought of him all during the rest of Christmas break that year, wishing she'd given him her phone number, or at least her last name.

Drawn back to the present, she followed him down the concrete steps to the main office, where he handed in his clipboard. "I only wish it was more," he said as they left. "Every kid should love hockey the way I do. It kept me out of trouble more times than I can count." He offered his arm. "Let's go put on some skates."

She balked. "Aren't you supposed to be out chasing muggers or car thieves?"

"I'm off duty. Come on, Elaine. For old time's

sake." He kept walking, pulling her along with him through the passageway to the ice level.

"Why would I want to remember old times?" she asked.

He stopped walking but kept hold of her arm as he turned to her. "Because they were good times," he said in a soft tone. "Mostly."

Before she could reply, he started walking again, bringing her to the rental kiosk.

"It's too crowded," she said. "No one can get ice time on Christmas Eve."

"A cop can."

"I haven't skated since…you know."

"You've got to be kidding," he said. "What, did you have an injury?"

She almost laughed at his assumption. "No, I had a life. A career. Who has time for skating?"

"Don't tell me you've been all work and no play the whole time."

"My work *is* my play. But ice skating is just not something I normally do."

"All the more reason to skate now. It's like riding a bike—you never forget."

She narrowed her gaze and took refuge in a lie. "I'm very good at forgetting things."

Unexpectedly, he took her gloved hand in his and squeezed. "I'm good at reminding people of things."

Despite her conflicted feelings about being with this man, Elaine found herself lacing up a pair of gamey-smelling size-seven rental skates and worrying about the way the attendant had eyed her designer boots. It felt strange, wobbling along on the rubber matting toward the entrance to the rink, grabbing Tony's arm for support. This was not at all how she had planned to spend her afternoon. She'd intended to visit Bergdorf's or Saks to buy Byron another designer sweater. Instead, fate had thrown her a singing elf, an old flame and a break from those parts of her life that were all too real.

When Tony led her to the ice, reality fell away. The piped-in music, blaring from speakers mounted on lightpoles, should have annoyed her but instead made her wistful. The huge Christmas tree, alive with thousands of twinkling lights, took on a diffuse, fairy-tale beauty in the flurrying snow. Even gold-chrome Prometheus and the parade of international flags surrounding the center seemed as charming and friendly as a scene inside a snow globe.

With a wink and a nod at the attendant, Tony stepped through the low gate and stood aside, motioning her onto the white expanse of ice, gouged by thousands of skate marks per hour. She pushed off and her legs immediately bowed out, blades heading in different directions until her knees started to scream. Sheer determination gave her the strength to reel her feet back in, and a moment later, she was gliding.

"You're doing great," Tony said, flashing the grin she'd never quite forgotten.

She lurched, then found her balance, and, in spite of everything—the terrible day she'd had, the stressful night ahead—she found herself grinning back at him. With exaggerated gallantry, he held out his hand, and she remembered something she'd learned the first night she'd met him—it was impossible to skate and not smile.

Clinging to Tony's hand, she raced around the ice, feeling the wind in her hair and the snow on her face. He skated with the power and grace she remembered. He darted effortlessly through the milling throng, bringing her along on a ride that made her feel as though she were flying.

Just for these few moments, she touched the sort of joy that used to be so abundant in her life. Where had that gone? Like an uninvited guest slinking off to avoid being ejected, it had slipped away when she wasn't looking. Now the feelings of hope and possibility returned and she refused to examine the reason for the change. Post-Byron euphoria, she told herself.

But a little inner voice whispered that her ex had nothing to do with the way she was feeling right now.

She soared over the ice with a man she'd never thought to see again. She even hummed along with the music. She had no idea who Wenceslas was, but she'd known his song forever, and she believed in his goodness. The crowd parted before them, some slowing down to watch—Tony, of course, not her. He was the pro, after all. Together, they probably looked like a Porsche towing a Volkswagen.

Tony matched his pace to hers, giving only a hint of the speed and aggression that had propelled him to the top of his sport, winning him scholarships and offers from the NHL. Now he swung along with an easy glide. He didn't even seem to be watching where he was going. He was watching her.

And she couldn't help but watch him. He had a face filled with character, a marked contrast to the conventional, vacuous good looks of the male models and socialites of her world. That was what had attracted her in the first place—that he was so different from the boys she knew. Through prep school and the early months of college, she'd dated slender blond young men with blasé attitudes of noblesse oblige and Roman numerals after their names. Unlike those pale, pampered boys, Tony Fiore had an unabashed appetite for life, a fiercely competitive spirit and something no one else had ever given her—genuine interest in Elaine herself, in her hopes and dreams, not her social connections and bank account.

As they skated, the edges of the rink elongated to streaks of color and light, and the smeared, surreal images revived all the sensations she'd felt years ago. She'd been giddy, filled with a sense of promise. Even though the first meeting was a chance encounter and they'd gone their separate ways, a part of her had believed it was the start of something special. How could it not be, when he gazed at her with magic in his eyes?

Yet the sturdy barriers between them had remained in place.

"We should date," he'd said.

"How?" she'd asked. "By phone? E-mail? No, thanks."

He had kissed her just once that night, but it had made every subsequent kiss thereafter pale in comparison. And then, only half joking, he had said, "Same time next year?"

Despite the futility of a romance between them, they'd both kept their promise. Christmas Eve, sophomore year. Elaine stealing away from the St. James affair, Tony making himself late for midnight mass. They spotted each other across the ice and met in the middle. Both of them knew that whatever spark they'd initially felt hadn't dimmed.

"So we're starting this forbidden Romeo-and-

Juliet thing, eh?'' he'd said, and then when he'd laughed and kissed her again, she'd had the strong and undeniable conviction that their attraction was something rare and not easily dismissed. But she was leaving for St. Kitts the next day, he had to go back to hockey, and it was all completely impossible. They'd even joked about the way the world was conspiring to keep them apart.

They'd indulged in a brief fantasy. She would transfer to Notre Dame, live in the sorority house across the street from his frat…. The very idea had made her laugh.

"What's funny?" he asked.

"The thought of my father paying for me to go to a Catholic college in the midwest."

"Hey, it's Notre Dame. People respect Domers."

"But they don't send their daughters to school with them."

Yet their lives had crossed a third time the following Christmas Eve. Elaine could still picture how he'd looked after waiting for her in the cold. Ears and nose red, eyes aglow with pleasure at the sight of her. This time, there was no pretense of surprise or coy declaration of "I was just passing by…" Each admitted that they'd come looking for the other, that the past year had been endless, the urge to track the other down almost irresistible. But they hadn't wanted to disturb the magic that happened each Christmas Eve. Meeting in between was like knowing what your presents were early. They were young. It was a game. But they both knew it was turning into something more.

Naturally, they'd discussed meeting between Christmases—but they never actually did it. There was magic at work. They hadn't understood it. They were almost afraid to mess with it. Until that third year, when Tony had news. He was going pro. He had an agent, he'd told her with an endearing sense of wonder. The New York Rangers wanted him, offering the chance of a lifetime, a shot at a life he'd only dreamed about. For the sake of his proud, adoring parents, he would stay in school and finish his degree, because no Fiore had yet earned a college degree. They wanted Tony to be the first. The wait would be excruciating, but he owed it to them. He wouldn't think of doing it any other way.

That night, he'd given her a gift—a key chain attached to a silver skate. Elaine, accustomed to receiving tokens from Tiffany and Harry Winston from other boys, was reduced to tears. At the gift kiosk, she'd bought a little snow globe with two tiny figures skating arm in arm, and told him to think of her every time he looked at it.

She became obsessed with Tony. His new status as rising professional sports star had changed everything. He was becoming someone her parents would adore. She'd dreamed about him, fantasized about him. He would be the next Wayne Gretzky. They would keep a condo in the city and a summer place on Long Island, maybe one with an ice rink.

By the time the fourth Christmas had rolled around, she'd been convinced. After only three encounters, she knew she was going to fall in love with him. Never mind that he was an Italian-American from a working-class family, that he had attended public school and worked summers for the sanitation department to earn extra money. Never mind that her parents would immediately enroll her in therapy sessions and try to convince her she was delusional. She was falling in love with Tony Fiore. She'd never been in love before. That fourth year, she showed up early at the ice rink.

Even now, she felt flushed with embarrassment as she recalled how long she'd waited for him. How many times she'd paid for ice time, how many wobbly ovals she'd skated around the rink, how cold she'd gotten from being outside for so long. When she could no longer feel her feet, she'd turned in her skates, trudged out to the street and flagged a taxi. At her parents' annual affair, she drank too much champagne and danced with too many men she didn't care about. The very next day, she'd embarked on the annual vacation with her family.

When she returned, she called her college counselor to accept an overseas internship that had been offered to her. Numb with disillusionment, she went to London to work for a prestigious magazine and embark on a fabulous life. Whether or not she'd succeeded at the latter depended on whose yardstick was used.

For the next year, she became an avid browser of the sports pages, seeking news of the NHL. She dug for information about rookie players but found nothing on Tony Fiore, only that he'd graduated with distinction from Notre Dame. She refused to let herself dwell on him, though she burned with curiosity. What had happened to his dreams? His big plans to become a star on ice?

What did it matter if his plans didn't include her? Eventually she'd forced herself to stop wondering. Stop caring.

A musical chiming noise, like the sound of silver bells, startled Elaine, drawing her back to the present. Apparently the bells signaled the skaters to clear the ice for grooming. The blocky Zamboni machine emerged from its tunnel and pushed out onto the oval to methodically smooth out the ice that had been chopped up by the blades of the skaters. Perched like a toy high on the seat, the driver wore a bright red muffler that streaked like a banner down his back.

Elaine did a double take.

"What's wrong?" asked Tony.

"I'm being stalked by an elf."

"Come on." Laughing, he grabbed her hand. "I'll buy you a hot chocolate."

It was lousy hot chocolate from a machine, but the watery sweetness had a strange, simple appeal. "So you became a cop," she said. "How did that happen?"

"It was my backup plan, in case hockey didn't work out."

"I take it hockey didn't work out."

He took a gulp from his white cardboard cup. She waited, but he didn't address her comment. Instead, he asked, "So what about you? I figured you'd be an ace reporter or something. Didn't you study journalism in college?"

She had a fleeting recollection of her idealism. By becoming a reporter, she'd wanted to make a difference in people's lives, digging out the facts and holding up a mirror to society. Instead, she made dinner reservations and threw parties and pushed luxury products. She convinced women who couldn't afford subway fare that they must not be without a certain seventeen-dollar brand of lipstick. As the writer of overwrought press releases, she practiced a strange, hybrid form of reporting and publicity.

Tony's question was still hanging in the air.

She sipped her drink. "So I became a publicist, okay? Maybe I don't protect and serve, but it's a living. Look, Tony, you caught me on a bad day."

"So tell me what a good day is like."

She hesitated. "When my clients are all happy and the firm bills them for hours well spent, I have fun at my job," she said, feeling a bit defensive. "That's no crime. Working in my field is like going out on dates and to parties. People pay me to attend movie premieres and celebrity galas. How bad is that?"

"Doesn't sound bad at all. Unless it makes real dates and real parties feel like work."

Ouch, she thought. She stared down at the table, trying to talk herself out of asking what she knew she would ask. But she couldn't stand it a moment longer, couldn't keep in the bitter accusation that had been pressing at the back of her throat from the first moment she'd spied him today. "You didn't show up that last night."

He didn't even ask which night she referred to. "I'm here now."

CHAPTER SEVEN

THE ZAMBONI DRIVER had worked on the ice forever, it seemed. More than an ice tech or maintenance drone, he was a vital part of the skating operation, practically a celebrity in his own right. Sometimes kids even asked for his autograph, which he obligingly gave. He even put up with the tedious "Zamboni Song," which some smart aleck invariably belted out now and then.

When his big Lego block of a machine chugged out onto the ice to enact the hourly ritual of renewal, he attracted as much attention as the amateur figure skaters practicing their double axels. The sight of the surface being groomed satisfied on a deep level; rough imperfections disappeared almost instantly. There was a mesmeric, Zen-like appeal in watching the resurfacing of the ice. In perfect, overlapping oval swaths, the machine scraped off the gouged and pitted epidermis of the rink, washed the shavings and then laid down a slick, smooth mirror of perfect ice in its wake.

Reaching a top speed of nine miles per hour, the

Zamboni crept along so slowly that the driver had plenty of time to study the crowd, studying him. This was what kept him in his heated vinyl seat each winter, year after year—the opportunity to watch people. He had all the time in the world to observe the way they looked at the world, weathered storms, slammed into walls and picked themselves up after a fall, the way they raced out to embrace life.

He'd seen all sorts of people come and go. The crowd here was made up mostly of tourists and occasional regulars. Every once in awhile, someone interesting was swept up in emotional turmoil—that sort of thing always caught his attention. He'd never tire of watching a mother arguing with her almost-grown daughter. A newly divorced man working up the courage to ask a woman out. A young couple on the brink of falling in love.

They were tantalizing, those glimpses of lives, flickering across his ice. Some disappeared forever, leaving their resolution to his thoughtful imagination. Others came back, their stories deepening, darkening or sometimes turning out all right.

He had one hard-and-fast rule. Never meddle. He was here to smooth out the ice, not mess up people's lives. But it was tempting sometimes, like right now.

There was no forgetting Tony Fiore and the girl he loved, some society debutante named Elaine. Some years back, Fiore had been a hot prospect in hockey, maybe the best ever to cross the ice here. His explosive speed and unfailing coordination had made him a good bet for any team. But it was his love of skating, that rare and genuine feel for the ice beneath his blades, that sharpened his edge. The overcrowded tourist mecca wasn't his usual place to skate, of course, but one Christmas Eve long ago, he'd stopped in on a lark. And so had the girl named Elaine. Maybe they'd been lonely that day, possibly frustrated by last-minute shopping or needing to kill time before some engagement, yet they'd both shown up within minutes of one another.

It happened all the time, but these two, they were something. From the first moment they saw each other, they practically melted the ice beneath their feet. They were youth and spirit and hope personified, and anyone watching them could tell they were seeing something special.

When the hour was up, they went their separate ways, of course. The Zamboni driver hadn't been surprised to see them back the next year, and then the year after that, their interest and passion deepening perceptibly each time. They'd changed, as all young folk do. But there was something about this pair that had never wavered. They'd looked at each other as though they were the first to discover the true meaning of love. It was all there in those young, good-looking faces, those glowing smiles, those hands clasped tight.

And then…nothing. It was no big deal and certainly none of his business, but the ice groomer had taken their disappearance as a personal failure. Deep down, he knew what had happened, and he always wanted to believe he was wrong, but he wasn't. Life had interfered with these two, and they'd been foolish enough to allow it.

Now they were back, and he was anxious to see if they'd finally figured out what he already knew— that they belonged together, not just once a year, but always. After finishing his rounds, he parked the machine and headed over to the concessions area, which consisted of a few tables and benches arranged on a large mat of interlocking rubber squares. At a cheap metal table, they sat across from each other, hands cradling paper cups of thin hot chocolate, gazes anxious with everything the years had done to them.

"Well, if it ain't the lovebirds," he said. "So what is it with you two?"

Elaine glared up at him. "Do you mind?"

"Not at all." He had a seat at their table, unsnapped the top buttons of his coveralls and let his red scarf hang loose. The name Larry was embroidered on his shirt pocket.

She gasped, then pruned up her face into a frown.

Probably trying to figure out if he was the same Larry from the carolers, not that he'd care to enlighten her. "You don't remember me, do you?"

"You're the Zamboni driver," Tony said.

"The question is," Elaine said, "why are you behaving as though you remember us?"

"Because I do."

She laughed a little nervously. She was even prettier than she'd been years before—more sophisticated, sure of herself. Yet there was something about her, something a little wistful.

"Right," she said.

"Three years in a row I see the two of you meeting like you invented love at first sight, and then the fourth year—"

"He didn't show," Elaine said, and Larry heard the sudden spike of hurt in her voice. Then she looked a little queasy, probably regretting that she'd said exactly what was on her mind. He sometimes had that effect on people. He wasn't surprised when she left her hot chocolate on the table and headed off to the rental kiosk.

"Sure, he did," Larry called out after her.

She froze like an ice sculpture, then pivoted slowly back to face him.

He winked at Tony, who shot him a look of fury. "I guess you got some explaining to do."

CHAPTER EIGHT

"THANKS A LOT, pal." Tony glared at the Zamboni driver.

"You don't have time to thank me." Larry jerked his thumb at the rental booth. He was compact and spry, a blunt, friendly man of indeterminate age. He had a froth of white hair, but the light in his eyes sparkled with an ageless mingling of wisdom and merriment. "So, what are you waiting for? An engraved invitation?"

Tony followed Elaine, who barely looked at him as she put on her boots, then stood there tapping her toe in impatience. Okay, he thought. Party's over even before it started. He led her back to the car and held open the door for her, catching a whiff of sweet cold air in her hair as she got in.

"You want to explain that?" asked Elaine, clipping on her seatbelt.

No. He really didn't.

He slid a glance at her, then concentrated on his driving. The car surged into the string of taxis, limos and private cars. Tony stole another look at her.

Elaine St. James. He couldn't believe he was seeing her again after all this time. He'd never forgotten her. How could he? All that cool blond beauty, that smart-alecky sense of humor, and the almost-hidden sweet vulnerability he noticed when she didn't know he was watching. The passage of time had added polish and sophistication to a woman who had been polished and sophisticated to begin with. And in spite of all the ways he'd reasoned with himself over the years, he still wanted her. Bad.

She was the reason he had never married and settled down. Thanks to her, he would never be happy with any other woman. She didn't know that, and he wasn't about to tell her. Yet what he had done—rather, what he'd failed to do—the last time he'd seen her had had ramifications he never could have predicted. Because of that moment of decision, just that one moment, his heart had been stuck in the same place. He was beginning to think maybe this was true for Elaine, too.

As he navigated the flow of traffic, he could feel her watching him. Waiting for his answer. "I got no idea what that guy was talking about," he said.

"Simple. He knew we met there every year on Christmas Eve—"

"Every year, Elaine?"

"Okay, for three years. There was a pattern. Even the Zamboni driver realized that."

He said nothing for a few minutes. A crooner on the radio made "Little Drummer Boy" sound like a timeless love ballad. "Okay," he said at last. "I showed up that night."

A small intake of breath. "I didn't see you."

"I changed my mind." He figured she was too proud to ask why, but the question shouted through the silence. "I couldn't even get down to the rink level. I was just out of the hospital, recovering from surgery. I had to use a wheelchair to get around."

"A wheelchair?" She leaned forward to get a closer look at his legs. "What happened?"

"Wrecked my knee and couldn't skate. I was looking at months of physical therapy, and then God knew what."

Incredulous silence pulsed through the car.

He had not wrecked just his knee. He'd wrecked his shot at the pros, his plans for the future and his chance to offer something to a girl who had everything. He still remembered sitting at the rail above the rink, his knee throbbing, his eyes smarting as he watched her circling the rink below. He'd tried to imagine what was going through her mind. Or did skating blank everything out as it did for him? Even now, he remembered everything he had seen and felt while she'd skated around the ice, alone, a slender figure moving in and out of the skaters. Anger. Grief. Frustration. Shame. *Love.*

"I watched you for a while," he said. "You were wearing a long white scarf."

"Let me get this straight. You showed up after knee surgery and you couldn't be bothered to speak to me?"

"We were brand new. I didn't want to blow it."

"Well, you did."

"No excuse." Except stupid male pride. The shattering realization that everything he'd worked for all his life was gone. "I didn't even know what I was going to say to you. I was still trying to figure out what to say to myself. I had to figure out what to do with the rest of my life. I was a little preoccupied with that. I told myself I'd get in touch with you later, when my head was in a better place—"

"Your head? What about mine? I was frantic with worry."

"I figured you'd move on."

"How could you figure that? You didn't know me at all. I would have understood." She almost admitted that she'd been heartbroken, but she was too angry to give him that.

"So tell me this, Elaine, and be honest. If I'd come rolling up to you in a wheelchair and said, 'Gee, I may be on permanent disability and I might not even walk again, but how about we plan a future together?' What would your reaction have been?

Would you have stood by me in rehab and helped me learn to walk again?''

She blanched, but didn't look away. "You'll never know, because you made up my mind for me."

He couldn't dispute that. He hesitated, then opted for honesty. "I made a big mistake that night. I don't want to make it again."

"Tell me one reason why I should give you another chance."

He pulled up to the curb in front of the address she'd given him. It was a luxury building from the 1930s, complete with a liveried doorman.

This was nuts, he thought, eyeing a career dog walker following a pedigreed pack up the tree-lined street. He and Elaine were from different worlds. They ought to forget the whole thing. Instead, he slid his arm along the seat behind her. "Because," he said, "you've never been in love."

"I never said that."

"Sure you did."

"What's that got to do with us?"

"Maybe nothing," he said. "Maybe everything."

She parted her lips a little, and he thought about kissing her. He didn't let himself act on it. Later, he told himself. Definitely later.

"Thanks for the skating," she said, then studied him for a few seconds. "Would you like to come up?"

CHAPTER NINE

As she greeted the doorman, Elaine felt a beat of unease. Maybe it wasn't such a good idea, letting Tony Fiore into her life. They'd only had three dates, after all, and they hadn't really been dates as much as accidents. They barely knew each other. It was probably best to leave it that way.

Yet what he had just revealed to her could change everything between them—if she let it. She hated that he hadn't told her about his injury. But what she hated even more was a deeply shameful realization. If he'd told her, she would have wept for him. She would have raged with him at the injustice, mourned the loss of his lifelong dream with him. But then she would have slunk away in fear. That was the sort of person she was, back then. And it struck her that she didn't want to be that sort of person anymore.

"Some building," he said.

"Thanks. It's a co-op."

"Places like this are tough to find," he said.

"The Board knows more about me than my gynecologist, my therapist and the IRS." She gritted her teeth, wishing she hadn't admitted she was seeing a therapist. She opened the door to her apartment and led the way inside. The answering machine had a welcome message—Jenny had arranged for some talent to take Bobbi's place tonight. That was something, at least.

Her apartment was exquisite. The spare white-on-white decor imparted a mood of space and cool elegance. She found herself wishing it was a little more…whimsical, maybe. Some colorful throw pillows on the designer sofa, or artwork that actually represented something recognizable. She turned to see Tony studying an array of silver-framed black-and-white photos on a glass-and-chrome étagère. Maybe the pictures conveyed a personal touch, Elaine thought. But no. There were no warm portraits of a laughing family, but merely souvenirs— pictures of her with celebrities, socialites, rock stars, company executives.

As though feeling her stare, he smiled at her. "Nice—"

"Please don't say nice place."

"Why not?"

"It's not nice."

"It's not?" He picked up a small Baccarat bowl and carefully set it down. "So why do you live here?"

She blinked. "No one ever asked me that before." She'd never even asked herself that question. She lived here because it was on the Upper East Side. The brushed-steel-framed Italian sofa was there because the designer had chosen it for style, of course. Not for comfort. The Venetian glass-top coffee table was there because it matched the sofa. Everything in her apartment went together perfectly. Her designer wouldn't have it any other way.

The only thing out of place at the moment was Tony Fiore himself. He was too earthy, too real.

"It's a great apartment. People wait for years to find an apartment like this." She gestured at the tree-framed view out the window. The snow had rendered the world more brilliantly white than her stark interior.

"You didn't answer the question, Elaine."

"Can I offer you something to drink?" She went into the gleaming kitchen and he followed. She swung open the fridge. "Soda? Beer?"

"Thanks." He helped himself to a soda.

She tried to put herself in his place that night, the night she'd stopped believing in Christmas.

He'd lost something, too. What must it be like to have a dream as powerful as the dream he'd had, and then to have that taken away? She pictured him watching her from the upper level, trying to figure out what to do now that his entire life plan had shattered to pieces. The horrible truth was, she was afraid to contemplate what her reaction might have been if he'd come rolling toward her in a wheelchair. She'd been young and self-centered and focused on glamour and success. She'd built up such fantasies around the sort of life they would have together, with Tony as a famous hockey player, and she as an international journalist. Maybe, just maybe, he had made the right choice, turning his back on her that night. The person she was back then could not have dealt with him. She'd simply had no resources to love a man who didn't fit her idealized view of what the future would be. Now, years later, she knew the problem of living a life that looked perfect on paper. It was as one-dimensional as the piece of paper itself.

It felt so strange having him here, where she lived. Where she slept and showered and talked on the phone. He was seeing her in a different context, and she desperately wanted him to like what he saw. But how could he, when *she* didn't even like it?

"Look," she said. "About tonight...you don't have to—"

"Are you kidding?" He set his soda on the counter and turned to her, and when he smiled, it was like glimpsing a dream she thought she'd forgotten. "You think I'd pass up another chance to spend Christmas Eve with you?"

CHAPTER TEN

"MA, IT'S NOT the end of the world," Tony said, wedging the phone under his jaw as he stood back and surveyed the contents of his closet. If he didn't have a clean shirt, he was going to shoot himself. "It's just a change of plans."

"Change of plans, he says. You hear that, Salvatore? He abandons his family on Christmas Eve, and he calls it a change of plans." Gina Fiore always had two-way conversations with people—one on the phone, the other in her warm, yeasty-smelling kitchen.

Tony's father, Sal, mumbled something indistinct. He was used to the fact that his wife thrived on drama and, like Tony, secretly found her entertaining.

"Tell you what…" Tony said. He spotted a crisp white shirt, still in the cleaner's cellophane, and pounced. "I'll try to get back in time for midnight mass."

"Mass, he says."

"It's the reason for the season, Ma."

"What about supper, eh? You're going to miss the *torta di spinaci,* the *bauletti di maiale,* the *pandoro.*"

He dragged five different ties from the rack on the back of the closet door. "I'll live, Ma. I'll eat the *pandoro* for breakfast tomorrow morning."

"Oh, so now we don't see you until breakfast. What's going on, eh, Tony?"

He took a deep breath, then said, "Well, there's this girl—"

"I knew it! *Ringrazi il cielo,* did you hear that, Sal? Tony's got a girl. A Christmas Eve girl."

He grinned, shaking his head. "Look, Ma, don't get too exci—"

"Ha. Don't you tell me. I know what it means when a man spends Christmas Eve with a girl. Didn't your father and I get engaged on Christmas Eve, eh? Didn't we?" She paused to blow her nose. "It's just like when you were in college, and you kept promising to bring someone to meet us. It always broke my heart that you never brought her home, Tony."

He knew he should explain that this was a casual date that happened to fall on Christmas Eve. He knew he should explain that Elaine St. James was out of his league, that they'd probably go their separate ways after tonight, that she was no more cut out to be a cop's wife than he was to be a society husband. He should tell his mother that he'd stood in the middle of Elaine's designer apartment today and felt like an alien life-form.

But he didn't say any of that. Because there was something stubborn about his heart, something that made him think that maybe, just maybe, he and Elaine could get it right this time.

"Are your shoes polished?" she demanded, businesslike now.

"Huh?"

"Your shoes, your shoes. You shine them until you see your teeth reflected, you hear me?"

Grinning again, he excavated his dress shoes. "No problem, Ma."

"And your suit—the one you bought for Uncle Rico's funeral, yes?"

"An excellent choice."

She rattled off a string of instructions while he held up each tie, looking for the perfect match.

"I got to get in the shower, Ma," he said after a while. "I don't want to be late."

"Go, go," she urged him. "But…Tony?"

"Yeah?"

"Bring her home this time, eh?"

He ripped the cellophane off the white shirt. "I'll do my best, Ma."

CHAPTER ELEVEN

ELAINE'S WORK on the St. James affair had long been finished. What she was supposed to do, at this point, was relax, enjoy the party and make sure everyone had a fabulous time.

But tonight was different. It was Christmas Eve, the clients were her parents and she was getting a shot at her biggest account to date. In the midst of all this, she was supposed to forget her troubles, forget that her best friend had betrayed her, forget that her boyfriend had dropped her.

But that wasn't what was making her nerves jangle on the swift, thirty-one-story rise to the St. James apartment. Smiling tautly at the elevator man, she admitted to herself that the source of her apprehension was something—someone—altogether different.

There was no denying it. Just being near Tony Fiore, even the very thought of him, made her tingle with an awareness that was actually embarrassing in its intensity. She wasn't a naive girl anymore, yet with Tony, she felt young and light and full of feelings she had long thought lost to her.

Catching a glimpse of herself in the smoke-tinted elevator mirror, she detected a splotchy blush on her neck. It was like a red map of the former Soviet Union rising up from the décolletage of her perfect cocktail dress. She hadn't blushed like this in ages, though it used to be a common and embarrassing trait of hers. The red rash of rapture, she had once jokingly called it when her college roommate had asked her if she had a fever. Agitated, she raised the collar of her coat.

As they arrived at the thirty-first floor, the elevator man tipped his cap. "Merry Christmas, Miss St. James."

"What? Uh, thanks. Same to you."

Flustered, she stepped out of the elevator and into the place where she'd spent her over-privileged childhood. It was gorgeous as always, in the gleaming-marble, sleekly chic way of the city's finest old money roosts. It had a special holiday sparkle imparted by the subtle, elegant touches of the floral designer she'd engaged for the event.

Graceful and minimalist, the seasonal decor avoided the usual swags of holly and mistletoe in favor of simple elegance. In the foyer, a pair of beeswax tapers flanked a single calla lily in a crystal vase, artfully displayed atop the Louis XVI side table. The living room had been arranged for conversation and dancing. She and the designer had talked her mother out of putting up the traditional twelve-foot tree because it would take up too much space. Instead, the designer had insisted that the "suggestion" of a tree—an abstract stainless-steel sculpture of a branch over the mantel—would suffice.

Elaine found herself wishing she had argued more with the designer.

Sinbad, who had no last name and whose talents were booked for years in advance, was warming up on the white Steinway. Elaine surrendered her coat to one of the caterer's uniformed staffers, who bore it away to the guest room that tonight would serve as a cloakroom.

Elaine took a few moments for a quick tour. In the vast, well-equipped kitchen, Armand orchestrated the preparations like an air traffic controller. He paused only long enough to greet Elaine, assure her that everything was perfect and on time, and insist that she sample the tamarind-perfumed seviche.

"Outstanding," she assured him, savoring the lime-cured raw fish. Secretly, she yearned for Chex Mix and little cubes of cheese.

The familiar tap-tapping of her mother's footsteps drew her back to the huge, beautiful living room, which had been designed by Mongiardino. But the room itself faded to obscurity when Elaine's mother walked in.

The press had always been especially kind to Freddie St. James, and for good reason. She had married Banner St. James, whose roots and wealth were sunk deep into the mythos of the city, and she was everything the media wanted from a woman like her: graceful, educated and generous. She was admired by everyone from her bookkeeper's assistant to the attorney general.

Tonight she wore a Vera Wang original and Cartier jewels. An invisible fog of Gucci Rush surrounded her.

"Wow," said Elaine. "If I didn't know better, I'd swear you were from central casting. You look perfect, Mom."

Freddie smiled and held out both hands. "Hello, sweetheart. Merry Christmas."

They leaned toward each other but didn't touch except for their hands. Both were conscious of not wanting to disturb the other's porcelain-perfect makeup. Freddie stepped away from Elaine and subjected her to a shrewd study. "Wow, yourself," she said with genuine admiration. "That dress is fabulous."

Elaine had thought so when she'd first put it on. Over a long-sleeved tunic of black Sea Isle cotton, the designer had draped a shimmery mesh of baby-fine gold cord.

"You think?" she asked, realizing how much she had always sought her mother's good opinion by trying to appear just right. "It reminds me of chains. Didn't Marley's ghost wear chains?"

"Merry Christmas," called a jovial voice. Banner St. James joined them, timelessly handsome in his crisp Armani tux.

Elaine greeted her father with cordial warmth, and regarded both her parents with a certain diffuse wistfulness. Despite that she was an only child, they weren't really a close family. Her most cherished Christmas memory was the year of the biggest blizzard in the history of the city. Socked in by a record snowfall and extended power outage, the three of them had slept together under duvets in the living room around the fireplace. They'd fixed canned soup and crackers for supper, then played board games by candlelight. Something about the slow rhythm of that magical day had fulfilled her more than any international ski trip or luxury cruise.

She did not doubt that her parents loved her, or she them, but they had never shared the sort of easy, natural affection she sometimes observed in families that were less busy, less self-conscious, less preoccupied with appearances.

As she smiled with confidence and assured them

that the party was going to be wonderful, there was so much she wished for. She wished she could tell them about Bobbi and Byron. She wished she could explain that she'd run into Tony Fiore and was totally confused by him. She wished they could spend Christmas doing something quiet and cozy rather than over-the-top entertaining. But, of course, she couldn't say those things to them.

Melanie and Jenny arrived, setting off a chain reaction of preparatory events, followed by the arrival of the guests in convivial clusters. Within a short while, the St. James affair was underway. With Sinbad's expert playing as a sound track, the party burst into a flurry of celebration that seemed to Elaine to be as staged and visually busy as a music video.

When Tony Fiore walked into the room, there seemed to be a subtle pause, like a collective intake of breath. Even as Elaine hurried to welcome him, the speculation started, an insistent current of whispers flowing beneath the surface small talk. He was a rising young star, a socialite's lover, an Olympic athlete.

As he removed his parka and gloves, he was either oblivious or took the attention in stride, focusing solely on Elaine. He looked wonderful in a dark suit and white shirt that set off a burgundy-colored tie.

She took his hand, grimacing a little. "You're freezing."

"My hands are always cold. Even when I remember my gloves." He handed the gloves, along with his jacket, to an attendant.

Elaine's parents greeted him with their usual poise, but also silent questions they couldn't quite conceal.

"Byron's not coming," Elaine said, taking the coward's way out and breaking the news in the safety of the public eye. "Tony's my plus-one tonight."

"It's very nice to meet you," Freddie said, her voice perfectly modulated.

"He's an ex-hockey star," Elaine added, easing into the familiar phony party patter she'd developed into an art. She was an expert spin doctor, adept at making people and products seem larger-than-life. With a simple verbal twist, she changed out-of-work actors into rising stars, has-been artists into cutting-edge visionaries.

But the trouble was, Tony seemed amused by her spin. When she said, "He's in law enforcement—"

He burst out laughing and said, "I better get you out on the dance floor before I find out I'm a Kennedy cousin." He offered her parents a jovial smile, and led Elaine into the midst of the milling couples.

"I get it now," he said.

"Get what?"

"The reason it wouldn't have worked out for us."

"Really. And why is that?"

"Your folks. I'm sure they're great people but I'm not exactly their idea of the perfect guy for their daughter."

"Back then, maybe."

"And now?"

"Now that so-called perfect daughter has a mind of her own."

"I was counting on that, Elaine."

She found herself swept against him, and something incredible came over her, as it had when he'd taken her skating. He moved with the grace of an athlete, his hand firm and secure at her waist. There was magic in his embrace, in the hard bulk of his body and the soft smile that curved his full lips. She was engulfed by his nearness, his warmth, the heady essence of his masculinity.

As the music filled her, so did memory and emotion, warmed by a contentment deeper and more real than anything she'd felt in years. She'd been out in the cold too long and had gone numb in vital places. Now she was thawing out and she welcomed the surging tingles of pain that reminded her she was alive.

When was the last time she had danced just for the pleasure of it? Just for the feel of a man's arms around her and the mindless delight of moving to the rhythm of the music? She couldn't remember, because these days when she danced in a man's arms, it was to entertain or conduct business or impress someone. Tony Fiore couldn't know it, but this was such a gift, to simply be with him for no other reason than to dance. She wasn't stupid. She knew the reason for this newfound sense of fun and freedom was Tony. He had that effect on her. That was why she'd fallen for him the first night they skated together, and why she'd kept coming back.

She tilted back her chin to gaze up at him. And to her astonishment, a tear slipped from her eye. She prayed he wouldn't notice. He did, of course.

"Hey, what's this?"

What the heck, she thought. He already knew far too much about her. He always had. She saw no point in hiding her feelings. "This is fun," she said. "I love dancing with you. It's sort of like skating, but *I'm* better at it."

He grinned. "If this is your idea of fun, I guess I don't want to see you depressed." With infinite gentleness, he brushed his thumb over the crest of her cheekbone, wiping away the tear. His smile softened, and she was startled to discern a hint of genuine, uncomplicated affection in his regard. It was so different from the way others looked at her. With interest, perhaps. Ambition, undoubtedly. Wariness or respect, occasionally. But straightforward, no-strings-attached caring was something she rarely encountered. He made her feel important and valued, not for her social pedigree but simply for being in the world.

"The women in my family get all choked up over Christmas, too," he said, misinterpreting her tears. "My Aunt Flo can't even look at a manger scene without turning into a leaky faucet."

Elaine decided to leave it at that. Her unexpected reaction was too complicated to explain. Nor did she want to try explaining that she didn't like Christmas because she was afraid to let it mean something to her. She couldn't bring herself to confess that the last time she'd tried to let someone into her heart, she'd been so hurt that she'd simply stopped trying. And she would never admit that the someone had been him.

"He's here," Jenny hissed, breaking in on their dance without apology. "It's showtime."

"We're in the middle of a dance here," Tony said, his voice neutral but firm.

"Sorry, but we're in the middle of a deal here," Jenny said, flashing a smile designed to dazzle.

He wasn't dazzled. Elaine could see that immediately. "Give us a minute, Jen."

"Half a minute," she said curtly.

Elaine pretended to be amused as Jen hurried

away. "So you've got thirty seconds, and then it really is showtime."

"Elaine, even I'm not working on Christmas."

She tried to forget how much it meant to dance with him, how it had felt when he'd wiped away her tears. She reminded herself of the importance of landing this account. And not just to her. Jenny and Melanie needed it, too. The three of them had built the business and rose or fell with the firm's success or failure. And her partners didn't have room to fail. Unlike her, they had no trust fund spread out like a safety net below them, ready to cushion them when they failed or simply got bored and walked away.

"Look," she whispered to Tony, "I gave my word I'd help out with this guy. And we're short-handed tonight." The thought of Bobbi tugged at her spirits. She pictured her former friend alone in her tiny walkup, fretting over unpaid bills, wishing she'd gone home for Christmas. The image of Bobbi's misery gave Elaine no sense of justice or moral victory. It was merely depressing.

"Okay," Tony said good-naturedly. "I'll go help myself to more of those liverwurst sandwiches."

She couldn't help smiling as he headed for a waiter holding out a tray of *pâté de foie gras en croute*. For the next hour or so, Tony mingled effortlessly with the glittering company, his friendly, genuine manner endearing him to everyone, from the bartender to the ambassador of Uruguay.

There was an artful pause in the music and conversation when Axel entered the room. The subtle hush was different and more dramatic than it had been for Tony, because Melanie had arranged for Sinbad to pause dramatically in his playing. Axel and his Euro-chic entourage were so cutting-edge sharp that they resembled fashion mannequins. Their close-cut hair was slick and glossy, their black suits glovelike around starving bodies that probably subsisted on Campari and Dunhill cigarettes.

"So there he is," Melanie murmured in her ear, "the holy grail of accounts. Let's hope you can snag him without Bobbi's help. Get going."

Elaine turned on the charm with no more effort than flipping a switch. She made introductions and drew the somber Swiss man into the center of the action. He was stunningly handsome, his slender body impeccably clad in an Italian suit, his face as perfectly smooth and gleaming as carved and polished wood. He had a reputation as a fabulous but demanding lover, and was nearly always found draped in supermodels. That was where Bobbi came in. Without her, they'd have to improvise. Jenny came forward with the hired escorts, a pair of bony, bright-eyed actresses in borrowed designer dresses.

Axel was suave and low-key, greeting everyone

with continental panache. Elaine's parents were as taken with him now as they had been at Parents' Day at school in Lugano. He was precisely their type. Despite the trendy moniker, he had a family tree hung with European royalty. Anyone who could call Prince Rainier "Uncle" was certainly welcome in their home.

She felt his attention on her like a beam of cold light.

"Your daughter has always charmed me until I cannot see straight," he declared in an accent more delicious than melted chocolate.

It was all Elaine could do to keep from rolling her eyes. Although just thinking about Tony could summon up a blush, blatant flattery from a Swiss billionaire blew past her like dust bunnies.

She caught Tony's eye and motioned him over. The moment he joined their group, she saw the contrast between them. Side-by-side, they were almost comical, with Tony the picture of the all-American male, big and brawny, exuding self-confidence and a tangible amount of testosterone. By contrast, Axel was a svelte and polished European import, his sculpted mouth taut with a condescending smile. Clearly they both sensed an undeclared rivalry afoot.

"May I have this dance?" Axel said to Elaine, offering his hand. The nails gleamed from a Japanese manicure. His laser-whitened teeth flashed as he smiled.

Winning his business was the sole purpose of the night, she reminded herself. She said, "Of course," then turned to Tony. "Jenny and Melanie will take good care of you."

"That's okay. I need to get going anyway."

She felt a stab of panic. How could he leave her when she'd only just found him again? "But—"

"I always go to midnight mass with my family. 'Night, Elaine. Thanks for having me." He gave her a brief peck on the cheek and then turned away. "I'll see you around, okay?"

Before she could say another word, he was gone and she was dancing with the holy grail, unthinkingly maneuvering him in front of the photographer from *W*, insincerely offering a blissful smile for the camera. Old habits died hard. It was pointless to think she could spend a successful Christmas Eve with Tony Fiore. She'd tried that in the past and it had never turned out well for her.

She heard herself chatting blithely with Axel, heard him laugh with sensual appreciation as he led her around the dance floor. He was a flawless dancer, she conceded. But he didn't sweep her away. He didn't make her feel glad she was alive. He didn't make her wish she could love Christmas again.

At the end of the dance, he handed her a white business-size envelope. "This is for you."

The envelope contained a printed travel itinerary.

"I want you to come skiing with me," he said. "Just give your passport information to my service, and they'll take care of the reservations and tickets."

Skiing. In Gstaad. With European royalty. It was a moment, Elaine had to admit that. So why did she feel so underwhelmed?

She glanced at the departure date. "This is for tomorrow."

"Yes."

She shoved the paper into the envelope. "This is so unexpected—I don't quite know what to say."

He sent her a practiced smile. "Come now. You expected it. I'm sure your parents will be delighted. If we're going to do business together, we might as well have fun doing it, yes?"

He was all but offering her his business. It should have been the biggest moment in her career—her life, maybe. But it wasn't.

She smiled brightly, falsely, spying her reflection in the slick black glass of the picture window. "I'll let you know."

Without another glance at him, she headed for the foyer.

Jenny and Melanie hissed questions and protests

in an undertone. "What are you doing?" Jen demanded.

Elaine filled them in on Axel's invitation.

"Don't tick him off," Melanie warned.

"Are your passports current?" Elaine asked them both.

"Mine is," Melanie said. "But what—"

"I'll tell you what." With a little laugh, Elaine handed over the envelope. "It's your lucky day. You're going skiing in Switzerland tomorrow. Staying at the Hotel Grande Suisse. Just contact this agency, and they'll take care of the paperwork."

Leaving them gasping and sputtering—Melanie with a broad grin breaking through her surprise she headed for the cloakroom. "The Gallignani," she said, indicating her coat, which hung from a portable rack set up in the guest room. She felt light and free. "The gentleman who left a short while ago—did he mention where he was going?"

"No."

Well, of course he hadn't. But he lived in Brooklyn. That narrowed it down.

"He forgot his gloves," the girl added, holding out a large, lived-in pair.

Elaine shoved them in her purse. "Then I'd better take them to him."

On her way out, she found her parents to say good-night.

Startled, her mother studied her. "Are you ill?"

"I've never felt better." Elaine leaned forward for the customary makeup-preserving air kiss, then impulsively hugged her mother close and embraced her father. "Merry Christmas," she said to them both, and realized it was the first time she'd said those words in years.

CHAPTER TWELVE

OUTSIDE, the world had gone white; the streets and sidewalks were smooth and clean. Sable, the doorman, who was actually a woman, phoned for a taxi and they waited together in the gleaming, mid-century-era lobby.

"So, the man who just left—Mr. Fiore—didn't take a taxi?" Elaine asked.

"No. He had his own car." Sable studied the thick fall of snow on the pavement outside. "Bad night for driving."

"Did you see which way he went?"

"Toward Roosevelt, I guess."

Nervous, Elaine studied Sable. The unflattering double-breasted uniform had not changed in generations, and on a young woman, it looked particularly absurd. At least in winter, the traditional warm coachman's cloak helped conceal the two-toned fashion crime. "Do you have plans for tonight?" Elaine asked her suddenly.

Sable glanced behind her to see who Elaine was

talking to. "Me?" She put a hand to her chest. "I got to play Santa Claus to my two kids."

Until now, Elaine had never realized Sable had kids. "Sounds like fun."

"Oh, it is." Her glance crept almost imperceptibly to the lobby clock. "This year, there's a bike and a dollhouse to put together. I imagine my husband made a good start on the bike, but he doesn't know the first thing about dollhouses." She smiled, and there was a special quality to her smile, a softness made of love and pride and wistfulness. "He'll have his hands full getting them to bed."

"Then you should go home and help him," Elaine said, surprising herself with the words.

Sable glanced at the lobby clock. "Ravi doesn't come in for another hour."

Despite her urgency to find Tony, Elaine felt a keen sense of sympathy. She hesitated, the dilemma weighing heavily on her.

She'd lost Tony for a long time. Now she knew where to find him. Yet here was a woman who was working rather than tucking her babies in on Christmas Eve. How could anything in the world be more important than that? True giving meant sacrifice, didn't it? "I'll cover for you."

Sable laughed. "I don't think so, Ms. St. James. I could lose my job if someone found out."

"Oh, for heaven's sake. Things like that don't

happen to good people on Christmas. Now, hand over the cloak and hat and whistle.''

Sable looked torn to the point of breaking. Elaine put a hand on her arm. ''Please. This is as much for me as it is for you.'' She gestured outside. ''Look, your cab's here.'' Seizing the doorman's accessories, she pushed and bullied Sable out through the cold night and into the waiting taxi. Then she prepaid the driver and stood on the sidewalk, watching the yellow car pull away. Sable turned and waved through the rear window until the snowy night swallowed her up. The woman's smile was the last thing Elaine saw, like the grin of the Cheshire cat before he disappeared.

As she returned to the lobby, Elaine felt the satisfying weight of her mission. Maybe Christmas was a disaster for her, but that was no reason for anyone else to give up on it. Christmas really meant something to women like Sable, who worked hard all year and deserved to spend time making their kids happy.

With a dramatic flourish, Elaine flung on the crimson and dove-gray cloak, fastening the ornate frog closures down the front. Turning to the gilt-framed lobby mirror, she donned a matching flat cap, angling the patent leather bill jauntily down over her eye. She looked ridiculous. An overgrown organ grinder's monkey. What were the building managers thinking, making the doorman work in this getup?

They were thinking residents like the St. Jameses wanted it that way.

A movement outside caught her eye. A party of well-dressed couples emerged from a Town Car at the curb. Clients! She hurried to let them in, holding the brass-and-glass door wide for three couples. It was on the tip of her tongue to greet the Wyndhams, the Blantons and the McQuiggs, old friends of her parents. Over the years, she had attended school and summer camp with some of their kids.

They swept past her in a laughing, babbling mass. No one looked at Elaine. No one greeted her. She didn't feel hurt, but mystified. Was it just this group of guests or did everyone treat the doorman this way? *Everyone,* she thought, answering her own question. In her world, the help was invisible, and friends were chosen for their social value as much as for their personal qualities.

After the next group swept through, she realized it was no fluke. They ignored her, too, even though she'd sent one couple a Tiffany bowl as a wedding present not so long ago. Then a man she recognized, a famous orchestra conductor who had come to dinner several times while she was growing up, alighted from a taxi. Certain he would be delighted to see her, she arranged her face in a smile. But his eyes barely flickered in her direction as he gave a curt, dismissive nod and headed for the elevator. These people, Elaine realized, treated the doorman with no more regard than a potted fern.

As she stood watching the polished-steel elevator doors closing, Elaine made an even more disturbing realization. She was one of ''these people.''

When Ravi arrived for his shift, she made a hasty explanation he clearly didn't understand, then called a cab for herself. She slid into the back seat, shivering as her thighs touched the hard plastic upholstery. She tucked her warm designer coat more securely around her and thought for a moment. The fact was, she had no clue where she wanted to go.

She wanted to find Tony. She wanted to tell him that seeing him again had caused her to step back and take a hard, painful look at her life. She'd left the best party in town and put her career in jeopardy to work for an hour as a doorman. All because she'd seen him again and realized the dream was still there, hiding, waiting for the right moment. So she was either losing her marbles or turning into a different person.

She felt the driver eyeing her in the rearview mirror. ''Brooklyn,'' she said. Ordinarily, even an hour ago, she wouldn't have given a second glance at a cabbie. Now she frowned as she detected something—a flicker of recognition?—in his glance.

"Got it." He turned south on Roosevelt Drive. "You probably want to be more specific."

She thought hard. "Do you know of a Catholic church in Brooklyn? One that holds midnight mass?"

He narrowed his eyes in the mirror. "That'd narrow it down to a couple dozen."

"Maybe I'll think of the name on the way over."

As it turned out, she had plenty of time to think because traffic came to a standstill a few blocks north of the bridge.

"Great," Elaine said. "I'm going to throw myself at a man for the second time in my life, and I get stuck in a traffic jam."

"The second time in your life? What happened the first time?"

"He didn't show." The chime of bells shimmered from the radio speaker. There was a silvery quality to the chimes that made her shiver.

"I thought he explained all that." Something in his voice caught her attention, and she studied him with more than passing interest. He was just a cabbie, she told herself. He wore a cap with earflaps and a bright red muffler.

The back of her neck prickled. Clutching the back of the seat, she leaned forward to read the driver ID affixed to the meter box. Lawrence E. Simms.

"Larry?" she said.

At last, they reached the bridge. The normally busy span was oddly deserted. "That's me."

"Larry the elf? Larry the Zamboni driver?"

The cabbie seemed not to hear her as he cranked down his window and stuck his head out. "Hey, lady. Do you see what I see? Oh, man."

She craned her neck and squinted, straining to see through the foggy curtain of snow lit by the headlamps of the taxi. "What?" she asked.

"There's someone on the bridge."

"What do you mean?"

He slowed and pulled over. "There. Isn't that a jumper?"

A woman stood alone on the wrong side of the bridge rail. She had somehow gone around the protective chain-link fencing and was facing out over the river. She wore no coat, and the wind whipped her hair around her face.

Chills zipped down Elaine's spine. "What's going on? Is that woman…" She stopped, unable to voice her fear.

"They say this is the time of year for it."

She wrenched open the door of the taxi and got out. Eerily, there was no one in sight—only the taxi…and the woman on the bridge rail.

Elaine walked through the snowy night, feeling the cold feathers of snowflakes on her face. She headed toward the woman, no longer intent on finding Tony but on trying to help.

It was absurd, of course. What could she possibly do to help? She whipped a glance around, but still no cars emerged from the storm. "This is the busiest bridge in the city," she muttered through chattering teeth. "How can it be deserted?"

Down on the river, the heartbeat rhythm of a boat motor pulsed into the ghostly stillness of the night. The winter wind off the water smelled cold and harsh. Shuddering with apprehension, Elaine approached the woman. The misty glow of a sodium vapor light illuminated the slender form, the delicate profile, her features seemingly frozen by the wind off the water. She wore nothing but a suede skirt and cashmere sweater—no coat, no hat, no gloves.

An icy sense of recognition raced over Elaine. Her heart jolted. Numbed by dread, she stepped to the chain-link fence and clutched at the cold wires. "Bobbi," she said, obeying an instinct to keep her voice low. "It's me, Elaine."

Bobbi didn't seem startled, so that was something. Nor did she seem in the least surprised to encounter Elaine. As fragile and brittle as a snowflake, Bobbi did not move. She simply stood there, like a figurehead at the prow of a ship.

"Go away," she said simply, her voice clear and firm.

"Not on your li—not in a million years. I'm so glad I'm here," she said. "Please don't hurt yourself, Bobbi. Please."

"What does it matter to you?"

"Well, for one thing, I didn't get a chance to tell you how sorry I am about today."

"Oh, that's great, Elaine. Let's make this about you."

Elaine was slightly encouraged by Bobbi's anger. "That's not what I'm doing."

"Then what are you doing, Elaine? Trying to improve my life for fun and profit?"

Elaine was wracked by guilt, as well as fear. In the frigid night, she was forced to truly see her relationship with Bobbi. They'd made friends for all the wrong reasons—Elaine had "created" a media figure, nothing more. Their friendship had never had any depth or genuine intimacy. It had been, like all of Elaine's other relationships, a business arrangement.

"I was wrong," said Elaine. "I was awful to you. Bobbi, please. Think what you will of me, but don't hurt yourself. For heaven's sake, it's Christmas."

"Another work day, as far as you're concerned. What's suddenly so special about Christmas?"

"Well, there's…" Elaine's voice trailed off. Suddenly, at the very worst possible moment, she had absolutely no idea what to say.

"There's what?"

"The Christmas tree," Elaine said. "What other time of year can you put such a large home fashion accessory in your living room and actually feel good about it?"

"That's only because you know you're going to take it down. And if that's supposed to give me a reason for living, you'll have to do better. You wouldn't know the true meaning of Christmas if it slapped you upside the head."

"Then maybe I'm the one who should be out there on the bridge," Elaine snapped. She was still terrified, but keeping Bobbi engaged in conversation was at least stopping her from doing a swan dive into the East River. "And I do, too, know the meaning of Christmas. It's to celebrate the birth of Christ. Everybody knows that."

"Actually, Christmas is not the birthday of Christ," Bobbi contradicted her. "He wasn't born in the middle of winter."

"How do you know that?"

"Well, for one thing, the sheep were out in the fields. It would have been very cold at night in the hills of Judea, and shepherds in that area never keep sheep in the fields after the end of October."

"What's that got to do with—" Elaine shut her mouth.

"Besides," Bobbi went on, "Herod never would

have ordered people to travel to their hometowns for tax registration in the middle of winter.''

"I can believe that," Elaine said. "Everyone knows you pay taxes in the spring." This was nuts. She was supposed to be convincing Bobbi of the true meaning of Christmas so she wouldn't take a flying leap off the bridge. Keep her talking, Elaine told herself. That was the key. "But listen," she said, "December twenty-fifth is as good a time as any to honor Christmas."

Bobbi hugged herself against the cold. "Jesus wouldn't have celebrated his own birthday because it wasn't a Jewish custom to do so."

"Anyone with half a brain ignores birthdays," Elaine said. "Look, Christmas is not just a time for people to be extra nice to each other, to make ourselves feel good by giving gifts. Christmas is to celebrate the fact that we don't have to shoulder our own burdens alone, that a humble child can be our salvation. It's a joyful thing, Bobbi, and what better way to show joy than to share it? I'm not doing such a good job giving you a reason to come down off this bridge, but here's something I know. I've been awful. I need to learn kindness and generosity again. I'm learning it from people like you, Bobbi. The world needs you in it.''

"What, more thieves?" Bobbi's voice broke.

"More people like you to show people like me

what desperation really is. You were desperate, and I didn't let myself see that.''

For the first time, Bobbi turned her head to look directly at Elaine. ''That's a little more like it. But it's still about you.'' She turned back to stare at the river. ''This isn't the life I wanted for myself. I need to be with people I love, with family. I need for my life to mean something more than a media opportunity. You didn't give me anything, Elaine, except the chance to live a phony life. Today I finally woke up to that.''

''Fine, then let's get you home for Christmas. Your mother wants to see you on Christmas, honey. She needs you. We can get you to the airport and on the next flight to Raleigh Durham. You'll be home by Christmas morning.''

''All right,'' said Bobbi softly, and a ripple of relief moved through Elaine.

''Perfect.'' Elaine rummaged in her purse. ''I'll call my service. There's someone on 24/7.'' As she took out the phone, her key ring came with it. Her special key ring, the one with the silver skate. Before she could catch it, the trinket fell through the iron grating, disappearing into deep blackness.

She imagined the small splash as it hit the water. She shut her eyes briefly, telling herself it didn't matter, it wasn't a portent of bad luck. Then she speed-dialed her twenty-four-hour travel service and secured a seat on the next flight out. "You're all set," she said to Bobbi. "It's time you headed for the airport."

Bobbi stared down at the river, seemingly fascinated by the descent of the key ring. Finally in a tiny, pathetic voice, she said, "I'm scared."

Somewhere behind her, Elaine heard traffic sounds. A car, coming from the other direction, she thought. She was terrified Bobbi would panic and fall.

Bobbi's designer boots wobbled on the slippery narrow ledge of steel. How on earth would she ever turn around?

Elaine heard a car stop but didn't dare turn to look.

"I got her." A tall, swift-moving man strode past her.

Elaine nearly melted into a puddle of relief. "Tony."

He barely glanced at her as he approached Bobbi. He was totally focused on saving her. He squeezed through an opening that had been bent in the fence, then climbed over the rail and edged toward her.

"We're both going to fall," Bobbi wailed.

"No, we won't. Don't even say that."

Elaine held her breath. The shiny cold steel framework was encased in ice. Tony wrapped one arm around the pole and reached out with the other.

"Take my hand," he said. "There you go. I got you."

Trembling with panic, she reached back blindly. Tony took hold with his bare hand. "It's okay," he said quietly. "You're okay now." Safe in his grip, Bobbi turned and let him coax her along the pipe, feet scraping along. She slipped, and her arms flailed. Elaine crushed her knuckles to her mouth to keep from screaming. Tony grabbed Bobbi and tugged, until she pitched forward into his arms.

Elaine rushed forward and hugged Bobbi. Heartsore, she took off her coat and settled it around Bobbi's shoulders. "I'm so sorry," Bobbi said. "What I did was wrong."

"But I was wrong, too," Elaine admitted. "I didn't listen to you."

Bobbi shivered uncontrollably. "No kidding."

Elaine remembered looking at the glossy black window in her parents' apartment. She'd seen a reflection of herself at the party, with her perfect career and perfect clothes and perfect jewelry—and a loneliness in her eyes that reminded her of two empty bowls.

The cabbie tapped the car horn. "Let's go already," he called. "It's another fifteen minutes to the airport."

Elaine bundled Bobbi into the cab and pressed a

wad of cash into her hand. "Should I come to the airport with you?"

"No. I'll be all right," Bobbi said with a sniff.

As the taxi pulled away, Tony scratched his head. "That cabdriver. Isn't he the guy—"

"Don't ask," Elaine said. "He's magic."

Traffic started up again. Tony settled his jacket around Elaine's shoulders and held it in place with a firm embrace. She could have stayed like that all night, warm and safe and protected.

"How did you know?" she asked. "How did you know to find me?"

"I was driving to church, and a dispatch came over the radio."

The cabdriver, she realized.

"What are you doing here, Elaine?" he asked.

"You left your gloves." She fished them out of her purse and handed them over.

"You were coming all the way over to Brooklyn on Christmas Eve to give me my gloves?"

She nodded.

With a laugh that was deep and pure, he brought her to his car and turned on the heater full blast. "So I guess you need a ride home."

She started to nod her head, then looked him in the eye. "I don't want to go home."

CHAPTER THIRTEEN

ELAINE ST. JAMES was the last person Tony thought he'd be spending Christmas Eve with. At the same time, she was the only person he wanted to spend Christmas Eve with. He led the way out of the underground parking and up the block to his building, situated on a quiet Park Slope street. He glanced at the silent woman beside him. She was coming into his home, into his life. He hoped he hadn't left the place too much of a mess.

The old brownstone wore garlands of holly on the stair rail and around the door. In the foyer, someone had suspended a sprig of mistletoe over the mailboxes. There was a Santa hat on the newel post. The scent of bayberry candles spiced the air. It was late, so they didn't speak until they were inside his third-floor apartment.

He let her in and watched her, trying to gauge her reaction. At some point in his life he had figured out how not to be a slob. The place didn't look too bad or smell like a hamster cage.

But it also didn't look like the kind of place

Elaine St. James belonged in. She was like some exotic flower standing there, completely out of her element. But then she smiled.

She took off his parka and handed it over. "Thanks," she said. "I would have frozen without it."

The fancy coat she'd given her friend was probably worth a month's rent.

"So...am I keeping you from something?" she asked, surprising him by seeming a little nervous.

"I skipped mass tonight," he said. "But I suppose that can be forgiven, seeing as how we had to help out your friend."

She nodded and gave a little shudder. "I hope she's going to be all right."

"Helluva thing, seeing your friend like that."

"I'm not sure she was ever my friend, but I'd never want to see her hurt herself."

"That's up to her. You did a good thing, Elaine."

"Did I? What about at lunch, when she asked me for an advance and I turned her down? That's what started this whole mess."

"You don't always get it right the first time. Nobody does. How about you have a seat?" He indicated the brown corduroy sofa. His scrawny Christmas tree was set up on a table in the window, a little lopsided thing sagging with too many colored lights.

He left a message on his parents' answering machine as he poured two glasses of wine—he hoped she liked red—and handed one to her. "So, are you all right?" he asked.

"I guess." She wandered through the apartment, much as he had hers. When she studied his collection of framed photos, the expression on her face broke his heart. Glancing up, she saw him watching her. "Pictures of friends and family," she said wistfully, sitting on his rumpled sofa. "It's nice."

She deserved friends and family of her own, Tony thought. She was a good person. Yet, somehow, she'd wound up stuck in a life that was less than she deserved and more than she wanted.

He wasn't to blame for that, but he'd played a part. Years ago, he'd abandoned her because he felt that, without a pro hockey career, he didn't measure up to her standards. He'd really believed that. But then he'd come to terms with the end of his dream and made a new life for himself.

It occurred to him that Elaine was still rich and sophisticated. But he no longer considered her out of his league. Life had sent him a bum shot, and he'd made his peace with that. Now life was giving him a second chance.

He watched the way her throat moved as she took a swallow of wine. She had the kind of face that would always be beautiful, at any age, glowing with youth or softened and lined by years. He knew he wanted to be there for that transformation, no matter how crazy it seemed and how different their worlds were. And he wanted it all to start now.

The air between them was hot, electric. Some things never changed.

"Elaine." He took her glass and set it with his on the coffee table. "What are you doing here?"

CHAPTER FOURTEEN

ELAINE wasn't sure how to answer him. She clenched and unclenched her hands as she watched him, his attention focused wholly on her. Even though they weren't touching, she could feel his warmth; he glowed with it. She wasn't sure how to answer his question. *What are you doing here?*

She wanted nothing. She wanted everything. And he would never understand.

Silently, deliberately, she slid toward him on the sofa, pressed her hands to his chest. He took in a quick breath, then grabbed her wrists. At first she feared he was going to push her away, but he gripped her hand and lifted it to his lips. Then his mouth lowered over hers, brushing lightly and finally pressing, exploring. It was the kind of kiss she didn't experience anymore. It was fierce and deeply honest, sharing emotions that could not be shaped into words.

She felt as though someone had touched a flame to a fast-burning fuse. Everything welled up inside her and spilled over, as though all her longing and desires converged in this single desperate moment.

She clung to him, her hands smoothing the big shoulders, fingers tangling in the thick hair curling against his collar. She had not realized she could feel this way anymore. She was young and giddy and hopeful again, filled with the knowledge that she was, finally, in the right place with the right man.

He stood and drew her up with him, holding her by the upper arms and gazing intently down into her face. "Just so you know," he whispered, "I don't do one-night stands."

"That's not what this is," she said.

"So what is it?"

Oh, she needed him. Not just in her arms, but in her life. Not just for tonight, but forever. She needed soft searching kisses and warm flesh against warm flesh. Endless conversations about things only they understood. The simple joy of building a life together, moment by moment. It was amazing, the way she and Tony seemed to know and crave each other. They were intimate strangers who had been dreaming of this meeting for years, moving toward it without knowing it.

"It's what should have happened years ago."

He smiled. "That's what I thought, too." He kissed her again, keeping their mouths joined even as he walked her slowly backward. The hardwood floor changed to carpet under her feet, and she pulled back briefly to gather fleeting impressions of his bedroom. King-size bed. Old-fashioned dresser with a framed photo of his family. A shoeshine kit left out. Several neckties draped over the back of a chair.

He grinned sheepishly. "I wasn't sure what to wear tonight. I was a little nervous."

She took his hand, held it over her thumping heart. She was so glad he'd admitted it. "I'm nervous now."

"Yeah," he said, his thumb tracing the line of her collarbone. "Me, too. I've been thinking about this for a long time." He plucked ineffectually at her dress. "I didn't picture you wearing chain mail, though. Geez, Elaine, you got a chastity belt under this?"

She laughed softly and reached back to unclasp the mesh overdress, letting it slide down her torso and pool like fallen coins around her feet. She stepped toward him, into his arms, and when she looked into his eyes, she saw herself reflected there, and the love and wonder on her face was startling.

After that, there were no more awkward moments between them, not even as they undressed. She felt only a searing anticipation and breath-held awe at the realization that finally, unexpectedly, she had rediscovered something real, something to give depth and resonance to her life, to fill the empty spaces where cold loneliness had taken up residence, to make her matter in a way she had never mattered before.

He turned back the covers and brought her against him. Shivery heat coursed through her. She reached out and caressed him, discovering the shape and texture and warmth she had only imagined before. He returned the caresses with exquisite tenderness, wringing wonder and emotion from her as her lips formed a wordless cry of startled joy. She couldn't believe how deeply she felt each intimate stroke of his hands, his mouth, how profound it seemed with him. Her heart was engaged, hopelessly tangled, and it made all the difference. When their bodies joined, she clasped him tighter, wishing for a way to bring him closer still. And then she found it, whispering love words into his ear while ecstasy lifted her up, transported her and held her high and light in some exalted place she thought she would never have reached. When after long blissful moments she returned to herself, Elaine knew she was a different person.

She felt the change deep in her bones. After this night, she knew, nothing would ever be the same.

CHAPTER FIFTEEN

THE SMELL of freshly brewed coffee teased Tony awake by small degrees of awareness. *Elaine.* The thought came to him like the last precious shred of an almost forgotten dream, and for a second he thought maybe he *had* dreamed her. But no. She'd been with him. Her presence was still there, a faint warmth in the hollow in the bed next to him where she had slept in his arms all night. The smell of her hair lingered on his pillow.

And in his heart lived the feeling that no morning in the history of the world could ever be as good as this one.

Elaine St. James. Finding her again was a small miracle, like coming across a diamond glittering in the snow.

She stood in the kitchen, seemingly mesmerized by the fragrant drip of the coffeemaker. She wore a pair of his socks and an ancient hockey practice jersey. Her makeup was gone and her hair was a mess. She looked like a goddess.

''Merry Christmas,'' he said, coming up behind

her. He slipped his hands around her waist and kissed the side of her neck.

"It is," she said softly, pressing herself back against him. "I was going to find some Christmas carols on the radio."

He reached across the counter and clicked it on, then fiddled with the dial. "God Rest Ye Merry Gentlemen," drifted through the room.

"Good idea," he said, turning her in his arms and pulling her back toward the bedroom, where the bed was still warm and inviting. His heart soared, because he knew exactly what he was going to do—in the next few moments, and for the rest of his life. He had never been more sure of anything.

"I was trying to make coffee," she protested.

"That thing takes forever."

She started to protest again, but then her face softened, and she looked up at him with her heart in her eyes. "Good."

"DO YOU THINK it's ready now?"

"What's ready?" Elaine felt a smile spread across her face. It simply would not go away. It was as though she had been born this way and would live the rest of her life this way.

"The coffee."

"I think it must be. I started it over an hour ago."

He rolled to one side, offering a tantalizing

glimpse of all of him, and grabbed the clock from the bedside table. "Oh, man."

"What's the matter?"

"I'm supposed to be at my folks."

She deflated a little but hid her disappointment by looking away, shaking her hair across her face. Just because everything had changed for her didn't mean it had for the rest of humanity. One of the painful discoveries she'd made as an adult was that the world did not revolve around her. And, this morning, reality lay in wait, ready to spring like a predator on her happiness.

"You'd better head for the shower," she said, being practical. "I'll phone for a taxi."

"It's walking distance."

"For you. I've got to get going."

He turned back to her, pulling her against him. "Going where?"

She hesitated. Her family usually slept late on Christmas, exchanged tasteful gifts, had a champagne brunch and then took off on vacation, to ski or sun themselves somewhere exotic. They liked to travel on Christmas Day, because it was less crowded than just before or just after the holiday. This logical program did not appeal to her in the least and hadn't for a long time. She simply went along with it because there was nothing else to do.

"To my parents' apartment, I suppose," she felt obliged to say.

"Call them and say you can't make it."

"Why can't I make it?" she asked, eyeing Tony.

"You're coming with me," he announced. "You're going to love my family. They're going to love you." His face, shadowed by the night's growth of beard, wore a lopsided smile that took all her willpower to resist.

"No way," she said, getting up from the bed. One by one, she retrieved articles of clothing, feeling tingles of remembered pleasure as she picked up each discarded piece.

"Remember what I said." He stood and pulled her against him. "I don't do one-night stands."

"I remember." She shuddered in his arms, now feeling the burden of her decision to change her life. She was different. She was brand-new, she reminded herself.

"So," said Tony, "that's what it'll turn into if you leave now."

A HALF HOUR LATER, in her couture dress minus the chain mail, and a shapeless borrowed coat from Tony's hall closet, Elaine stepped out into Christmas morning. Church bells clanged with joyous abandon and, somewhere in the distance, carolers sang. The snowstorm was over, and the sun peeked through a crack in the clouds. A sparkling carpet of dazzling white lay over everything, turning parked cars to anonymous giant marshmallows, heaps of garbage to glistening ivory sculptures. Laughing children played in the streets while their parents, cradling steaming mugs in their hands, looked on from stairways and stoops. Kids tried out new sleds and skis and radio-controlled trucks.

They encountered a dark-eyed girl with a shy smile who carried a large box as she walked along with her mother. "Tony," she said, "look what Santa brought." She lifted the lid to show off a brand-new pair of hockey skates. He winked at her mom and tugged at the end of her stocking cap. "You must have been extra good this year, kiddo."

"We're going to Prospect Park to try them out right away."

He waved at them as they headed for the bus stop. "She's one of my best left wings," he said.

"So she's in your hockey league?"

"Yeah. For the time being." A troubled crease appeared on his brow.

"The lack of funds is a big problem, isn't it?" She watched the girl and her mother at the bus stop, their faces glowing with excitement. "It doesn't have to be that way."

"I know. Better PR, bigger donations. But we can't afford better PR."

"You can if it's free."

He lifted an eyebrow. "Yeah? When are you going to have time for that?"

She smiled, suddenly sure of herself, more sure than she'd ever been in her life. "From now on, I'm going to make time. My firm's going to open a nonprofit PR division and take on some pro bono clients."

He grinned and put his arm around her. "It's good to be the boss."

As she walked at his side, she felt lighter than air. She felt as though she'd been roused from a long sleep of numbness and was finally waking up to life. This was Tony's world, this colorful, noisy, imperfect place, and it made more sense to her than her own. He was a part of this neighborhood, this tree-lined street filled with families and laughter.

There was a quality of belonging here, and as she walked through the winter morning with him, it encompassed her like a vast embrace. She heard herself singing along with the carolers and laughing at a family playing with a frisky new puppy with a bow around its neck. Everything warm and real bubbled up inside her and spilled over and, at last, after the long, strange night, she knew what it was. And it was so simple, so very simple. It was happiness, pure and unpretentious and more real than the fresh snow squeaking beneath her feet.

"'I am as merry as a schoolboy'," she said with a laugh, quoting half-remembered lines from Dickens. "'As giddy as a drunken man!'"

Tony laughed with her and pulled her close. "Good thing you smell better."

The sweet yearning she had felt for him all those years ago had never gone away. It had only grown, nurtured in the dark, secret places of her heart. The things that truly mattered had been buried under the smothering press of ambition and expectation and all the other business that had taken over her life when she wasn't paying attention. But she was free now, and she could tell her joy shone in her face when she looked up at him, because she could see an answering joy reflected in his eyes.

They didn't speak as they walked the next few blocks to the classic Prospect Park West townhouse where he'd grown up. Finally, as they stood on the sidewalk in front of the handsome, blocky building, she couldn't stay silent any longer. "You wouldn't believe how nervous I am."

He stopped walking and turned to face her, seemingly oblivious to the pedestrians who had to go around them. "Hey, do you know how long my family's been waiting for me to bring home the love of my life?"

She couldn't breathe, couldn't think. She had never, ever felt this way before, but somehow she recognized the emotion. It was the feeling of a dream coming to life. Her dream. The time stretching out before her was her own. It was up to her to decide how to spend it. She could forge ahead, fueled by ambition, toward the shadowy fate she'd glimpsed in Bobbi's desperate eyes as she'd hovered on the edge of the bridge. Or she could choose a different path to a new and unexpected destination.

"About as long," she said, "as I've been waiting to meet them."

Tony's smile turned slightly shy. "Before we go in, I need to give you something."

She frowned. "What?"

He rummaged in his pocket. "I meant to give it to you last night."

Her heart quickened. "So why don't you give it to me now?"

Right in the middle of the snowy sidewalk, he went down on one knee and handed her a small box. "Elaine St. James, this means more than you think it means." Passersby were trying to be polite and not stare but they did anyway, grinning and whispering and nudging each other. But it didn't matter. Nothing mattered but this moment, the two of them, the warmth flowing between them.

Her hands trembled as she opened the box. She gasped, taking out a key ring with a silver skate. "How on earth did you get this?"

"Don't ask," he said with a grin. "It's magic."

She stared at him and her heart started to sing every carol and love song she'd ever heard.

"One of these days," he promised her, "this is going to be a different kind of ring," he added, getting to his feet. "And you're going to say yes, Elaine. Because, well, I love you," he said. "I always have."

A warm wash of tears fell down her cheeks, and a hush of reverence gripped her. "I know," she whispered. "I know that. Tony, I love you. I'll love you forever."

She clasped the silver skate in her hand, knowing the real gift was something she hadn't expected and maybe didn't even deserve—a chance to change her life.

She buried her face against his shoulder and inhaled. A thousand hopes and dreams gave birth to a thousand more, and all the cares in the world slipped away. *I promise,* she thought. *I promise I won't blow it this time.*

They stood like that for a long time, with Christmas exploding all around them, and finally Tony pulled away and walked up to the blocky brownstone.

He opened the door to a big, loud, cluttered kitchen that smelled of baking bread and rang with laughter and conversation. Everyone turned to them when they stepped inside.

"This is Elaine," Tony said, drawing her into the room with him. "We're home."

A CATERED AFFAIR

Nancy Warren

CHAPTER ONE

MARINA SHIELDS gazed at the bite-size vol-au-vents, each flaky pastry shell containing a thumbnail of fresh Dungeness crab, a soupçon of lemon, a heady froth of crème fraîche and a festive julienne of red and green pepper.

So much was riding on such tiny dainties.

Her business, her self-respect, her bank balance. She sighed heavily. Her entire life.

Rapidly, she dotted the silver tray with the crab vol au vents among an assortment of Swedish meatballs, goat-cheese triangles, stuffed cherry tomatoes and snow-pea-wrapped prawns. Not until the balance of color and shape looked perfect to her critical eye did Marina replace her kitchen apron with one of the frilly server's aprons.

"I'm going out front," she said to her assistant, Liz. As the president, CEO and literally the chief cook and bottle washer of her catering company BonBon, Marina always spent time out front serving. It helped her gauge customer feedback about her food and—she patted the pocket of her black skirt to make sure she had a good stock of business cards—the practice allowed her to promote her fledgling company when the chance arose.

She pasted a festive, carefree smile on her face and cruised through the swing door of the small kitchen and into the main boardroom of Archer and Co.

Her professional caterer's gaze swept the room, filled to overflowing with the property management company's clients and staff. From the noise level and bursts of laughter, everyone seemed to be having a good time.

She noted a balled napkin that needed removing from the boardroom table. The ice should be checked and possibly replenished at the sushi bar, and she must remind her new waitress, Janet, to smile more.

Through the laughter and chatter Marina heard the strains of ''White Christmas.'' Anyone hoping for a white Christmas in Vancouver was indeed dreaming. In the five years she'd lived in this city, the closest she'd seen to snow on Christmas Day had been sleet. Mostly the rain was unadulterated. Not that she minded. She was always so exhausted by December twenty-fifth that she usually holed up in her apartment, munched leftover hors d'oeuvres and stayed as far away from eggnog and Christmas carols as she could get.

Last year, she and Pierre had enjoyed a lazy brunch in bed....

Fighting the pain that jabbed her in the chest, she forced her smile wider, slapping a Do Not Enter sign across Memory Lane. That had been last Christmas, when she'd been the food half of a successful catering team, engaged to her business partner and in love. A woman on the rise.

This year she was disengaged, out of love and very much alone. She was still a woman on the rise, however, only she was starting from a lot lower down. The bottom. Building a catering business from scratch for the second time.

The enormity of her task staggered her at odd moments like this one. But Marina was an optimist at heart. She knew she could make a success of her own company given half a chance. Besides, there was the small matter of revenge.

Pierre had not only cheated on her with another woman, he was also doing his level best to cheat her out of her share of the catering company they'd built together. While she now realized she'd been criminally foolish to trust that he'd honor their informal agreement, she wasn't completely without resources. If he wouldn't act honorably, she'd take what was hers by building a competing business and whipping his butt in the marketplace.

She continued to smile as she offered the tray,

thinking it must have been a caterer who'd said revenge is a dish best served cold.

Passing the boardroom table, she twitched the napkin into her pocket, glanced at the trays of ice on the sushi buffet and decided they were fine and managed to get close enough to Janet to whisper, "Smile."

Then she headed for a pair of suits, one of whom was the man who'd hired her, the other was someone she didn't know. Aaron Lepinsky was a VP and right hand to Clayton Archer, who headed the company that bore his name. Aaron had hired her after attending a similar cocktail party she'd catered a few weeks ago. That's how her success was beginning to build—slowly, through word of mouth. She hoped if she wowed Archer and Co. with this small do, she'd be asked to quote on their bigger parties.

Gliding smoothly up to the men, she offered her tray of goodies and her best smile. Beside Aaron was a tall athletic type who glanced at her as she approached. Their gazes connected and—*oh, my*—the impact almost made her stagger.

It wasn't that he was good-looking, exactly. It was more that attitude of command that drew her attention and caused her to notice the sensuality lurking in his eyes. He had dark-brown wavy hair, a little shaggy in back as though he were a week or two overdue for a trim, the kind of nose that says *I'm in charge,* a strong mouth and chin that announced *and don't you forget it* and eyes that held a person and wouldn't let go. Their color was hazel, she supposed: green and gray, a touch of blue here and there, the irises ringed with black. Gorgeous eyes that sent her messages that made her pulse flutter.

As she took a breath and got a tighter grip on her tray, Aaron smiled and said, "This is Marina Shields. It's her company doing the catering for us. Everything's great so far, Marina. Thanks." He reached for a goat-cheese triangle.

"Glad you're enjoying the food," she said weakly, wishing the man beside him would stop staring.

Wanting to give the guy a reminder about manners, she deliberately returned the stare. And immediately wished she hadn't. The pull of attraction was as strong as the first time.

"Marina, this is Clay Archer." Aaron's voice broke through and she blinked.

Clay Archer took his time selecting a vol-au-vent, and she noted how strong his hand looked, the fingers long and blunt-tipped.

Her smile went a little rigid as she watched that firm, commanding mouth devour one of the vol-au-vents. He never broke eye contact, making the act of eating an hors d'oeuvre seem both sensual and intimate. "Delicious," he said at last. "What's in it?"

"Oh, um." She was usually so polished and smooth around clients. What was the matter with her around this guy? And what on earth was in her food? "Um…some crab and crème fraîche."

One side of his mouth tilted in a crooked smile that was far too attractive for her blood pressure. There was a time when she'd have happily engaged in a light flirtation, but not anymore. Given her recent history, she was staying as far away as she could get from attractive, bossy men.

"Excuse me," she said smoothly, and moved to the next group.

Clay watched the dishy caterer strut a couple of steps and offer her tray once more. He liked the way she moved. His gaze roamed her figure and he liked that even better, noting that her sexy gait was exaggerated by a pair of strappy black stilettos—something he'd never seen before on a caterer. Those spike heels and the frilly apron could give a man ideas.

With her short, sleek shiny black hair, elfin face and men's-magazine body, Marina was at least as tasty as whatever he'd just eaten. He realized that his entire being, including his taste buds, had been so concentrated on the woman, he could have been eating toenail clippings for all he'd have noticed.

"Well, what do you think?" asked Aaron, following the direction of his gaze.

Clay said exactly what he was thinking. "She'd look better in nothing but the apron and those stilettos."

In one of those bizarre instances that sometimes occur, at the moment he'd spoken the song had ended and everyone in the room either ran out of things to say or paused to sip a drink. He hadn't bothered to lower his voice, thinking the noise would cover his unguarded remark, but there was a moment of crystal silence when his words rang out louder than the "Hallelujah Chorus."

He heard a couple of snickers near him, and the long, elegant back of Marina Shields went rigid for a second. He tensed automatically, half waiting for her heavy silver tray to come sailing at his head. But she didn't so much as glance at him, merely carried on serving while conversation heated up once more and the next Christmas carol crooned through the speakers.

"Chestnuts roasting on an open fire…" He wished it were a song about peace on earth instead. A man in trouble with a woman didn't want her getting any ideas about flame-broiled chestnuts.

Just as he was beginning to think she was going to ignore his faux pas—hell, maybe she hadn't heard him, after all—she turned, her sparkly blue eyes like frozen sapphires, an equally cool smile on her plump red lips. Slowly, she walked toward him and held out her tray.

"I saved this one for you, Mr. Archer."

There was one item left on her tray. A solitary meatball.

Clay hoped he could appreciate an ironic gesture as well as the next ignorant ape. Giving her what he hoped was an apologetic, rueful grin, he took the meatball.

"Listen, I didn't mean—" He got no farther. She'd turned on those knife-sharp heels and was already clicking her way across the Italian tile floor toward the kitchen.

He couldn't take his eyes off her.

He had a pretty shrewd idea there was an extra twitch to those sensational hips for his benefit. In spite of the knowledge that she was punishing him and he deserved it, he admired her attitude. Politely handing out goodies, she'd been gorgeous. But angry and disdainful, she was magnificent.

It was clear that he wasn't the only one who'd noticed the meatball incident. He was being regarded with expressions from outright smirks to disdain.

Swallowing a little pride, along with the meatball still clutched in his fingers, seemed to be the order of the day. With a half shrug, he tossed it in his mouth and chewed.

No one would ever know what it cost him not to spit the thing out right then and there. Because he had his pride, and he'd already damaged the caterer's, he kept his expression pleasant, but he felt like an accidental extra in one of those god-awful TV shows where they make the contestants eat insects.

He didn't know what was in this meatball, but under the savory flavors he'd expected was something sickly sweet and gooey that made him want to gag.

Manfully, he swallowed as he came to an obvious conclusion. Marina Shields might be sexy as hell, but she needed to find a new line of work. The lady was one terrible cook.

Marina fumed as she swung through the kitchen door. Why was she not surprised that Clayton Archer was nothing but a patronizing womanizer? She'd found him attractive, hadn't she?

The minute she entered the kitchen her imitation smile went south. *Jerk.*

Well, Pierre hadn't ruined her life, as hard as he'd tried, and Mr. Archer wasn't going to ruin her party. All she wanted from him was that he pay BonBon's bill in full and on time.

Passing off her empty tray to Liz, she took a deep

breath. Leaving out men she found attractive, there were loads of wonderful people in the world. Witness the loyalty of some of the staff who'd chosen to take a chance on her new company when she and Pierre split. They were all gambling, just as she was, and she wasn't going to let them down. She would build the most successful and innovative catering firm in Vancouver.

One hors d'oeuvre at a time.

Instead of handing her a full tray, Liz gave her a funny look. "Are you trying out a new meatball recipe?"

"No. I know the Swedish meatball isn't exactly cutting edge, but people like a mix of old favorites—"

"You'd better taste one," Liz interrupted.

She glanced at Liz, not liking the expression on her face. Please let it not be more bad luck. For someone just starting out, she'd already had more than her fair share of that.

She bit into the meatball and felt her eyes bug out. She chewed and almost gagged. "Water!"

Liz handed her a full glass, obviously having foreseen the need, and she gulped it trying to clear her mouth. "What was—"

"Maraschino cherries somehow ended up in the middle of the meatballs instead of capers. I'm guessing the new cook misread the recipe."

Horror buckled her stomach. "How could any-body possibly think—? Never mind. We don't have time for that now. Throw away all the meatballs. Get them off the trays. I'll get Janet's tray back and...oh, no," she moaned, realizing she'd just given her last meatball to the CEO of the company.

Now what?

CHAPTER TWO

CRÈME FRAÎCHE. What the hell was crème fraîche anyway? Clay wondered, hoping that focusing on the peculiar ingredients of a caterer would help take his mind off the utter fool he'd made of himself last night.

Normally, he considered himself smooth around women, but he had to admit, his charm had gone down with the caterer about as well as her meatball had gone down his throat. What had that been about? It was clear to him now that his assistant had been wrong. It wasn't Marina Shields who'd been the genius behind Delicieux, but her ex-partner the Frenchman. Too bad, he'd have liked to throw some more business her way, but he had to face facts. She topped the chart in beauty, but anybody who could make a meatball taste like that was rock-bottom on the catering scale.

She sure was sexy, though. He worked all morning trying to put Marina Shields out of his mind. When that didn't work, he tried at least to shake the feeling that he'd been a prize ass at the cocktail reception—but the notion wouldn't leave him. She might be a terrible cook but she didn't deserve to be embarrassed while she was working.

While Clay scrutinized the lease of a law firm that was proposing to move into one of his buildings downtown, visions of that plump-lipped mouth, firmed in anger, rose to taunt him. Marina Shields was the most attractive woman he'd met in months and he wanted to see her again.

After reading one section of the lease three times and still not taking in a word, he tossed the document on his desk, picked up his phone and punched in the accounts department. "Jan," he said, "did the catering company last night leave an invoice?"

"BonBon? Sure did. With a box of her chocolates just waiting to be devoured." Jan sighed. "I wish all invoices came with chocolate."

He chuckled and squelched the impulse to suggest she toss the candies in the garbage. God knew what they'd taste like. "Did you pay it yet?"

"No," she sounded puzzled. "I put it in the payables file to be processed. It should go out in the next batch."

"Could you cut the check today?"

"Today?" Surprise lilted her voice.

"As a favor to me? Long story, but it would help me out of a jam."

"Good thing there's chocolate involved," Jan

said, in her usual breezy, unflappable manner. "I'll have it on your desk by the end of the day."

"Thanks," he said. "I owe you one."

MARINA SLIPPED into her black woolen coat, pulled on black leather gloves and took a quick peek out the window to see if an umbrella would be required. The evening was dry for a change so she left her umbrella in her bag. A frown creased her forehead as she locked up and turned out the lights.

Her discussion with Alexei, one of her new kitchen hires, hadn't gone well. He'd been given the job of making the meatballs for last night's event and he swore to her he'd followed the recipe and included capers, not cherries in the center. He'd looked revolted when she'd suggested he might have made such an error and she'd ended up completely confused. She wanted to believe him, but if she did, then how on earth had such a mistake happened?

She decided she'd better keep a close eye on him for signs of drug or alcohol abuse, and wished there were someone she could share her troubles with, which only reminded her of Pierre. It was with a heavy heart that she turned the deadbolt on her front door and let herself out, locking up behind her.

She'd chosen the premises partly because they gave her a Robson Street address for her letterhead, though in truth this wasn't the best part of Robson.

She shared her block with a tattoo parlor, a seedy-looking discount furniture place and a social housing office. But the rent was cheap, the industrial kitchen huge and, until she could afford better, it suited her needs.

However, she hadn't worked in this neighborhood for several months without developing keen survival instincts. From her peripheral vision she saw a lone man pull away from the front window of the furniture shop and move toward her. She grabbed her purse strap tight and flipped her key ring until the pepper spray was in her hand, then turned to face him.

"Ms. Shields?"

The closest streetlight was burned out so his face was in shadow. All she saw was the breath turning to puffs of fog as he spoke. The voice was familiar though, cultured and crisp, and he knew her name.

"Yes?" She still held her pepper spray at the ready and knew she could be back inside her premises with the door locked in a matter of seconds. Even so, this tall stranger made her heart pound.

"It's Clay Archer. We met last night." He remained a couple of paces away, his hands behind his back.

Smart fellow not to come any closer. She felt like giving him a good squirt of pepper spray anyway, just for being the kind of man who made lewd comments about women. "What can I do for you, Mr. Archer?" she asked in a frigid tone.

"You can accept my most humble and abject apology for my inappropriate remark last night."

"Humble and abject." She rolled the words around, considering. "Yes, that's exactly how you should feel. Your behavior was unprofessional and embarrassed me."

"I know," he said softly. "I'm sorry."

The shorter, simpler apology sounded much more sincere and she could tell he really meant the words. He'd come all this way to apologize, and from a certain stiff way he held himself, she had a feeling he was cold.

"How long have you been standing here?"

"A half hour or so."

"You should have come inside."

"I figured if you were going to slap my face, or whack me with your purse or something, I'd just as soon not have an audience."

She smiled. "You underestimate me, Mr. Archer. I was about to blast you with my pepper spray." She opened her palm so he could see the small canister before dropping her keys into her pocket.

From behind his back he produced a florist's bouquet of white roses, which looked ethereal in the dimness. In the other hand was a business envelope.

The envelope came toward her first. "Your check for last night's event. Thank you."

Having the CEO abject and humble could certainly speed up the accounting cycle she mused as she took the envelope and dropped it in her bag.

He stepped closer and handed her the flowers. "Since it is the season of peace, I chose the white ones."

In spite of herself, she was charmed. Their scent was slight, but enough to bring thoughts of summer in the middle of winter. "Thank you."

A bus rolled by, belching exhaust.

"Will you have dinner with me?"

"Really, the flowers are enough. I accept your apology, Mr. Archer."

"It's Clay, and I was hoping we'd moved beyond the apology stage to the starting-over stage. I was thinking of dinner as a date."

"I see," she said, dipping her nose toward the roses once more. "So abject and humble are behind you?"

Even in the darkness she could see his eyes twinkle. He was too sure of himself, too successful, too damned seductive. "I'll be as abject and humble as I've ever been if you'll say yes."

"I'm sorry, Clay, I can't."

He nodded solemnly, his smile fading. "There's someone else?"

Clearly, lack of self-confidence was not his problem.

"No. This is my busy time of year. I'm booked almost every night between now and Christmas with catering jobs."

He rocked back on his heels. "How about tonight?"

"Is this how you built your company?" she asked. "By never taking no for an answer?"

He laughed softly. "It's worked, hasn't it?"

"Not with me. I've got to plan menus and get my produce orders completed tonight."

"How about breakfast then? Tomorrow."

He was impossible. "Thanks for the flowers," she said, turning away.

"Lunch?"

"Good night."

"Can I drive you home?"

"No."

She headed for the panel van emblazoned with her company logo. She had parking in the back, but the van had been broken into twice and then the tires slashed. Now they had to keep moving it every two hours to avoid parking tickets.

Clayton Archer fell into step. "I really am sorry, you know. I could give you character references."

She fought a laugh. His tone was just goofy

enough to make her forget how truly angry she'd been with him. "Character references for a date?"

"If that's what it takes."

"I'm not sure how that would work. Would you give me the phone numbers of former women in your life? Let me ask them questions about you?"

He squirmed visibly, but managed a semi-confident reply. "Absolutely. I've got nothing to hide."

"I am almost tempted." She wondered what women would say about him. *Persistent* would no doubt top the list. "But I really have to put my business first. Thank you again for the flowers and the prompt payment of my bill." She shifted things so she could shake his hand, then unlocked her van door. He opened the door and held it for her while she scrambled in. He was still standing there when she pulled into the sparse traffic.

It would have been nice to go to a decent restaurant with an attractive man, and she was fairly certain she wouldn't be bored. But, after Pierre, she was allergic to attractive, dynamic men.

CHAPTER THREE

"PASS ME some more of the chocolates, will you Liz?"

Marina adjusted her serving apron and prepared to go back out with her signature chocolates, the final item on tonight's menu for the accounting firm's reception she was catering.

CBF Accounting had opened the whole of their corporate headquarters on Pender Street to their clients and staff. People were clustered in the foyer, meeting rooms, individual offices and the hallways. She walked through, passing out chocolates and checking that everything was fine.

She rounded a corner and almost dropped her tray.

Clayton Archer stood chatting to the senior partner, a glass of red wine in hand. He glanced up and smiled at her, the kind of smile that turned her innards to the same consistency as her champagne truffle. He did not appear surprised to see her.

"Hello, Marina," Gordon Blake, the B in CBF, greeted her heartily, his gaze falling greedily to her tray. Clay's eyes were also greedy, but they stared at her, not her chocolates.

Mr. Blake said, "My wife hasn't stopped raving about these chocolates since she tasted them at the last do you catered for us."

Marina smiled, glad she'd spent the extra money on having her company name embossed on gold gift boxes for her chocolates. "I've got a box all packed for you to take home to her."

He selected a nut cluster then turned to Clay. "Have you met Marina Shields, Clay? She's terrific."

"We've met," he said, with a smoldering glance her way. "I think she's terrific, too."

"Try one of these candies. They're sensational."

Clay looked as though he'd rather throw himself out of the window, and, with a pang, she realized the last thing she'd fed him had been that revolting meatball. He selected the smallest thing he could find, which turned out to be a dark chocolate truffle. He bit into it and seemed to sigh in relief. "You're right. It is terrific."

"Would you like a box for your wife?" she asked him sweetly.

"I'm single," he said, and helped himself to another truffle.

She murmured an excuse and turned away. So he

was single. He hadn't said, and she was cynical enough to wonder.

She was rearranging a buffet table when she felt his presence behind her. There must have been a hundred people there, but she knew instantly that the man standing behind her was Clay.

"Great party," he said.

"I didn't know you were a CBF client," she replied.

"Actually, they're one of my clients. I own this building."

Clay had planned to drop by for fifteen minutes tops, but the quarter hour had turned into a half and then an hour. He could barely keep his eyes off Marina. She was wearing those high heels again, which did amazing things for her legs, and a black skirt that fit her curves with tantalizing faithfulness.

It wasn't merely her sexy look that drew him, however, it was the indefinable way she managed to work the room, laughing and chatting as she went, but always keeping the food circulating, the clients happy.

She was, he realized, a great hostess. He'd love to see her in her own home, presiding over dinner parties or cocktail parties. An image flashed in his mind of her in a long black gown, no apron, hosting an elegant dinner party. With a start, he realized he'd projected her into his own home.

Not that it was all that surprising he should imagine a good hostess in his home. That was why he'd bought that barn of a place in Shaughnessy, wasn't it? To entertain clients?

He shifted uncomfortably. Clay had never been any good at lying to himself. The truth was, he'd bought the house because it represented everything he'd never known growing up. Permanence, stability, wealth, social position—and most of all, it was a home for building a family. Oh, he'd had a happy home. He was luckier than a lot of kids he'd grown up with, but his parents had been the working poor, always struggling, never getting ahead. They'd have been a lot happier with some money to fall back on.

He'd bought the mansion more than a year ago, and once renovations had ceased to occupy him, he'd started to rattle around the great place like a lone silver ball in a pinball machine.

Truth was, he was ready to settle down, and there was nothing like the Christmas season to make a man long for family. The right woman would be a start. Maybe that's why Marina appealed to him so strongly. She was, he realized, a little like his mom. Strong, independent, gorgeous and hellishly hard on him.

"You're staring at me," Marina admonished him. She'd walked bang up to him to whisper the criticism, and her color was heightened, which gave him the uncomfortable feeling he'd been staring for a while.

"I'm sorry," he said. "I was thinking about something else."

She laughed, but it wasn't the most carefree sound he'd ever heard. "That's not very flattering."

"I was thinking about my mother. You remind me of her a little."

"Do you practice these stunningly effective pickup lines or do they just come to you like magic?"

He shook his head, wondering why he was only oafish with the one woman he so wanted to impress. "That came out wrong. I meant it as a compliment. My mom is amazing."

She raised her brows slightly and he could see he had to apply the spade a little harder if he was going to dig himself out of this one. "I didn't mean you look like her. Well, you're beautiful," he said stating the obvious. "My mom was, too, but she faded. Too much manual labor, too much worry, too little money."

At least he'd been able to take his mother's burdens on at last. He'd settled his parents in Florida, happy to ease them into a retirement of comfort after they'd worked so hard all their lives just to scrape by.

Maybe she didn't feel as complimented as he'd

intended, but he saw interest light her eyes. "Really? For some reason I assumed you'd come from a privileged background."

"No ma'am. I'm from the working poor. Will my disadvantaged background soften your opinion of me and encourage you to change your mind and give me a chance?"

She shook her head, but he liked the small smile playing over her lips. "You never give up, do you?"

"Not when it's something I really want." He touched her wrist, where the skin was soft and smooth, and he felt her shiver. "And I really want you."

Her blush delighted him. Despite her standoffish attitude, he'd caught her gaze on him several times when she'd thought he wasn't looking. Unless he missed his guess, the powerful attraction went both ways.

"THIS ISN'T a coincidence, is it?" Marina didn't know whether to laugh or be angry as she bumped into Clay for the fifth time that week. She glanced around at the jugglers, mimes and balloon artists who'd just put on a charity show for kids. Now they were at a reception hosted by the corporate client who'd sponsored the event.

Clay grinned down at her, looking more pleased

with himself than abashed. "I told you I wanted to see you again."

"Do you always get what you want?"

"If I want it badly enough, pretty much. Yes."

A shiver of…something danced up her spine. She couldn't identify the emotion. Apprehension? Flattery? Irritation? She was aware of all three, but it was none of them that had her skin feeling ultrasensitive and her breath hitching slightly as she inhaled. No. That was desire.

And it was the last thing she wanted to feel with a man who pushed all her *never again* buttons. Besides, although he seemed like a normal enough man—if a little on the pushy side—she didn't think it was clairvoyance that had him gravitating to her parties day after day. "Are you having me followed?"

He chuckled. "Nothing so drastic. My secretary simply sorts through the invites and finds out which ones you're catering."

"You were invited to all these events?" The business socials she could understand, but a charity gala?

Clay rubbed the end of his nose, probably to check if it was growing longer. "Janice, my secretary, has an amazing network. I don't question her information. You should be flattered. Normally I only go to the events I absolutely have to, but this week I haven't eaten anything bigger than a poker chip. And, by the way, what is crème fraîche?''

She forced herself not to respond to the teasing note in his voice, or the seductive gleam in his eyes. He'd been totally up front with her about his intentions; she had to be as clear in her refusal. She needed to stamp out the sparks of desire just as Smokey the Bear would stomp out a burning cigarette in a tinder-dry forest.

She donned a cool smile. ''I'm sorry, Clay, but you're wasting your time—and your secretary's. I have to devote all my time and energy to building my business.''

He nodded. ''I respect that. I'm a selfmade man. But here's a piece of free advice from a guy who's been there. Don't work so hard you lose all the fun in life.''

Not knowing how to answer him, she didn't, and moved mechanically away, taking a full tray back to the kitchen in her preoccupation with his words.

She expected that her clear refusal would be the end of it, and she forced herself to believe she'd done the right thing.

SURPRISE HELD her motionless when she saw Clay the following day at an art gallery board members' Christmas luncheon.

''Are you on the board of the art gallery, too?''

she asked him curtly as she put his salmon in front of him none too gently.

"No. One of our vice presidents is, but he wasn't able to make it at the last minute, so I came instead."

"Really. Why couldn't he come?" Her question was rude, but she didn't believe a word of Clay's story.

She knew she was right when he leaned closer so he could whisper in her ear. She didn't want his confidence. Didn't want him so close she could smell the spicy scent of his shaving balm. Didn't want him so close his cheek brushed against her hair. So close his lips were in kissing range of her ear when he whispered, "He's representing me at the board of trade luncheon."

It was difficult not to be flattered when a man running a multimillion-dollar firm was taking time out of his schedule to attend events BonBon was catering, when he knew damn well they'd be lucky to have five minutes together.

Not only was she flattered, but she began dressing for work as though for a date. Even as she cursed herself for doing it, she took extra pains with her makeup and wore a few of her sexier tops.

Apart from flirting with Clay, she was passing out a lot of business cards. As she'd hoped, she was starting to get calls to quote on jobs for the spring and summer. With luck, she could be operating in the black by this time next year.

Perhaps Clay was right, she thought, and she should stop working so hard. Maybe give him a chance. What could one date hurt? She wasn't so busy she couldn't spare a few hours with an interesting man.

She pondered the idea as she headed for a meeting with a society matron in West Vancouver. The woman's daughter was getting married and they wanted a garden wedding in their own home.

It wasn't an enormous job, but a prestigious one, and Marina knew from her experience with Delicieux how profitable weddings could be.

She was a few minutes early. She parked and headed up the path to the house, a smile on her face as she wondered what strings Clay would have to pull to score an invitation to the wedding.

But the smile froze when she saw the handsome man with meticulously styled black hair coming down the path toward her, jotting something in a black leather binder.

She saw him first and had a moment to register that her biggest competition, her former fiancé, had also been invited to quote on the job. She was pleased to note that she felt nothing but vague disgust when she saw her former lover.

He saw her and she felt his recoil before his

smooth charm covered his face like a mask. "Marina, *ma chere,*" he said, and pressed a Gallic kiss to each cheek. "You look wonderful."

"Hello, Pierre," she said, wondering how she'd ever believed herself in love with his slick looks and the phony charm he dished up like an overpriced gourmet meal. On the menu was *charm à la français* with a dollop of *je ne sais quoi* served with an enormous side dish of hand gestures and cheek kissing.

He was as bright and showy as the Eiffel Tower in Las Vegas. And as authentic. He passed himself off as a Parisian, but Marina knew he came from a working-class suburb of Montreal—which reminded her of something that irked. "You're going to have to take the Cordon Bleu hype out of your ads, Pierre. It's me who earned it. Not you."

His smile grew even more charming. "Marina, I am waiting for you to come back. Delicieux needs you." He stepped closer, touching a finger to her cheek. "I need you."

She snorted. "You should have thought of that before you played hide the cocktail weenie with that temp waitress."

"Don't be provincial, darling. You know that meant nothing."

Her blood was pounding against her temple. "We agreed when we went into partnership that if it didn't work out, the remaining partner would buy the other out, or we'd sell the business. I expect you to honor our agreement.''

She didn't know why she bothered even bringing up the subject. She'd asked him, her lawyer had become involved, but the bottom line was that without any written agreement, there was nothing she could do.

She still hadn't decided whether she was angrier at Pierre for his personal betrayal or for his lack of business integrity. However, the person she most scorned was herself for being so naive. She'd loved their arrangement; she'd looked after the cooking and staff, and he handled the business side. They both did what suited them best. Never again, she promised herself. From now on she handled everything.

''Come back to Delicieux where you belong and stop making a fool of yourself trying to upstage me,'' he said with slightly less charm.

''Excuse me. I have an appointment,'' Marina said, and continued to the front door, deciding right then and there that she'd provide twice the meal at half the cost in order to get this job. She'd lose money, of course, but she'd eat a loss to beat Pierre.

If he wouldn't honor their agreement, she'd take her half of the business the hard way. By the time she got to the front door, she was designing a meal at a price this woman would be a fool to turn down.

By the time she left a little over an hour later, she knew her client was no fool, and she had a signed contract.

Take that, Pierre!

As she drove the winding Marine Drive, enjoying her small, if costly triumph, she noted Christmas lights on one of the container ships sitting in port waiting to be unloaded. Village shop windows sported elegant Santas, party dresses that made her drool with longing, bright-colored toys for kids.

An elderly woman walked a white poodle, which minced along wearing a bright red sweater and matching beret. Rhinestones glittered from the dog's collar—at least Marina assumed they were rhinestones, though for all she knew they were diamonds. The animal had an attitude as it strutted, nose in the air, that suddenly reminded her of Pierre. She laughed, and the next thing she knew she was singing along to ''Little Drummer Boy'' on her car radio.

It was a beautiful, clear day and she felt the urge to celebrate both her new contract and the fact that she'd confronted Pierre about his philandering and dishonesty.

She didn't want to celebrate alone. She'd show Clay Archer she wasn't all work and no play.

Pulling into the first parking spot she could find,

she called Liz on her cell phone. "We did it! Mrs. Braithwaite signed the contract."

"Hey, that's great," Liz cried.

"Best of all, I met Pierre as I was going in, so he'll know I know we beat him. How are things there?"

"Everything's under control for the Ashton dinner tonight. The crab cakes are all assembled, the lamb's ready to roast, the vegetables are done. François is making the tiramisu now."

"Can you manage without me for a couple more hours?"

"Sure."

"I'll be in around four. I'll keep my cell on in case you need me."

While she had her phone in her hand, and before she could think of all the reasons why this was a bad idea, she followed her impulse and called Archer and Co. She asked for Clayton Archer and gave her name, leaving it in fate's hands as to whether he'd be in the office and take her call.

Fate handed him to her with gratifying speed.

"Marina?" He sounded as though he thought the call might be a hoax.

"You sound more shocked than delighted to hear from me."

"I'm both. What's up?"

She swallowed and did her best to sound casual.

"I'm taking your advice and playing hooky for a few hours. I wondered if you could get away."

"Now?"

She felt like an idiot. He was a busy man and this was a stupid idea. "Well, yes. But of course I'm sure you're busy. It was an impulse."

There was a short pause and she knew he must be mentally cataloguing everything on his schedule, trying to work out if he could get away. "Give me half an hour," he said. "And tell me where to meet you."

She'd been so sure he'd have to turn her down that when he said yes, she realized how much she needed him right now. Her confrontation with Pierre had thrown her, and somehow Clay seemed like the antidote to her former fiancé.

Where to meet? She didn't have a clue. She gazed up across the water at Stanley Park plunked in the middle of the city and thought of how long it had been since she'd been inside the park. "Lost Lagoon," she said.

The half hour gave her time to drive over Lion's Gate Bridge to pick up a loaf of whole-wheat bread and some wild-bird seed. She hadn't fed the ducks and swans in the park since she'd first moved here. She couldn't wait.

Clay was right on time, striding into view in his

business suit and a navy overcoat and looking so drop-dead gorgeous her stomach gave a funny lurch.

He stepped close and studied her unabashedly. She did the same, understanding his behavior. This was the first time they'd seen each other outside of her work. The first time she'd admitted she returned his attraction. And the nervous quivers in her stomach were telling her she'd tacitly agreed to change their relationship from caterer and client to woman and man.

His eyes were serious as he contemplated her. "You've got some color in your cheeks. The fresh air is already doing you good."

She didn't bother telling him it was his nearness and the way he was staring at her that heightened her color.

"I'm glad you called," he said.

"I'm glad you came." And she was, she realized, even if she was going against her own best interests. But, somehow, seeing Pierre today made her realize how foolish and cowardly she'd been to refuse to get involved with one man because of the sins of another.

Clay reached for her gloved hand and she didn't protest. They set off hand in hand around the lagoon with its enormous Christmas tree in the center.

She was aware of the quiet, steady swish of traffic along the causeway, of the chatter and squawk of

Canada geese, and the frenzied flapping of wings, the quacking, honking and hissing as she scattered seed for the waterfowl. But mostly she was aware of the quiet warmth of their clasped hands.

"What did you do today?" he asked.

"I snagged a new client and a very nice wedding catering job." She paused, wondering if she should stop there, but the thrill of her victory was too great to keep to herself. "And I beat out my old…partner, Pierre—the scumbag."

She wished she hadn't stumbled over how to refer to Pierre. She was certain Clay had noticed, as his next words proved. "Partner? Or lover?"

Cold air filled her lungs as she took a deep breath. "Both."

"I take it things didn't end too well."

"He cheated me both personally and professionally." The last thing she should be doing was telling Clay the story. She'd never told anyone all the details—it was too humiliating at the time. Now, she was ready to unburden herself. They stopped for coffee at an outdoor vending booth and found a park bench. Without quite knowing how it happened, she told him the whole story.

"Is Pierre the real reason you've been avoiding me?"

She nodded. "I suppose so."

"I am nothing like him."

She studied him. The wind had brought ruddy color to his cheeks, and mussed his hair. His eyes were the colors of the park. The deep green of evergreens, the soft browns of winter earth, the silver gray of the clouds rolling in overhead. Christmas lights twinkled and she felt the same foolish twinkle within her.

"Finished?" he asked almost gruffly as the moment stretched.

"Yes," she said and handed him her empty cardboard cup. He tossed both in the nearest trash can and then pulled her to her feet.

She knew what was coming and didn't fight or turn from it; in fact, she smiled slightly as those intense eyes bored into hers. He pulled off his right glove and touched her cheek then slipped his fingers into her hair as he leaned forward and closed his mouth over hers.

And she knew in that instant exactly why she'd called him. She'd wanted this. Maybe even needed it. Pierre was behind her. She realized with a start that even the idea of revenge was behind her. Her company, her very own company, was going to make it. Pierre and Delicieux were in the past. BonBon was her future.

She leaned into the kiss. Exploring this intriguing attraction to Clay was also her future. His lips were cold on hers and then rapidly warmed as they shared body heat. More than body heat, there was some kind of current passing back and forth between them that made her moan softly, deep in her throat.

He pulled her tighter, wrapping his arms around her and deepening the kiss, and she opened her mouth to him greedily, tasting coffee and potent male animal.

Just before she fainted from lack of breath, Clay raised his head. She felt his gaze questioning her as he studied her face. He dragged in a breath. "Marina…" he said huskily.

Her lips felt much too cold and bereft without his warm mouth on them. She rose on tiptoe to indulge in a little more kissing, pushing Pierre even farther into her past and this man more firmly into her present.

"When can I see you?" Clay asked roughly when they broke apart. "I mean really see you."

She felt so breathless and churned up inside simply from two kisses; she didn't dare imagine what he could do to her if she let herself go completely.

She knew herself. If she got involved with him, she'd fall into that wonderful spell of not being able to get enough of each other. She'd obsess about Clay when she needed to concentrate on her business.

She shook her head. "I can't. I have to focus on my business, at least until after Christmas," she all but wailed. If he couldn't respect that, she knew they had no future. "It's only a couple of more weeks."

"I know I shouldn't push you, but I'm not known for my patience."

She smiled up at him. "I've noticed."

"Promise you'll call me like you did today if you get a break in your schedule."

"What about your business?"

"Unlike you, this is my quiet time."

"Oh." She glanced at her watch and gasped. "I've got to get back. I've got an event tonight." Deliberately, she gave him no information. It was becoming a game, she realized, to see how many of her events he could attend. She wondered if he was enjoying playing cat and mouse half as much as she was.

They walked back to their cars hand in hand. "Need a lift to the Ashtons?"

She laughed, not at all surprised that he'd be at her catered dinner tonight. "Do you have a spy in my camp?"

"No. My secretary enjoys the challenge."

"You need to give that woman a raise. She's amazing."

"She is. Plus, she knows I'm smitten."

"Oh, well…" She trailed off, feeling a blush rise. He was so absolutely in-her-face honest about his attraction to her that she didn't know how to reply. She was a lot less certain of her own feelings.

He didn't seem to expect an answer, merely tipped her chin and gave her a last quick kiss before holding open her van door.

"See you tonight," he said after she'd scrambled in. She found herself looking forward to it.

She belted out Christmas carols along with the radio as she headed back to her commercial kitchen, feeling excitement and optimism bubble through her veins.

She walked into the kitchen still singing "Deck the Halls," then ground to a halt at the sight of Liz's face. "What is it?"

Her friend and assistant was near tears. "I don't know how it happened, but a fuse must have blown in the oven and no one noticed. Nothing's baked."

Panic gripped Marina's throat in a stranglehold but she swallowed and forced herself to stay calm. She glanced at her watch. "We still have time—"

"That's not all. Our order got lost somehow at the produce place."

Anger bubbled in Marina's stomach more violently than the water in the industrial stockpot. She focused on the anger. It stopped the despair from floating to the top.

CHAPTER FOUR

SHE KISSED like an angel, Clay thought, then grimaced at himself in the mirror as he shaved. It must be the seasonal fixation with angels getting to him. He had no idea how an angel would kiss, but he doubted it would be a bit like the way Marina had kissed him. That had been more earthy than heavenly, and she was definitely more woman than angel.

She might not realize it yet, but she'd also answered a question that had been bothering him. She was as wildly attracted to him as he was to her.

Her kisses told him so.

Marina was too busy with work to get involved with him. He could respect that. But maybe he could drive her home after work tonight. Maybe they could treat the next couple of weeks like extended foreplay. They could spend what little time she could spare together, and that would give him an opportunity to make her want him as much as he wanted her.

Because on one point he was determined. When

he finally took her to bed, she was going to be as eager for the event as he was himself.

Well, since that might not be humanly possible, he'd settle for close.

He dressed with more care than he'd usually waste on such an evening. He even took a couple of minutes to vacuum his car, hoping someone from her staff could drive home the kitchen van and he could drive her home.

He had high hopes when he entered the Ashtons' gracious home, only to have an unforeseen disaster greet his eyes the minute he was ushered into the ballroom-size living room. Meghan Riley was staring at him with the same delight a black widow spider might accord a juicy bluebottle that has tangled its feet in her sticky web.

Damn. He should have figured she'd be here. Truth was, he'd been so caught up with one woman he'd forgotten former lovers existed.

Well, Meghan had seen him now. He'd have to make the best of it. He wished he had some acting lessons behind him and could pull off a convincing *nice to see you but we won't be picking up where we left off.*

''Meghan,'' he said, walking toward her with his hand held out.

She ignored it and planted a good one right on his mouth before he could evade.

"Merry Christmas," she said.

"You, too." From the unpleasantly sticky sensation on his lips, he had a feeling she'd just shared her bright-red lipstick with him. He resisted the impulse to wipe his mouth. Breaking off their relationship last year had been far from easy and he knew he'd hurt her.

She took his hand and pulled him down beside her on the couch, then snuggled closer so her hip, clad in silky gray pants, brushed his. She had a shiny silver tank top on and leaned forward a little, giving him a great view of her spectacular cleavage. "It's so wonderful to see you."

She'd obviously seen him come in alone and appeared delighted with the prospect.

While he tried to think of a graceful way out of this couch, he said, "Great to see you, too."

A hand settled on his thigh, a little higher than necessary in his opinion, and he shifted, trying to move away.

The hair prickled on the back of his neck and he knew, just as early humans had known when there was a saber-toothed tiger after them, that Marina had entered the room.

Yes. That was her low, musical voice not far behind him. Any second now, she was going to see him sitting on this couch with a woman all but perched on his lap, her lipstick staining his mouth and her hand sitting cozily on his thigh.

"So, Meghan. Are you seeing anyone?" He asked in a voice loud enough that the Ashtons' next-door neighbors would hear him.

Instantly he realized his error. Meghan squeezed even closer. "No," she said, giving him a sultry look. "I'm not."

A pair of stilettos, red this time, came into view. "I am," he said quickly. "Seeing someone, I mean."

He raised his gaze and found Marina heading over, but where he'd expected some kind of feminine outrage, he saw worry. Had he done that to her? Had that lowlife Pierre left her believing all men were unfaithful?

"You're seeing someone?" Meghan's smile dimmed. "Where is she?"

"She had to work tonight." He let his gaze meet and linger on Marina's while he chose an appetizer at random.

The woman beside him waved away the tray irritably. "Is it serious?"

Oh, damn. How to answer that one with Marina standing right there, her brows raised slightly as though she was just as interested in his answer.

He decided the truth might scare Marina, but she deserved it anyway. "I think so." He bit into one of those little pastry things with cream and crab that he'd come to love. "I think it's very serious."

What was he doing? Practically admitting undying love to a woman too busy to spend an evening with him? A woman he'd kissed for the first time this afternoon?

Hell, yes. That's exactly what he was doing. There was nothing scientific or planned about his feelings, but he'd watched Marina for weeks now, and he'd seen how hard she worked, only guessing at how many hours she put in before he saw her at the various functions. She was professional, charming and, apart from her meatballs, he had to admit her food was terrific.

She was terrific.

He had a strong notion that she was the woman he wanted permanently in his life. Now, all he had to do was wait patiently for a few weeks and ask her out sometime in January.

Oh, yeah. That was going to happen. He and patience weren't exactly on intimate terms.

Meghan excused herself from his side and he watched her cross the room to join a group that included at least two men he knew were single.

With a sigh of relief, he rose and decided to indulge in some serious flirting with the caterer. Maybe he could find out if it was Meghan who'd put the lines of stress between her brows or if he was responsible, or if, hard to believe, this had nothing to do with him.

"I had a great time this afternoon," he said. He

hoped she'd tell him what was bothering her so he could fix it.

Handing him one of the red-and-gold Christmas napkins, she leaned forward and dropped her voice. ''You might want to wipe the red lipstick off your mouth. It clashes with your tie.''

He wiped his mouth. ''That was…'' He shrugged helplessly.

''I know,'' she said. And somehow he believed she did know that though Meghan and he had been lovers, they'd never been serious.

For all her soft assurance, that slight worry frown was still pulling her brows together. He longed to kiss the spot and soothe her troubles away. ''What's the matter?''

Surprise showed in her eyes. She didn't bother to deny that she was worried, but she didn't answer his question, either. ''You're perceptive,'' she said.

''Are those crab cakes?'' a male voice boomed at Clay's elbow. Immediately, Marina put on her hostess smile and offered the tray. ''They sure are. Made from local Dungeness crab.''

Recalled to her duties, she moved on once his meaty paws had scoffed three of the crab cakes. ''Jim Bennett,'' he said, offering Clay his hand. ''I'm not supposed to eat anything good anymore with my high cholesterol. Have to sneak the stuff when my wife's not around.''

Clay introduced himself and they continued chatting, but all the while he watched Marina make her way around the crowd. It struck him that she was always smiling, always charming, but, as the hired help, she was on the outside looking in. Damn it, he wanted her to join the party for once.

She disappeared into the kitchen and he waited impatiently for her to reappear. Two waitresses were cruising the room so the food kept circulating, but he'd been to enough of these affairs to know that once Marina swapped aprons, she remained a server. What had happened to her?

Deciding that this afternoon had changed their relationship to the point where he could go into the kitchen and check on her—something he'd never before done—he followed the path Marina had taken earlier, deciding he'd ask for a glass of water if anybody challenged him.

No one did, and he soon found himself in a kitchen straight out of *Gourmet* magazine, with stainless appliances, acres of black marble countertops and fancy tile floor. He didn't know what a catering staff was supposed to look like behind the scenes, but this one didn't look good.

A young man with a white kerchief tied round his head and a white chef's coat was muttering angrily, his face alarmingly red. One woman he'd never seen before was crying, and Marina didn't look far behind. She'd turned a startled, almost guilty countenance his way when the door opened. "Can I do something for you, Clay?"

"Yes." He strode forward and stopped just short

of taking her in his arms. If he'd ever seen a woman who needed a hug, she was standing in front of him now. "You can tell me what's wrong. Are you sick?"

Her laugh was bitter and verged on hysteria. "I'm sick all right. I'm sick of disasters and bad luck."

"Tell me," he urged.

She looked stubborn for a moment, and he waited for her to toss him out of the kitchen with a thanks but no thanks. But she didn't. She gazed up at him and her eyes went watery.

"Honey, what is it?" He was barely aware he'd used the endearment, so focused was he on her distress.

The flesh around Marina's eyes had a pinched look, almost as though she were squinting. He rather thought it was the effort not to cry.

"Tell me," he said again, more urgently this time.

"The cakes, the desserts, my signature bonbons." She shook her head and gestured helplessly behind her. He immediately saw the problem. Open bakery boxes revealed smashed chocolates, a cake dented in on one side and little puffy things with chocolate and cream that appeared stomped on.

"Someone loaded the van wrong," she said, her voice wavering. "Those boxes should have gone on the top, but they ended up under the chafing dishes."

"I loaded the boxes. I already told you I put them on top," the guy in the white hat grumbled.

Marina opened her lips, and Clay felt the tension buzzing in the room. "Okay," he said. "Forget about blame now. We need to fix this." He pulled Marina close, seeing the dark circles under her eyes, the strain. She might hit him over the head with a frying pan for what he was about to do, but he'd take the chance and help her.

"You," he said to the grumpy guy in the hat. "Find a bakery that's open—a grocery store if there's nowhere else—and buy some cakes." He pulled out his wallet and passed over some bills.

His decisiveness seemed to breathe life back into the woman in his arms. "I'll pay for those," she protested.

"We'll sort it out later."

She nodded and suddenly seemed to pull herself together. "And while you're out, Miguel, stop in at the shop and bring six more boxes of chocolates. And pack them all carefully."

The guy looked as though he were about to bluster, so Clay turned to him and barked, "Go."

CHAPTER FIVE

"I DON'T THINK I could have made it through to-night without you," Marina said. They were in her shop sipping brandy. She'd told him it was the good stuff that she kept for the Courvoisier truffles.

"You would have been fine without me."

"Oh, I know. But," she stared at him and her blue eyes were clear and direct, "I liked having you there. I liked being able to lean on you, just for a minute."

He understood. She was telling him something akin to what he'd told Meghan in her hearing. In some bizarre fashion, over bits of shrimp and dainties with goat cheese, over the ubiquitous crème fraîche and caviar and toast points, they'd become important to each other.

He sipped cognac, feeling the warmth spread through him. He wanted to make love to this woman, sitting across the beat-up countertop, so badly he had to grit his teeth to stop himself from asking her to come home with him.

She'd probably say yes, if only because she had

had a lousy night, was feeling grateful to him and was in a vulnerable state. He didn't want her on those terms. He wanted her in his bed because she was crazy about him.

To get his mind out of his trousers, he went back to something he'd filed away earlier.

"You said when I first came into the kitchen, that there had been other cases of bad luck."

"Beginner's luck, I guess. Only I'm having nothing but bad luck."

"You've never said anything about it," he said.

She grimaced. "I don't want to obsess over the negative. We pulled another one out of the fire. That's all that matters."

"Indulge me. Tell me what's been going on."

Slowly, she sipped her drink, licking a drop from her lower lip. She could have no idea how much the gesture made him want to make love to her right here, where they probably chopped vegetables and kneaded bread. Or up against the stainless-steel industrial-size fridge.

He simply wasn't going to be able to wait until the New Year. But he sensed that now was not the time to tell her that. Besides, something else was bothering him, and by concentrating on the series of unfortunate coincidences, he was able to sidetrack his lust—temporarily.

As she detailed the van break-ins, the switched

ingredients in the food—which explained the inedible meatballs—the oven failure, the lost orders and finally today's broken chocolates and desserts, his amazement at her resilience grew.

What she couldn't see—probably because she was too stressed out—was that there was something suspicious about so much "bad luck" hitting one fledgling enterprise.

"Those things could seriously mess with your reputation, you know."

"Yes," she agreed. "I know. The only one I didn't catch in time was the maraschino meatballs."

Her eyes twinkled as she stared at him.

His disgust must have shown on his face because she snorted with laughter. "I was going to apologize and explain it to you but I decided I couldn't imagine a more fitting punishment than to make you eat one of those meatballs."

"That was one of the worst things I've ever eaten. Who made those meatballs, do you remember?"

She seemed surprised by the question. "Alexei, but he swore he'd put capers in the meatballs."

"And who was on shift when the oven stopped working?"

Her expression darkened to suspicion. "Why do you want to know?"

"You've been so busy you can't see the forest for the toast points, but after what you told me today about your former partner…'' He let his words trail off, not wanting to make any accusations. He knew she was smart enough to pick up on what he was implying.

She'd joked earlier about him having a spy in her camp, but he wondered if it wasn't Pierre who had the spy in her camp.

''You think Pierre is behind this?'' Shock was plainly written all over her face. ''That he's…what? Sabotaging my business?'' She rose, went for the bottle and refilled their glasses. ''Why would he do that?''

Clay shrugged. ''I don't know the guy, but he's the only one I can see who has anything to gain if you fall on your ass. He's proven himself dishonest since he won't honor your partnership agreement. Your success is hurting him professionally and making him look like a failure personally. He sounds to me like the kind of guy who cares about that stuff. Don't you think it's too much of a coincidence that you beat him to that contract today and then tonight all hell breaks loose in your kitchen?''

She was nodding, but he suspected she was only half listening. She was likely going over all the disasters in her head and trying to figure out who among her staff was working, not *for* her, but against her.

''If what you say is true, it has to be François or

Miguel. One or both of them was around for all the incidents. Alexei made the meatballs, but he wasn't there for any of the other incidents.''

''Is there anyone else? No matter how much you think you trust them?''

''No.''

''What about that woman who was crying in the Ashtons' kitchen?''

''Liz?'' Marina shook her head. ''Liz is the one who encouraged me to start my own business. She's my best friend. No. She wouldn't do something like this.''

Clay wasn't so sure, but he wasn't going to argue, not knowing any of the players but Marina.

''But how can we find out?'' She gazed at him with naked appeal in her eyes. ''What do we do?''

He wondered if she was even aware she'd said ''we.'' She was thinking of them as a team, an item, maybe even a couple. ''You'll have to confront the two you suspect.''

''I can't accuse those guys. They left more secure jobs to come and start up with me. How can I accuse them of betrayal?''

''If someone who works for you is sabotaging your business, then it's the worst kind of betrayal. Did both Miguel and François come from Delicieux?''

She shook her head. ''No. Only François.''

"That makes him the most likely candidate, but I think we have to interview both of them. Pierre could have got to Miguel."

She muttered an obscenity, and then raised furious eyes to his face. "I won't let him destroy my dreams. Not again."

And Clay knew she didn't mean the sous chef, but her former lover and business partner. Personally, he thought a little rough justice meted out in a back alley was what Pierre needed. And he very much hoped to be the one dishing out that justice.

"Do you have a good lawyer?"

She nodded.

"Have him or her do the interviewing. Lawyers are good at that stuff. And if you can get it on tape—"

There was a knock on the door and a skinny young fellow with bad skin entered. Clay remembered seeing him earlier but didn't know his name. From the expression on Marina's face, however, it had to be one of the suspects.

He tried to catch her eye to warn her off, but she didn't see him—or wouldn't. She'd never win any acting awards, he thought, seeing the sadness on her face. "Come in, François."

"I forgot my smokes."

"How could you do it?" Marina whispered. "I trusted you."

Oh, great. He wished he'd kept his suspicions to himself or at least waited until she was less emotional before telling her. This was the worst thing she could do—it was as good as warning Pierre that they were on to him. They needed a lawyer, a taped confession, more evidence. He was still considering what else they needed when he heard a sob.

Startled, he glanced up to find the kid burying his face in his hands. "I'm sorry, Marina," he mumbled in a thick French accent, her name coming out Mareeena. "I didn't want to, but I owe Pierre money. My girlfriend's pregnant and I promised her I'd look after her and the kid, but Pierre, he tell me he'll need the money back if I don't do these things."

"Couldn't you have come to me? Told me? I'd have helped you."

"I did come to tell you." He gestured dramatically, sniffed, and said, "I didn't leave my smokes here. I was going to tell you, but then the guy was here."

Tears were running down the boy's face and he waved his hands as though conducting the Boston Philharmonic.

Clay could see the outline of a pack of cigarettes in the young man's back pocket, so perhaps he *had* been on his way to confess. "My girlfriend, I told her when I got home. I felt so bad and she told me

I had to come find you tonight and tell you what I done.''

Marina nodded. ''How much did you owe Pierre?''

''Five thousand. He said he'd give me another five grand when...it was done.''

''When you'd put me out of business, you mean?''

''I'm sorry,'' he said, more tears spilling down his cheeks. ''I've never done anything that make me so ashamed.''

''You'd better go home, François. I'll call you in the morning.''

The young man nodded and headed for the door.

Clay spoke for the first time. ''Don't say a word to Pierre or I promise you'll go to jail.''

''I won't tell him,'' François muttered and kept going.

''Will he keep his word?'' Clay asked after the boy was gone.

Her solemnity was broken with a swift smile. ''If the girlfriend has anything to say about it, I think he will.'' She sighed. ''Well, for what it's worth, at least we know the source of my bad luck.''

He chuckled, feeling the same burning excitement in the pit of his gut he felt before closing a big deal. ''Oh, it's worth a lot more than that. Once we get lawyers involved and threaten your ex-partner with criminal charges, a civil suit and a whole lot of media attention, it's worth the money you're owed at the very least. After that, it's up to you how much revenge you're after.''

''Revenge…'' She savored the word as though it were a sip of brandy, then slowly shook her head as though the flavor no longer pleased her. ''I think I've lost my taste for revenge. All I want is what's fair.''

His instincts hadn't been wrong about her, he was pleased to note. She was nicer than that French weasel deserved. But Clay was a big believer in justice, and he was determined to get it for Marina.

There were two kinds of justice. The suit-and-tie kind that involved lawyers and a lot of paperwork, and there was the justice system he'd learned growing up. The back-alley kind. Didn't matter what you wore, and there was no paperwork involved, but the results could be impressive.

He didn't much care which route he had to follow—although in his heart he kind of liked the idea of taking Pierre apart with his bare hands. He understood business competition, but he hated seeing anyone get ahead by cheating, lying and sabotage. Especially when it hurt a woman who was putting everything she had into her business.

She yawned and shoved her hand up a moment too late to cover the gesture.

"You're tired," he said, stating the obvious. "You should go to bed." She glanced at him and the expression in her eyes pulled him to his feet and to her side as powerfully as if she'd used a grappling hook.

She stumbled to her own feet and no power on earth could stop him from kissing her. Her lips were warm and a little sticky from the brandy. His body sprang to life and he felt her desire echo his.

He thought she was trying to deepen the kiss, then realized she was yawning against his mouth. Frustration bit deep, but he pulled back, looping his arms around her waist and holding her loosely against him.

"You should get home to bed," he said. Her skin was pale, and dark semicircles of fatigue shadowed her eyes.

"I'm not that tired," she said, holding his gaze.

He grinned down at her. "You need sleep and if—make that *when*—I take you to bed, I promise you won't get any."

"Braggart," she said softly.

"Lock up. I'll see you out."

He released her but she didn't move. She touched his cheek with her palm. "Thank you."

"That kid was coming to confess anyway. I didn't do anything."

She shook her head. "Not for that. Thank you for being there for me."

"Hey, it's all for the food. I love your cooking."

She smiled up at him. "One day, very soon, I'm going to cook you breakfast."

"I'll hold you to that."

CHAPTER SIX

"JAN," he said next morning. "You know that Christmas party at my place that Delicieux is catering?"

"Mmm-hmm." She turned her head from her computer screen and slipped her glasses down her nose.

"Cancel it."

She blinked. Didn't move, just blinked at him over the tops of her glasses. "We've had that date booked for six months. The menus are approved. Invitations have gone out. Any particular reason why you want to cancel?"

"Guy's a crook. He's not getting any business of mine."

Not bothering to suppress a sigh of long-suffering, his faithful assistant swiveled to reach the filing drawer behind her desk. In about one and a half seconds she had the file folder in her hands. He loved watching her retrieve files. It was uncanny.

She flipped it open and found the catering contract. "We've already paid a nonrefundable deposit."

Clay ground his molars. He hated that the greasy Pierre had a cent of his company's money. He'd make certain to take that out of Pierre's hide, as well. "Make a copy of that, will you? And arrange a meeting with Pierre." He couldn't prevent the sneer that twisted the word. He was thinking fast. Marina didn't have time to go after Pierre. What better Christmas gift could he give her but the money she was owed? "And get our lawyer on the phone, will you?"

Jan nodded. "You want your coffee first?"

"Yes, thanks." At first he'd told Jan he'd get his own coffee, but she was an old-fashioned secretary—and had kept bringing him coffee until he shut up and drank it. He'd go to almost any lengths to keep her.

"HERE'S WHAT we're going to do," Clay said later that day to Pierre, whose initial Gallic charm had dwindled to blustering incredulity, and, finally, when confronted with François's signed confession, to sullen fury.

"What?" he spat.

"We're going to have your company appraised, and you're going to give Marina a check—certified—for half the value."

"That's crazy. The bitch is lying. She never—"

"Watch your mouth." Clay's hands involuntarily bunched into fists and Pierre flicked an alarmed glance at them.

"This is nonsense. What are you? The judge and jury?" he scoffed.

"No. We could call the cops if you'd prefer." Clay shrugged and fingered the confession. "Up to you."

A sheen of sweat appeared on Pierre's forehead.

Clay flicked a glance to his lawyer, Allan, silently telling him to take over. "My client's preference would be to work this out among ourselves. You pay Ms. Shields what she's entitled to, and this goes no further."

Pierre spoke to Clay. "And if I spit in your face and walk out of here?"

"First, your face won't be quite so pretty when I'm finished with it, and, second, I'll tell your sordid little story to everyone I know in town. I know a lot of people. A few journalists, too."

It took another hour, and involved Pierre's lawyer joining the meeting, but in the end, the man knew he was beaten.

With a few mumbled curses, some in French and some in English, he signed the agreement to give Marina half the value of Delicieux.

As he and his lawyer were leaving, Clay said,

"Oh, and by the way, your contract for our Christmas party is cancelled."

He was whistling when he passed his secretary's desk. She raised her brows at him. "And I suppose I can guess which caterer you want me to call first with this sudden opening."

He grinned at her. "You are a rare and wonderful woman. Shuffle the dates if you need to, but I want BonBon catering the event. Set up a meeting with Marina and you two can figure out the menu."

"You sure you don't want to take that meeting yourself?"

He was in too good a mood to be needled. "No. You do it." He turned and started to walk away, then turned back. "But let me know when you're seeing her. I might drop in."

A most unladylike snort was his only answer.

Three paces past her desk, he turned and walked back. "Wait, I've got a better idea. Here's what we'll do."

MARINA OUGHT to feel elated—or at least relieved—to have her mysterious bad luck explained and presumably put to a stop. But instead of relief, she felt something closer to despair. How could she have shown such poor judgment with Pierre?

Why, she'd agreed to marry a man who'd turned

out to be not only a cheat, but someone who would stoop to criminal sabotage to ruin her.

She continued to beat the choux pastry dough before her by hand, needing the outlet for her rage and frustration.

François, accompanied by his visibly pregnant girlfriend, had visited her this morning. After another apology and his painfully uttered promise to pay for any damage he'd caused, she'd decided to keep him on, on the understanding that he'd work extra hours to pay off the damage. She had no idea if she was doing the right thing. She'd stopped believing in her own ability to judge, but she couldn't turn her back on the plea in their two sets of eyes, or on the poor baby coming into the world.

When she'd beaten so much choux pastry her arms felt like wet spaghetti, she felt imaginally better. The dough was light and ribbony, bulges of air bubbles telling her she'd beaten well.

The phone rang. Marina was closest, but she held up her mucky hands, so Liz took the call.

''It's a booking,'' she mouthed to Marina, giving her a thumbs-up.

A new booking usually filled Marina with glee. Each job was one more step on the path to success. Today, however, all she felt was tired.

She only paid the scantest attention to what Liz was booking. Some sort of Christmas party in a private home. They'd left it late to book, and only because Marina's business was just starting out did she still have openings in December. The way things were going this time next year that wouldn't be the case.

Liz walked to their master calendar on the wall and checked dates. They did a lot of their work on the computer, but Marina liked an old-fashioned wall calendar so she could see at a glance what was coming up. "You're in luck," Liz said. "The twenty-third is available.

"Absolutely. Of course the owner herself will be happy to meet with you to suggest menus, discuss pricing and look at the space," Liz said. Her blond ponytail bobbed as she nodded vigorously, even though whoever was at the other end of the phone obviously couldn't see her. Her best friend and right hand shot Marina a glance that appeared oddly mischievous.

"Yes. She'll be there at seven. I'm not sure. You'd better give me the directions." She pulled out a scratch pad and ballpoint and scribbled something.

As Liz hung up, Marina said, "Tell me you didn't book me a 7:00 a.m. appointment. You know I don't do perky and chipper before nine," she complained, knowing she had no choice and she'd be perky and chipper round the clock if it would save BonBon.

"Not 7:00 a.m.," Liz retorted, tearing off the notepaper. "Seven o'clock tonight."

Irritation pulled Marina's brows together. Did Liz need glasses? "We have an event booked for tonight." A private dinner for six that she had donated as a prize in a charity auction. The winner was claiming her prize tonight. Sure it was a freebie, but she considered promotion essential.

"Marina, if you don't give up these control-freak tendencies you're going to collapse. It's a simple dinner. Miguel and I can handle it."

Liz was right, of course. Most of the food was already prepared. She had to let go a little more. "All right." She nodded as Liz slipped the directions into her binder.

"I'll type up the details and print out the specs for you."

"Thanks." Marina filled a pastry bag with the choux pastry and began piping pale blobs of shiny dough onto baking sheets. "Seems odd to be doing business at seven o'clock at night," she said.

"I think the client is planning to mix business and pleasure."

"Pardon?" Marina glanced up, puzzled.

Liz typed rapidly at the computer, her back to Marina. "The client. You'll be seeing the CEO of Archer and Co."

As Marina cried, "What?" her hand squeezed

convulsively on the pastry bag, squirting choux paste until it resembled a triple scoop of soft ice cream toppling precariously above the neat little balls she'd piped earlier.

"Clayton Archer," Liz said breezily—just a bit too breezily. "He wants to have a dinner meeting at his house. His secretary said he has a party every year on the twenty-third and then closes the office until after the New Year."

Shock gave way to wrath. "Oh, he does, does he? He left it awfully late to book."

"Well, Jan, that's who called, said it had originally been booked with another caterer."

"Delicieux?"

"Bingo."

And he'd cancelled it. That was good. But dinner at his place she wasn't so sure about. "And I suppose he thinks I'm going to bring the dinner for our meeting."

"No. Jan says he's going to cook dinner for you."

She was trying to remove the mutant giant pastry glob but instead smeared the dough when her hand jerked once more. "Are you sure you heard right? He's cooking dinner for me?" No one ever cooked for her. She was a professional chef, trained at the Cordon Bleu in Paris. She always cooked.

For a second she let a shaft of delight into her dismal day.

She couldn't imagine what it would be like to have someone cook for her.

MARINA SWAPPED the van for Liz's compact car and headed out to Shaughnessy with mixed feelings. What game was Clay playing with her?

After their scorching kisses the other day, it seemed fairly obvious where they were headed—but she wanted it to be out in the open, and on her terms. She didn't care for being manipulated.

A frown gathered as she headed down Granville Street, ignoring the few flakes of snow that were making a pitiful pretense of falling, ignoring the lit up Santas, the icicle lights, the neon reindeer. The traffic seemed extraordinarily heavy and she wondered how much of it was headed for the airport.

She pictured families reuniting, kids flying home from college break, scattered siblings gathering yearly at the family home. She blinked. How many years had it been since she'd been home to visit her family? Ever since she'd started waitressing at sixteen, the holiday season might have meant peace and goodwill to other people, but for her it was the season of aching feet and not enough sleep.

Her family would call from Montreal on Christmas morning as they did every year. They'd thank her for her gifts. She'd thank them for hers, for the practical things and the silly gag gifts, which were so pathetic when there was no one around to share the joke. What kind of family Christmas was that? Maybe next year she'd squeeze out a couple of days and fly home. Or maybe her business would be successful enough that she could fly her parents out to spend some time with her. She snorted to herself. Well, she could dream, couldn't she?

She turned down the street indicated on her notes and headed into an area of gracious homes, some from the turn of the century, some much newer. Recent Hong Kong immigrants and dot-com millionaires were responsible for many of the newer mansions. She supposed Clay lived in one of those.

Surprise had her rechecking the address she'd been given when she pulled up in front of a Craftsman-style home that looked to be almost a century old, with soft blue shingles and aged stone. There was a large front porch supported by square pillars that made her think of rocking chairs and climbing roses.

A second perusal of her note proved that, unless Liz had written down the wrong address, this was it.

She stepped out of the car and felt a moment's desire to jump back in and peel away from Clay's house as fast as she could.

"Business, strictly business," she mumbled to herself as she trod up the curving stone path lined with privet hedging. Even in the middle of winter, she could see that the lawn would be velvety come summer, and the trees that graced the front yard were probably almost as old as the home.

She rapped on the heavy oak door and it opened with flattering speed.

It wasn't a housekeeper standing there, as she'd half expected, but Clay himself, looking more casual than she'd ever seen him in jeans and a moss-green sweater. On his feet he wore a pair of plaid bedroom slippers, which for some odd reason blew her dread away like so much dandelion fluff.

He didn't pounce as she'd half expected but, like her, seemed to be willing to treat this as a business meeting only. "You're right on time," he said, stepping back to let her inside.

"This is a beautiful home," she said, gazing around the entrance hall paneled in rich dark oak. The parquet floor gleamed in the entrance hall, which was big enough for a grand piano but held only a Duncan Phyfe table and a sofa. "I bet you say that to all your clients," he said with a lopsided grin.

"I do." She laughed because it was so true. "But in this case I actually mean it."

"Come in."

He took her coat, then led the way into a living room that made her feel as though she was stepping back in time. He'd clearly tried to suit the decor to the period in which the house was built. A fire crackled in the grate—real, not gas.

"This is absolutely gorgeous."

"Thanks. Well, I can't accept any credit. The decorator did it all."

It was so exactly what she would have chosen herself that she was amazed. "Didn't you choose colors or anything?"

He shook his head. "Not my area of expertise. I told them to make the house look as authentic as possible and they did. Drink?"

It was the kind of room that called for thimble-size glasses of sherry for the ladies and whiskey in tumblers for the gentlemen. However, she wasn't a lady of leisure from a century ago, so she shook her head. "Not while I'm working." She pulled out a file of menus and sat on a chesterfield with a low table in front of it.

He sat beside her.

Irrationally, she wished he hadn't. Of course it made perfect sense to sit beside her so he could see the menus, but she didn't want him so close she could feel his body heat, so close she could smell him and be reminded of how she'd felt in his arms.

She slapped open a menu at random. "Liz wasn't

entirely sure what you wanted. I brought along several menus.''

He didn't even glance at the printouts spread before her. ''I want a buffet dinner for sixty.'' His gaze felt like a lamp heating her face. ''Imagine you're the hostess and they're your friends. That's the menu I want.''

She smiled faintly. ''Is that what you said to the interior decorator, too? Imagine you're the hostess and decorate my house?''

''No.'' He ran a finger down her cheek. ''They were a couple of guys. It didn't seem appropriate.''

''Right.'' She scribbled ''carte blanche'' in her notebook, and then sent him a glance.

''Good. Now that the business portion of our evening is over, can I pour you a glass of wine?''

''Don't you want to discuss costs? Timing?''

''No. You can sort out the rest of the details with my secretary, Jan.''

She glanced at her watch. ''The business portion of our evening took six minutes.''

''Leaving longer for the pleasure part of the evening,'' he said softly.

''Pleasure?'' she answered sharply as though the very idea of pleasure were repugnant.

''Dinner.'' He held out his hand. ''Come on.''

She took it, liking the firm warmth of his hand surrounding hers. ''Liz said you were cooking.''

"That's right. Steak, baked potatoes, mushrooms, a decent red wine. Nothing frilly and not a scrap of crème fraîche."

"Sounds wonderful," she said following him into the kitchen. At first glance it had the look of the rest of the house, but at second it became clear it was as modern and technically efficient as any home kitchen she'd ever seen.

"Pull up a seat," he said, indicating the stools at the granite breakfast bar.

She put her bag down on the black-and-white tile floor and hoisted herself onto a stool. She was aware that her legs were aching from another day on her feet. It would be a novel experience to sit at a food prep area and watch.

In truth, she cynically expected the watching to last about three minutes. He was bound to pull that helpless-man-in-the-kitchen routine, and before she knew it, *she'd* be cooking dinner and *he'd* be watching.

But, as he'd begun to do too often, Clay surprised her. He was no expert and didn't pretend to be. He opened a Bordeaux and poured them each a glass, then washed his hands and set to work. The warm, homey scent of baking potatoes told her he'd had the sense to put them in the oven earlier.

While she sipped wine, he chopped mushrooms,

paying no attention whatsoever to uniformity of thickness.

"Who else lives in this house?"

"No one." He glanced up from under his brows, a humorous expression in his eyes. "I like to spread out. I've got seven bedrooms. One for shoes, one for ties, one for socks, and one for sleeping, naturally."

"Naturally." It sounded kind of lonely to her, but who was she to talk? One person in a one-bedroom apartment wasn't any more convivial, simply more compact.

And he might slice his own mushrooms, but she had a shrewd idea he didn't do all the cleaning and gardening work on a house this size, as well as maintain a hectic work schedule.

It wasn't long before they were sitting at a small round oak table by a lattice window. She imagined an English country garden out there in the summertime, but it was hard to tell now that it was dark.

He set a full dinner plate before her and her mouth watered. The steak still sizzled, the potato steamed and the mushrooms glistened with butter.

"This looks fabulous."

"Glad you approve. I was nervous working in front of a pro."

She chuckled. "You were not."

While they ate, she told him about the visit from

François and his girlfriend, and he surprised her by supporting her decision to keep François on when she'd imagined he'd tell her to fire him. But it turned out he believed in second chances just as she did.

It was so wonderful simply to have a night free. She couldn't remember the last time she'd enjoyed one. As she sipped the last of her wine, she leaned forward, enjoying the sight of him across the table from her, so urbane and yet wearing plaid bedroom slippers.

A little voice was telling her to run like hell.

"I always do the cooking," she said.

"Okay. You can cook next time."

"No. I mean, I liked it. Having you cook me dinner was wonderful."

Those hazel eyes stayed level on hers. "You don't look overjoyed."

"I feel out of my element with you. You pursue me and charm me, and I can't seem to hold my ground. I keep getting pulled in deeper."

"Do you want to get away?" he asked gently.

She shook her head. "I don't think so. But I'm scared." She rose and started clearing the table.

"I'm scared, too. You're a woman a man could lose his heart to far too easily."

She gave a harsh laugh. "I always fall for the wrong men."

"Maybe not always," he said gently. After taking

the dishes from her and putting them back on the table, he kissed her.

She sighed and looped her arms around his neck, kissing him back, hoping against hope that he was right. It felt so good to be wrapped in his arms. Their bodies fit together as though they'd been sculpted for the purpose.

"Would you like to come up and see my sock collection?"

She giggled softly and tipped her head back to regard him. "I don't know. I feel like you're always pushing me. I'm not sure…"

He took a full stride back, leaving her feeling chilled without his warmth. "I'm not pushing anymore. Not this time," he told her earnestly. "It's your decision. I'll just be over in the kitchen doing the dishes. Let me know." And he picked up the plates and walked into the kitchen.

She bit her lip, wanting him so badly her body ached. "Do you have any argyle socks?" she called after him.

He was back so fast she felt dizzy. "Come on up and let's see."

She breathed in and then out, knowing she had to risk this again sometime. "All right."

It wasn't as though her heart was involved. This was only going to be about sex. When she woke tomorrow she would no longer have to remember that Pierre was the last man with whom she'd made love. That alone made Clay's proposition irresistible.

He cupped her face and stared deep into her eyes, causing a nervous twinge in her belly. This might well be a very bad idea, but she was beyond caring. Okay, so she had lousy taste in men. She knew it. She accepted it. If she didn't hold on to high expectations for Clay, then she couldn't be hurt. Right now, she wanted some new memories, the pleasure of being with a man. Physical release would be nice. And, if his kiss was anything to go by, Clay wouldn't disappoint her.

He kissed her again and, this time, it was something more, something deeper and richer. He tasted like wine and red meat and butter—all deliciously potent treats she indulged in sparingly.

Her taste buds were sending her a warning. Clay, she thought, ought to be on that list of high-risk substances. He might end up causing her heart damage.

But he was a special treat. A splurge. And, oh, she intended to enjoy her treat.

His hands slid lightly over her shoulders and down her arms. His right hand grasped her left and, breaking the kiss slowly, he turned and led her from the room.

She barely noted the gleaming oak floors, the

muted rugs, and then they were climbing stairs in silence interrupted only by their breathing and the creak of a couple of stairs.

The room he led her to was enormous, masculine, and modern. French doors led to a small balcony, and through an open door she glimpsed a gleaming bathroom.

A lamp illuminated a king-size bed upholstered in black and gray. He might have six empty bedrooms, and had likely set one of them up as a home office, but he also had a mini office right here in his bedroom. In an alcove, where she would put a vanity table if this were her room, sat a small desk with a combination phone/fax and a laptop.

But clearly business wasn't currently on his mind. He moved up against her and kissed the nape of her neck, sending tendrils of sensation curling down her spine.

Her black silk knit turtleneck zipped up the back, and he undid the zipper with a slow, languorous hiss, nuzzling his way down the path of skin he bared.

Mmm. She'd never before noticed how sensitive she was there. Her body felt as though it had been in hibernation and spring had just sprung. Her skin was coming to lovely, sensual wakefulness, every inch anxious to be touched.

When he got to the end of the zipper, he didn't

yank the top up and off her as she'd expected. Instead he turned her slowly to face him and kissed her mouth once more.

It was a slow and easy seduction that gave her confidence she could pull away anytime. He'd even left the bedroom door open halfway. They were alone in the house, so they didn't need the privacy, but she liked the subtle message. The door was open if she wanted out.

She didn't, though. To ease Clay's mind on that score, she pressed closer to him, rubbing her body against his, surprising a quickly stifled groan out of him when she pressed her pelvis deliberately against his erection.

He managed to provoke a similar surprise reaction from her when he sneakily gripped her butt and pulled her forward. This time it was him doing the rubbing and he found her sweet spot unerringly, making her quiver. As desire roared to life in a body that had been denied too long, she felt as though there were a couple of duvets between them instead of clothing. Her sex-starved body was not happy at the encumbrance.

They undressed each other, but slowly still, each wanting to savor the experience. She hadn't wanted this to feel special, but it did. Because the very thought made her nervous, she banished it and concentrated instead on pleasure.

She was young, healthy and she liked sex. And she sure as hell could use the tension release. Why shouldn't she indulge? Clay was an attractive, single adult male.

This was good. He was exactly what she needed.

So she ignored the warmth in his eyes that was about more than lust, and the jerky response of her heart as she returned his gaze. She shut her eyes and let her fingers do the talking.

They didn't just talk, they teased—touching, rubbing, scraping as her desire built. There were ridges that intrigued her under his shirt, hair patterns she needed to explore so she dragged his shirt over his head and found his torso looked as good as it felt.

"You keep in shape," she said, impressed that a desk jockey had such nice musculature.

"I try," he said.

Her shirt came off next and he gave her biceps a playful squeeze even though his gaze was riveted to her chest. "You keep in shape, too," he said, his voice a trifle gravelly.

"It's carrying all those heavy trays."

She'd never intended him to see her underwear, of course. It had been the last thing on her mind when she'd run home earlier and showered. She'd slipped into a lacy emerald-green bra and panties set to get her into the Christmas spirit.

At least, that's what she'd told herself.

As his fingers trailed from her bare arms and over her shoulders, as he traced the green straps to the silky cups she felt her nipples tightening.

He used the silky material to caress her, cupping and toying with her breasts through the silk until she could barely keep still. While his hands were thus engaged, she went to work on his belt buckle and zipper, slipping her hand inside to find him hot and hard.

She felt her own body soften and open in anticipation. She felt the straps of her bra slip down her arms while he stripped her of it. She felt his gaze on her breasts and it was like another caress. His hands didn't go there, but slipped lower to give her the same attention she was giving him. Oh, how she gasped when his hand slipped into her panties and glided over her where she was slick and ready.

Their mouths fused as they toyed with each other and the slow seduction became torturous.

"I can't—" he muttered, pulling away from her mouth and, at the same time, pulling her hand out of his pants.

"No," she agreed softly, understanding his distress since she shared it.

By unspoken agreement, they stripped themselves of pants and socks and shoes and he tumbled her to the bed. He jerked the bedspread back at the last minute so she fell onto sheets so soft they must have had a thread count in the thousands.

Then his mouth was on her body and she couldn't have said she was on sheets or a bed. All she was conscious of was the burning heat of his mouth on her nipples. She thrust her hands in his hair, loving the rough texture, tracing the bumps and furrows of his skull as though they contained a Braille message just for her.

While his mouth was busy with her breasts, his hand tracked its way down her belly and found her heat, working her up to fever pitch.

When it seemed she wouldn't be able to hold back, and the sound of her own panting echoed off the walls, he reached for his night table and flipped open the lid of an ornate wooden box she hadn't noticed before. Inside was an egotistically generous supply of condoms. Blindly, he grabbed one and in seconds he was sheathed.

They were still sideways on the bed, but it didn't seem to matter. He parted her knees and slid between them until they were face-to-face and his erection was nudging her.

She didn't want to look into his eyes while he entered her. It seemed too intimate—and she didn't want intimacy, damn it, she just wanted some good raunchy sex. But she couldn't so much as glance away. His eyes compelled her. His expression was fiercely tender and far too serious as he slowly pushed into her.

For that long, sliding moment, she was transfixed, feeling emotion well even as her excitement rose.

No, no, no. She raised her head to kiss him, blocking out his too-serious face from her view. At the same time, she grabbed his hips and pulled him hard against her as she bucked up against him.

He didn't resist, and soon they had a nice slamming rhythm going that blocked out the nuances of feeling and left no room for soft emotion.

He rode her hard. She left him no option to do anything else, twisting and straining beneath him, pulling his hips toward her like a wild thing.

Blissfully, the tension release she'd craved was soon upon her and her climax rocked her to her toes.

Clay still seemed far too controlled as she gasped out the last of her orgasm into his mouth. If he was going to go back to tender and slow she wouldn't be able to bear it. She had no idea why it bothered her so, but she knew it was a bad idea. So she shoved against him until he obligingly rolled to his back, taking her with him.

Her goal was to make him lose control as soon as possible, but she was still so sensitive, her blood still pumping so hotly to supply her starved erogenous zones, and it had been so damn long that, as she moved above him, she felt another wave build.

She was on her knees, her hands clutching his shoulders, moving to her own rhythm, but he seemed to naturally rub that magical spot each time she came down on him, so that before she knew it, or quite believed it was possible, she was being swept up once again into bliss. Her head went back and she cried out to the ceiling, only to hear a hoarse cry echo her own. Beneath her, Clay began to buck wildly and it was all she could do to stay with him through his own passion.

She collapsed.

It wasn't pretty, but her body left her no option. Robbed suddenly of all bone matter, she simply slumped against him, dreamy and pliant as a jelly fish.

She thought she'd never felt more content. And on that alarming thought, she fell asleep.

She awoke suddenly wondering where she was and why one side of her face felt so hot. After blinking hard a few times, she realized she had her face plastered against Clay's naked chest and bits of him were tangled nakedly around bits of her, so she did the only thing she could think of.

She panicked.

Easing away from him, she glanced at her watch, trying to figure out from the eerie fluorescent green dots and lines what time it was.

Two in the morning.

She breathed deeply, smelling the last vestiges of good sex, the pleasant scent of the man sleeping warmly beside her, and the much sharper, far less pleasant scent of her own fear.

She wanted to slap him. All she'd wanted was some good sex. But the sex hadn't been good. It had been great. Fantastic, rock-the-house-down, great.

Nothing to worry about, she told herself as she gnawed her lip. Great sex could happen to anyone. She'd simply gather her clothes and sneak out to avoid any morning awkwardness.

No. No. No. Every part of her body not connected to her brain hollered at her to stay right where she was. Already, her body was aching at the thought of waking naked with Clay and enjoying another round in the morning.

Gritting her teeth, she forced herself to roll surreptitiously out of bed. He rolled with her and threw a hand over her chest. Those fingers dangling near her nipple had her wanting him again.

If she rolled into him and kissed him, she bet she could wake him. If kissing his mouth didn't work, she could always kiss his—*stop it*. What was she doing? She had to get home, get some sleep. Tomorrow was a busy day.

Once more she eased slowly out of bed, and this time her sleeping partner let her go.

She picked up her clothes as sneakily as though

she were a thief, and eased out of the still-open door like a shadow.

She didn't take a full breath until she reached home.

Home? Her apartment didn't feel like a home. It felt cold and empty. She brushed her teeth, washed and crawled into bed. Her sheets were so cold she shivered, curling herself into a ball. When she breathed in, she smelled fabric softener.

She'd never felt so lonely in her life.

CHAPTER SEVEN

CLAY WOKE feeling as though everything in his life was perfect.

Then he noticed the other side of his bed was empty and his day started to go downhill. Marina's clothes were gone and so, he soon discovered, was Marina.

He shook his head as he brewed coffee. Why couldn't he have fallen in love with a woman who was uncomplicated? A woman who didn't drag around enough baggage to fill a freight train. He supposed it was payback time for all the easy relationships he'd enjoyed over the years.

Once he fell, he fell hard, and he'd fallen for a woman who gave the term *high maintenance* new meaning.

He shouldn't be surprised that she'd run from him after a night that had left a goofy smile permaglued to his face. Oh, yeah. Last night had been something. It hadn't been just great sex. It had been making love for the first time with the woman he wanted to be with for the rest of his life. The woman with whom he wanted children. Grandchildren.

He drank the first cup of coffee leaning against the kitchen counter, staring at the granite top as though he could find the answers he sought in its pattern.

The woman he loved was running scared. He understood that. But she needed him. Her need was making her run. He understood that, too.

Likely his feelings had telegraphed themselves to her during their night together, and that had added a sprint to her gait.

He slumped onto a kitchen stool and his gaze fell on the airline ticket tacked to the bulletin board. He'd booked a flight to Florida to spend Christmas with his family. In her hurry, Marina had left behind the green bra, which he'd found tangled in the bedding this morning. He held it now, running a thumb over the fabric, wondering when he'd developed this Sir Galahad complex.

He couldn't desert Marina now, not even temporarily. She was badly shaken over the Pierre business. She was overworked and running on empty. And Clay wasn't going anywhere until every cent of the money owed her was in Marina's bank account. He also wanted to stay close to make certain nothing else suspicious happened to her business.

But it was her emotional vulnerability more than

her business predicament that had him making up his mind. She might not want to admit to anyone, least of all herself, that she needed him right now. But he knew it, and deep down he had a feeling she knew it, too.

He had to stay.

After pouring himself a second cup of coffee and gulping a couple of sips for fortification, he picked up the phone.

"Hi, Mom," Clay said into the phone with confident bravado when his mother answered. He figured he'd work his way up to the news slowly, butter her up a little first.

"You're not coming for Christmas."

"How do you do that? I was going to ease into 'I can't make it home for Christmas.'"

"I'm your mother. You've never been able to ease into anything with me."

"I'm really sorry. I know I promised."

"When are you going to learn that your company will run fine if you spend the holidays with your family?"

He cringed, knowing he recognized Marina's workaholic tendencies because he shared them. "It's not work, Mom."

"You're not sick? Are you?" Yep, he thought, always a mother.

"No. I'm fine. It's…there's this woman. She's

going through a tough time. She needs me right now.''

"So bring her to Florida. Some sun will do her good, and there's plenty of room in this oversized condo you insisted on buying us. I watch the weather channel. It's always raining up there.''

"Can't. She's a caterer. It's her busy season.'' Besides, Marina had no idea yet that she was spending Christmas with Clay, but he thought he'd best keep that information from his mother.

The woman who'd borne him huffed out a breath and he heard the puff of disappointment cross the continent. "So, some girl is more important than your family.''

"She's not some girl. I'm going to marry her.'' Another piece of information that would come as a surprise to Marina. He *was* going to marry her, though. He'd already decided. And she *did* need him. He didn't like the dark circles under her eyes or the look of despair when she'd learned how deep her former lover's deceit could be. No. She needed him.

"Getting married? When?'' That news changed his mother's tone as he'd known it would. Hope hovered like tiny grandchildren waiting in the wings.

"I haven't asked her yet. It's…it's a little complicated.''

"She's not married, is she?"

"Give me some credit." How did he manage to run a multimillion-dollar corporation with perfect confidence, he wondered, and then regress to an eight-year-old about to get grounded whenever he got on the phone with his mother?

"Unlike you, Mom, she hasn't completely fallen for my charm yet."

"Hmm. Would I like her?"

He thought about that for a minute. "I think so. You two are a lot alike."

"I baked all your favorites."

"I'm sorry, Mom. I'll come home for Easter. Promise."

"You'd better be engaged by then."

"How's Dad?" he asked, changing the subject. They chatted for a few minutes and he ended the call, hoping he'd done the right thing. Marina needed him, and he couldn't imagine Christmas without her.

Now to convince her of that.

He picked up the phone again to tell Marina good morning, in a much less intimate way than he'd originally planned before she'd hightailed it. Maybe he'd tease her about her missing underwear or— He returned the receiver to its cradle. No. Phoning her was exactly what she'd expect. And, of course, she'd throw verbal ice water, grenades and Scud missiles back at him—whatever she had to, to stop him in his tracks before she'd admit she'd fallen for him as hard as he had for her.

Much as he wanted to hear her voice, even if she used that frigid tone that pissed him off, he had to act strategically. He wanted this woman more than he'd ever wanted anything in his life, and he had a feeling he'd need all his business acumen, all the negotiating and persuasion skills it had taken him years to perfect, if he was going to get her.

And get her, he promised himself, he would.

CLAY DIDN'T PHONE the next morning.

Marina had rehearsed what she'd say when he told her he'd missed her on waking. She'd be casual, laugh it off, tell him she needed her sleep. Tell him anything but the truth—she hadn't slept a minute after she'd left him.

Her body trembled and her mouth went dry every time the phone rang—and it was ringing so frequently she was surprised the damn thing didn't get laryngitis.

But no Clay.

She spent a good long time on his menu, worrying her food choices to death before being satisfied and faxing them into his office. His secretary faxed back an approval.

His secretary.

Her stomach curdled as it began to appear that although she'd been so afraid he was going to get serious on her, the opposite was true.

Now he'd had her, he wasn't haunting her the way he used to. Three days passed and he wasn't at a single event she catered. She knew because she anxiously searched each one for him.

She saw him on the fourth day of an endless string of cocktail socials she'd catered. So unaffected and casual was she that she tripped over her heels and almost face-planted into the caviar and toast points. She managed to hang on to the food, but nothing could help her hang on to her composure. She felt the heat in her cheeks and she cursed herself for blushing.

"Hello, Clay," she said, trying at least for a cool tone.

She could have sworn his eyes were laughing at her, as though he knew exactly what she was thinking and feeling. As though he'd planned it this way.

"Hello yourself. I've missed your cooking." The way he said it, anyone in hearing would think she cooked intimate meals for him on a regular basis. Jerk.

"Sadly, we're out of your favorite meatballs."

She saw him twice more before his Christmas party, but he made no mention of their one memorable night together. No suggestion they should get together again.

In fact, she wasn't certain if he was at the events because of her or because they were functions he would have attended anyway. Every time their gazes connected, though, his scnt provocative messages that made her pulse skip. She felt toyed with and she didn't like it a bit.

She didn't know why his behavior prompted her to outdo herself on the food for his buffet dinner— but it did. She was determined that every morsel she served would have the diners weeping with pleasure.

Snow had been forecast for his big day, but it held off. With the food prepared and loaded in the van, François and Miguel set off to start the food prep at Clay's place and Liz and Marina went home to change.

She was nervous as she and Liz pulled up to his house. The last time she'd been here… No. Mustn't let her thoughts take that path.

Luckily, Jan, Clay's secretary and the woman who'd been her contact on the job, answered the door and led them through to the kitchen. From her quick peeks into the dining and living rooms, she could see the decorators had done a fantastic job. It looked like a Christmas fairyland.

A perfect backdrop for her best food.

''You'll need to put the lobster thermidor on no

later than seven-fifty,'' Marina said to François, going over her printed list of instructions for the third time. If he weren't currently in the doghouse, he probably would have protested, but he only said, ''I remember.'' She was determined this night would be perfect, so she'd drummed the schedule into everyone's head until they could recite it in their sleep.

She checked the next item on her clipboard. ''And the raw oysters—'' She stopped as the door opened and in walked Clay, gorgeous in a dark-gray suit that set off his broad shoulders and tall body to great advantage.

''I'm going over some last-minute things,'' Marina said over her shoulder. ''I'll be with you in a minute.''

''Not a problem,'' he said easily.

She tried to remember where she was on her list, ''Oh, yes, the oysters—'' She turned sharply. ''What are you doing?'' Silly question. It was clear what he was doing. He was untying her apron.

''I like this dress. I want a better look at it.''

''Really!'' she exclaimed, flustered. She'd never before chosen to wear the red dress with the plunging neckline for a work function. She'd told herself it was the festive color that drew her—a nice change from her usual black and white. The brand-new shoes she'd picked up on impulse when she saw them in the window of a Robson Street boutique were a perfect match and if she ended up with blisters at the end of the evening, no one needed to know that but her.

His low whistle of appreciation was worth every blister.

The next thing she knew, her apron was sailing across the room. "Get rid of that, will you?"

Liz caught it with a laugh. "Sure thing."

"What are you—?"

"Liz, can you handle everything in here? I want Marina to act as hostess."

Liz appeared so smugly pleased Marina had a feeling she'd known all along what he planned to do. Come to think of it, it was some chance remarks of Liz's that had caused her to wear the red dress in the first place.

Still, there wasn't a lot she could do about it—Clay was the client, after all. If he wanted her to act as hostess, she'd act as hostess. She knew everything was well under control back here, and they had more than enough serving staff. She'd simply keep an eye on things from front of house.

A thrill danced up her spine as Clay tucked her hand in his arm in a courtly gesture and led her to meet his guests.

"Are you sure about this?" she asked.

"Are you kidding? I've been trying to get a date

with you since the day I met you. Besides, you're always on the outside looking in. Don't you think it's time you joined the party?"

She glanced up, startled. "What do you mean?"

He squeezed her hand. "You wield that serving tray of yours like a shield. You can hide behind it, use it as an escape vehicle. You even use it as an offensive weapon." He winced as he recalled her serving him that single meatball. "I want to see you eating and drinking instead of serving, mingling instead of scanning for empty glasses and buffet tables that need replenishing."

Since she'd been doing the latter while he'd been speaking, she had to laugh. And he was more correct than he knew. She felt a little out of place without an apron or a tray. It had been a long time since she'd attended a party for fun.

And, surprisingly, it *was* fun. Even though she didn't know a lot of the people present, Clay, obviously, knew them all. He introduced her around, never strayed far from her side and acted as though she were his date instead of his caterer.

This was the first time they'd spent any real time together since she'd sneaked out of his house in the wee hours. He didn't act as though her behavior had been odd. In fact, if she chose to believe their incredible night was only casual sex, she supposed he'd given her that option.

What a kick in the ego! Here she'd been the one thinking she was calling the shots, so worried he'd get the wrong idea and try to trap her into a relationship she wasn't ready for, and the reverse turned out to be true.

He seemed perfectly content. Except there was that distinct twinkle of humorous understanding in his eyes that slipped under her skin like a splinter every time she met his gaze. She didn't like splinters. She tended to do her best to pluck them out.

She tried to keep a surreptitious eye on the food, drinks, general flow of things, but every time she did, he'd squeeze her hand.

"Stop it," he whispered at one point into her ear, then kissed it lightly in full view of anyone who cared to watch.

"I feel like a puppy being trained. You squeeze my paws when you don't like my behavior," she said with a chuckle, trying not to read anything into the fact that he'd kissed her ear in public. What did that mean? What did she want it to mean?

Even though she was barely allowed to glance at the buffet table without having her paw squeezed, the food was perfect. Drinks were replaced, empty plates vanished, the food was always plentiful and what was meant to be hot was hot and what was supposed to stay cold did. She was proud of her company, and, if there was a tiny pang that they could do such a great job without her, she stifled it.

She also stifled her feelings of misgiving as so many of Clay's friends and clients saw them together.

Aaron Lepinsky had a teasing grin for her when he came up to chat for a few minutes. "You two look good together. It's nice to see Clay with a woman."

She would have expected that a man like Clay always had women. She couldn't say that aloud, naturally, but something in her face must have given away her thoughts. "I'm not saying the guy's a monk," Aaron continued, "but he's the same in business. He waits until he finds the perfect thing before making his move. Then, watch out. Once he's made up his mind, he gets what he wants."

Thinking of his ruthless courtship of her, if that's what it was, she had to laugh. The laugh faded, though, when she wondered if he tired of his conquests, business or personal, once he'd bagged them. She didn't know, and his baffling behavior kept her on edge.

She decided she had a right to know where she stood. So, she waited until the end of the evening, when the food was all put away, the dishes and cutlery packed up and the van on its way back to the shop. The cleaners would be in in the morning, and by noon, you'd never know there'd been a party here. She loved that kind of efficiency.

He seemed to be waiting for her as she took a last walk through the main-floor rooms checking that nothing had been missed, and the twinkle in his eyes was pronounced.

"What?" she finally asked him.

"I'm wondering when you're going to stop fussing and let me take you to bed."

All her carefully planned words dried up. Immediately, his calm assumption irritated her and she stuck her nose in the air in a deliberately prissy fashion. "Is that all I am to you? A sex toy?"

"I think the shoe's on the other foot. You're the one who slept with me and snuck out at dawn. Not so much as a goodbye note."

"I..."

"You never even called." He sound wounded. She'd expected him to pursue her. Had never thought she'd hurt his feelings.

"But I... You haven't called, either." Damn, she wished he wouldn't look at her that way, as though he could see into her bruised and sorry past, into her insecurities and fears. She bit her lip. "You've got me feeling all mixed up."

"You know what you need?"

She could think of a dozen things, all of which required him to be naked.

"You need a nice hot bath. You've been on your feet in those sexy heels all night. In fact, you've been on your feet most of the time I've known you."

"In spite of how hard you've been working to get me off them."

He chuckled. "You bet. Come on, I'll start you a hot bath, and then I'll put you to bed."

"Are you going to tell me a bedtime story?"

He grinned at her in a way that made her toes curl. "We'll act one out. I think you'll like the ending."

It was time. Her legs ached something fierce and there were about half a dozen incipient blisters decorating her feet.

So, she followed him upstairs and let him fill the bath for her. She'd glimpsed the bathtub on her last visit. A claw-footed antique, it beckoned a person to soak. Okay, so once she'd had a bath in there, she wasn't going to haul on her clothes and go home. Sinking into that water was an admission that she planned to stay the night.

Maybe he'd even slip into the bath with her.

He didn't. He tipped some bubbling bath oil under the running faucet, explaining to her over the roaring water that his mother had left it on her last visit. Marina was too tired to care where it came from.

All she wanted was to be relaxed in there, with the scent of a French perfumery wafting around her.

Clay left, shutting the door behind him and she quickly shed her clothes, folding them neatly and placing them on the wicker chair his designer must have put there, with the steam-loving potted fern beside it.

Restful, she thought, as she sank into the tub, letting the bubbles cover and tickle her, enjoying the utter luxury of the moment.

She wiggled her toes and moaned softly as they throbbed in response. She let her head rest on the back of the tub and closed her eyes.

A soft knock had them flying open again.

"Come in," she said, feeling foolish to be so formal but secretly relieved that the bubbles covered her as completely as a duvet. As warmly, too. She probably looked like a TV commercial for bath products.

Clay entered with a single glass of amber liquid in one hand and a man's robe in the other.

"I thought a cognac might help you relax and here's my robe for when you get out of the bath."

"That will be sometime next year," she said. "You'll need dynamite to get me out of this tub."

He handed her the glass, dropped a kiss on her steam-damp forehead and left, closing the door behind him.

Marina allowed herself to relax, sipping brandy and wondering how her life had gone from so very bad to so very good in such a short time.

She set the glass down on the black-and-white tile floor with a quiet click and daydreamed a little. The rising steam seemed to conjure images that were pleasant and soothing.

In her bathtub version of the future, her business was stable and growing, her staff happy and dedicated. She had a little more time for herself—maybe a small house that she might actually own, with a garden where she could grow her own herbs. And always, as persistent as the steam in front of her face, Clay appeared in her reverie of the future.

She tried to banish him, but he couldn't be banished any more than the steam could. She'd blow it and watch it float back. Hmmm.

She yawned and let her eyes drift shut for a moment. It felt so good simply to relax....

"Mmmm." She was warm. Floating in warmth. Surrounded by warmth. Her eyes opened slowly and she frowned. What on earth?

She was in bed. Not her bed. She blinked and her heart fluttered in that second of confusion before she realized she was in Clay's bed. And the warmth surrounding her was his arms wrapped around her waist, one leg tossed carelessly and intimately across hers.

Warm comfort turned to claustrophobia in a heartbeat. She felt entwined by hot limbs that weren't hers. Restricted, confined.

With a tug, she freed herself, glancing around the room in vain for her clothes.

The last thing she remembered was the bath. Had they made love and she didn't remember? How disappointing. If it had been anything like their first time together, she wanted to savor every second, every detail, every nuance of feeling.

Making love with Clay and then forgetting was like slaving all day over a perfect meal and then burning it beyond recognition. Lost forever. Well, she supposed she'd enjoyed it. If she hadn't, she'd obviously blocked the experience from her mind.

"Morning," a sleepy voice mumbled in her ear.

She turned with what she hoped was a bright smile. "Good morning."

"How are you feeling?" His hand rubbed her thigh, warm and wonderful, bringing sensations rushing to the surface of her skin.

"Fine," she said. "I feel fine." Actually, she felt foolish, but she couldn't ask him if they'd made love. That would dash his ego like a fresh soufflé stuck in the freezer.

"I should have kept better watch over you last

night. I knew you were tired, but I didn't want you to think I was being a pervert hanging around outside the bathroom.'' He raised his head to gaze at her. ''You could drown falling asleep in the bathtub.''

She blinked up at him. ''I fell asleep in the tub?''

''Yes, you did. You never woke, even when I dried you off and put you to bed.''

''You dragged me out of the tub? Naked?''

''Uh-huh. But I kept my eyes closed the entire time.'' His eyes were grinning at her, she'd swear it, even though his mouth remained serious.

''Well,'' she said, trying not to squirm—after all, he'd seen her naked before. It was just that she'd been conscious at the time. The idea of Clay manhandling her while she was unconscious and soaking wet was… ''That's intimate.''

Now the grin spread to his lips. ''Not as intimate as I'd planned to be, believe me.''

''You should have woken me.''

''Honey, a twenty-one-gun salute across this bed wouldn't have woken you.'' He did his best to look hard done by. ''I went to sleep one frustrated man. This sexy beauty sleeping beside me and I couldn't wake her.''

His hand was making little circles now on her thigh, moving up in a seemingly slow, careless fashion, but she had a pretty good idea of his target, and it was already beginning to throb in anticipation.

"Seems I owe you," she said.

"We owe each other," he answered, leaning over to kiss her. She put a hand to his cheek and found it stubbly but appealing. In fact, he was an altogether appealing package to wake up to, she decided as she turned her body toward him to ease his access.

Her head tipped back with a sigh as his fingers reached their intended target. He toyed lazily with her until she was slick, her intimate flesh plump and pulsing with desire. She let herself go. It was so wonderful to enjoy a lazy morning in bed. Already naked, relaxed and still close to the dreams of sleep, she slid blissfully into a kind of waking dream as heat built within her body. She rolled closer, kissed his neck, enjoying the half-sleepy, half-aroused scent of his skin. Her own hands took a lazy tour meant both to acquaint her better with his body and to arouse.

Sleepy sexiness soon lost its lazy overtones and became sharper, more urgent, as desire flamed.

She traced his belly, the jut of a hip bone, the dense hardness of thigh where she felt a deep quiver in the muscle. Then finally, she let herself indulge, moving north, touching the silken hardness, wrapping her hand around him so he sucked in a breath and she felt his erection pulse against her palm.

"I need to be inside you," he whispered and she heard that need.

Smiling slightly with her own power and her own need, she reached for the ornate box on the dresser, took him in hand, with morning sun pouring into the room, and flipped back the covers to enjoy her task in the full light of day.

She pulled out the condom and then, just before putting it on, she couldn't resist the urge to kiss the tip of his penis, run her tongue once around the head. A groan rumbled, deep and desperate. She thought about taking him all the way into her mouth, but her lower body was sending her some pretty unmistakable signals. So she sheathed him quickly and then, since he was already so comfortably on his back, she threw a leg over and straddled him.

Their hands clasped, sweat beading their bodies, they moved together. She took him deep and still he thrust up into her, as though trying to reach even deeper. He was hitting some magic spot that had never been touched before and it was driving her crazy.

The bed was much too expensive to creak under the strain, but their ragged breathing was as noisy as screeching bedsprings. She was climbing so high she felt as though a climax might do her an injury— falling from such a height could hurt a person—and yet she couldn't slow down. Nor could she look away from the intense expression on his face.

"I love you," he said, hoarse and low, and it was the final spur. At the sound of those words her body gave a great shuddering clench. Sensation exploded inside her body, all over her, even seemed to shimmer in the air around her. Her cries were wild, free and barely human.

Her own enthusiastic response set him off and they bucked and shivered together until she slumped, spent and exhausted, onto his heaving chest.

He loved her. He'd said he loved her.

Hope quivered in her chest even as fear scoffed. *Love.* She'd heard that old joke before.

A minute passed while she kept her face hidden against his chest, while their breathing slowed. His hand was in her hair, tracing slow circles against her scalp. She wanted to stay there forever, which unnerved her so much she pulled away.

"How about I make us some breakfast?" she said, raising her head but deliberately not looking at him.

"Hey." He pulled her back down against him. "I just said words to you I've never said to another woman except my mother. Don't I deserve a response?"

She yanked herself away this time, wishing he

would leave her be. "I don't have a response. I don't know what to say."

She forgot not to look at him, and the expression in his eyes caused hers to fill with stupid sentimental tears.

"You might try, 'I love you, too.' That's always an appropriate one."

"And then what?" A tear slipped out and she wiped it with her wrist.

"We get married." His voice rose on the words, making marriage sound like a threat. Which it was—a threat to her serenity, her peace of mind, everything she was trying to build for herself.

"I tried that. It didn't work."

"The hell you did." He was really steaming now. So much for a romantic morning romp in bed. "You made a mistake and got engaged to a worthless piece of slime. It happens. Don't let him ruin your life and your shot at happiness. This is it, Marina. Can't you feel it? Hell, I know you do. I wouldn't have chosen you, either, but it happened. I love you and I know we can be happy together."

"You wouldn't have chosen me?" For some reason that made her smile, although in a slightly painful way.

"No. You're too complicated. Too much baggage. Too little trust."

"I had my trust stolen from me."

"I'm trying to give it back."

She sniffed, attempting to blink back another tear and failing. He touched the wet drop with a fingertip in a gesture that struck her as infinitely tender.

"Do you really love me?" she murmured.

"I knew after the first week," he said gruffly and pulled her back into his arms again, kissing her with such softness that tears pooled once more.

He hauled out of bed and walked to his desk. Since he was naked, she stopped crying to indulge herself in watching the long-limbed grace, the round butt and lightly furred legs. All she had to do was glimpse his backside and she wanted him again.

"I was saving this for later, but I have a present for you." He opened a drawer and handed her a sheaf of papers.

Puzzled, she took them. And read Pierre's signed agreement to give her half the value of Delicieux. Her stomach felt as though she'd eaten a couple of handfuls of gravel. "You did this."

"No. Mostly the lawyers did it. All I did was get hold of François and get him to write down everything."

"He never told me," she whispered through dry lips.

"Good. I made him swear he wouldn't."

"You did all this behind my back." She glanced up at him and flapped the papers in the air. "You gave me this on a silver platter. I didn't even have to lift a finger.''

''Honey, it's a gift.''

''But this was *my* battle to fight. *My* problem.''

''I thought you'd be happy.''

''I am,'' she sobbed. ''But I hate that you push me and manipulate me and take care of me when I'm perfectly capable of taking care of myself.''

Somehow, on some level, she'd known he loved her. That's why she'd worked so hard to stay away from him. He was going to destroy the world she'd rebuilt so carefully. The one where she was strong and tough, so independent no one could ever hurt her again.

He was back at her side in an instant, falling to his knees so her ducked head couldn't hide her face from him. ''Hey, I'm sorry if I overstepped. I only wanted to help. I love you. I'll always be there for you. I promise. You can be as strong as you want, but maybe you'll find we're both stronger if we work together.''

''And maybe you'll break my heart.''

''I can't promise it will be perfect, but make sure you're judging me for me and not some bastard who never deserved a second of your time.''

She wiped at her eyes, but it was pointless, the tears fell faster than she could keep up with them.

''I need some time. You know?''

He nodded and finally let her go. "Take as long as you need. We'll just hang out. We can spend Christmas together. Take things slow."

She rolled her gaze. This man didn't know the meaning of the word *slow*. Except at certain moments in bed.

She shoved her clothes on, stopping every once in a while to grab a tissue from the box beside his bed. The tears wouldn't stop flowing.

Clay was no help at all. He simply lay in that bed, sexy and rumpled and dear, watching her. She felt as though he could see right inside her and the fact that he understood her fears only made her cry harder.

She banged down the stairs like a kid having a temper tantrum, and, frankly, that's how she felt. It just wasn't fair! Why should he fight her battles—win her battles—for her without so much as asking her permission? And why the hell should he throw marriage at her when she wasn't ready? Why?

She got to the heavy front door and threw it open with a sob, only to give a yelp of surprise and jump back.

There were people there. Three of them. Tanned people. With suitcases.

While they all blinked at each other, Marina had a moment to take in the fact that the man standing there shivering in a pale-peach golf shirt was an older version of Clay. She wanted to slam the door and run out the back way. But, just as the craven thought presented itself, the older of the two woman stepped forward with a big smile. "You must be Marina."

She scrubbed at her eyes with her palms. "You know about me?"

"I'm Clay's mother."

Marina sniffed. "Oh. Hello."

"Bring in the bags, John. Find your son. I'm going to put coffee on. Damn flights. It was all we could get at the last minute. We had to overnight in Seattle and fly out at the crack of dawn this morning." As she spoke, the woman maneuvered Marina back into the house, and before she realized it, she was in the kitchen, trying to act normally. "But," she said, chucking Marina's cheek as though she were the one this forceful woman had come to see, "we made it."

Clay might look like his dad, but she realized a lot of his stubborn bull-headedness came from his mother. She was direct like him, too. "I hope these tears don't mean the wedding's off."

"How did you know about the wedding?" Marina shook her head violently. What was this woman talking about? There was no wedding.

"Clay told me on the phone, when he cancelled his plans to spend Christmas with us." His mother reached out and clasped Marina's hand. "He's never been in love before. I hope we can spend some time together over the holidays."

"But I'm not… He shouldn't have said… I haven't—"

"Mom!" Clay's voice boomed and Marina heard the thunder of far-from-tiny feet pounding down the stairs.

His mother's face lit up at the sound. Suddenly Marina pictured Clay as he must have been as a child. Then she imagined her and Clay's kids pounding down those very stairs. No! She was not filling her head with foolish fantasies. Not ever again.

Clay entered the kitchen and hauled his mother into a hug that looked as though it might break a few bones. She didn't seem to mind, though, and squeezed right back.

In another minute the rest of the crowd had joined them. Clay introduced Marina to his mother, whose name was Marge, his father, John, and his "little sister," Lizzie, who was five-eleven in her stocking feet.

Clay was in his bathrobe and she was wearing last night's creased evening gown. This wasn't exactly how she would have imagined meeting his parents for the first time—if she'd ever imagined such a thing.

"Coffee!" Clay said the minute the hellos and

handshakes were out of the way. "And breakfast. I cook a great omelet. It's too bad you didn't come last night. We had a party. Marina catered it. It was fantastic."

"I..." She felt like a cross between a scarlet woman in her sexy dress and Little Orphan Annie with her cried-out eyes. She knew they were red without glancing in a mirror. They always went hideously red and puffy when she cried. Sitting here eating an omelet with Clay's family was not going to help her recover her balance.

"I'm afraid I can't stay. I was on my way out when you arrived. I have to check on things at work." She pasted on her best smile. "I hope I'll get a chance to see you again before you leave."

"Count on it," said Marge. "And don't feel cramped by us. We're staying in a hotel. We only dropped by here first to surprise Clayton."

"That you did," he said, glancing from Marina's dress to his bathrobe and sending her the ghost of a wink. "But, of course, you're staying here. I've got seven bedrooms. What the hell's the point of them if my own family won't sleep here. Right, Marina?"

"Of course. Really, it's nothing to me... I mean, none of my business what... I mean... I really have to go." And with that she bolted once more for the front door.

This time it was Clay who left the crowd to stop

her, with a hand on her arm. "Come back tonight. We'll have dinner with my family. You should get to know them under more normal circumstances."

He seemed kind of jokey about the whole thing, but she was furious. "You told your mother you were going to marry me before you ever told me!"

He shrugged. "I didn't mean to. I just knew I couldn't go to Florida for Christmas, not when you were here. So I cancelled and, being my mother, she dragged the truth out of me."

"But that's just another example of how you're so presumptuous. And pushy. I never said I'd spend Christmas with you," she scolded in a furious whisper.

"So don't." His eyes darkened, and she felt his frustration. "Please yourself. I'm here. And I'm not going anywhere. Get used to it." Then he leaned in close and murmured, "I love you. Goodbye."

Her mouth opened and closed a few times and he took advantage of her complete inability to speak to kiss her thoroughly—which did nothing to restore her language skills.

He opened the door and held it for her politely as she left. She was still trying to decide how to answer him when the door closed softly behind her.

She drove home, showered, changed to go to work and then suddenly couldn't stand the thought of being cooped up and forced to use her thinking or cooking skills. She'd botch her recipes and muddle all the bookings for sure.

As she passed houses, buildings, even cranes lit for the holidays, she realized it was Christmas Eve. There was no cooking to be done today. No bookings until next week. She could go botch some paperwork instead, or she could take the day off.

So she followed the stream of traffic for a while, going aimlessly with the flow until she found herself on the causeway heading to Lion's Gate Bridge. Ahead of her the mountains were shrouded in cloud. She could drive to the North Shore or she could take the turnoff into Stanley Park. She took the turnoff, recalling that the last time she'd been here she'd been with Clay.

She parked by Lost Lagoon and walked the paved path with crowds of others, remembering the earlier walk when she'd phoned him on impulse and he'd dropped everything to meet her.

Things were going okay. Why did he have to jump all over her? Shoulder her problems without even asking her if she minded? Tell her he loved her? Talk marriage? It was too soon.

She was too scared.

A huge Christmas tree sat majestically on a barge in the middle of the lagoon. It wouldn't be lit until evening, but it was awfully festive. Thin ice laced the edges of the shore. She watched a little boy in a red snowsuit flap his hands in frustration as the crust of whole-wheat bread he was trying to throw to the birds kept sticking to his red woolen mittens.

Fed up with the wait, a goose waddled up and took the crust from his glove, yanking with its beak until the bread came free. Its head was almost level with that of the little boy who stared at the goose for a moment, uncertain whether to laugh or cry.

Marina laughed. He was so adorable and then, catching the sound, the boy laughed, too, turning his head her way. His cheeks were flushed with the cold, his eyes bright, his nose running. His mother rushed up to brush at the hand, and he told her the story in amazed halting sentences while she pulled a pack of tissues from her pocket and took care of the nose.

A father soon came into view with a little girl in a pink fuzzy hat strapped into a backpack. Marina gasped. Not from cold, but from the realization that that was what she wanted. A man to love. A family to take to the park on a cold clear day.

She kept walking. She'd tried that before. Believed in love and it had failed her. No, she realized, it was Pierre who had failed her. He'd taken her love and stolen her money.

But Clay had helped her get her money back. And Clay had given her love, not waiting to get hers first.

Clay was not Pierre. He wasn't anything like him.

And what she felt for Clay was nothing like what she'd felt for Pierre.

She walked faster as the truth hit her. She loved Clay.

She really, truly, till-death-do-us-part loved him.

He'd asked her to marry him and she'd run. He'd stayed home for Christmas because he wanted to be with her.

What was she, an idiot? The love of her life was giving her everything she wanted on a silver platter and she was turning up her nose.

Walking turned into a jog and then a sprint.

She reached her car and threw herself behind the wheel like a Formula One racer and headed for her shop.

For Clay, Christmas Eve passed in a blur. An awful lot of brightly wrapped packages appeared beneath his tree, including the ones he'd sent by courier to his family and they'd hauled back with them on the plane. He took his mother to the market and they bought turkey and all the trimmings. Once back home, she started cooking.

He lit a fire, played backgammon with his father, argued politics with his sister, and always in the back of his mind he wondered. What was Marina doing? Where was she? How badly had he scared her?

He didn't call. His hand itched to grab the phone a hundred times, but at least he didn't make the mistake of hounding her. He'd put his heart at her feet. Asked her to marry him. He'd even made a stop at a jeweler's and bought some ruby-and-diamond earrings. They weren't under the tree, though. He couldn't stand the possibility that they'd still be there, in a tiny, lonely, Christmas-wrapped jeweler's box after the rest of the gifts had been handed out. One more reminder that Marina had turned him down on every level.

He had a heart-to-heart with his mom, which helped somewhat.

"I like the look of that one," she told him. "She's scared, sure, but if she's smart, and I think she is, she'll know that you're the one for her."

"How are you so sure?"

"Because *you're* so sure. And you're a pretty smart boy." She patted his cheek, then pulled him into her arms for a hug.

Around five the doorbell rang. Clay told himself it was probably a last-minute gift delivery or a partier at the wrong house, but still his heart beat a little faster as he pulled open the heavy door.

It stopped entirely when he saw Marina standing there, dressed for dinner and gorgeous. She had an overnight bag in one arm, which looked very promising. And a tiny box of her chocolates, which suggested she'd brought dessert and so planned to stay for dinner.

"Merry Christmas," he said and opened the door wide.

She remained on the doorstep looking nervous. "Can you come out here a second?"

"Sure," he said, feeling puzzled. He stepped out and pulled her to him for a long, deep kiss.

"Oh, Clay," she said, putting her head on his shoulder. They stayed like that for a good minute and he barely noticed the cold through his shirtsleeves. He felt only the warmth of the woman. "I have a gift for you."

"Great. I have one for you, too. Put it under the tree."

"No. I want you to open it here. Now."

She took a step backward and presented him with the box. He felt absurdly disappointed. "Chocolates. Fantastic."

"Open it." She was wringing her gloved hands.

He untied the pouffy bronze ribbon she'd used and eased the gold lid off the small box.

And his heart swelled. The center three chocolates were piped with white icing and spelled Y-E-S.

"Is that the answer to the question I think it is?"

She nodded, eyes brimming, but sparkling, too. "Yes, I love you, too." She stopped and took a deep breath. "Yes, I'll marry you."

"My mom was right. She said you were one smart lady."

Then he pulled her into his arms and kissed her again. And he knew he would never receive a Christmas gift that meant more than those three chocolates.

A PHILADELPHIA AFFAIR
Jule McBride

CHAPTER ONE

I will honor Christmas in my heart, and try to
keep it all the year. I will live in the Past, the
Present and the Future. The spirits of all shall
strive within me! I will not shut out the lessons
that they teach.

—Ebenezer Scrooge after his transformation

"BAH, HUMBUG," Timothy Toye whispered under
his breath as he followed Kim Winkler down a long,
red-carpeted hallway. "She's avoiding me again."
Not that it surprised him. He'd rarely seen Smart
Markets' CEO since they'd quit sleeping together
and, just now, she'd fled after their meeting. He
wasn't going to let her get away, though. After the
hot three months they'd shared in the sack, he deserved some answers.

She was ten paces ahead, and every gorgeous inch
of her seemed to call to him. He'd once stripped off
the gray tailored suit hugging her willowy frame,
just as he'd slipped those same high heels from her
feet and had thrust his fingers into that short golden

hair. He sighed. He should probably head for his office across town. Instead, he made an abrupt right turn and strode into hers. And then he shut the door behind him.

Color crept into her cheeks. "Timothy," she said.

He smiled. "That's good. You still recognize me."

She playfully rolled her eyes. "Of course I do."

"I never see you anymore." They'd gone at it hot and heavy during the phase when their business relationship was getting off the ground. Once things were up and running, she'd broken things off. Because phone contact usually sufficed, today's meeting was a rare opportunity to see her again.

She said, "We broke up, remember?"

"You broke up."

"Hmm. Is this about work?"

"Nope."

She tried not to smile, but her lips tilted upward and he registered the awareness in her gaze as she surveyed him. Why would a woman who obviously wanted him decide not to spend time with him? He watched as she circled the desk, clearly determined to put some distance between them. It was a bad sign.

"What can I do for you?" she asked.

Despite the warning signals that he wasn't going to get lucky, looking at Kim warmed him. He couldn't help but broaden his smile. "It's Christmas and I'm lonely."

"Poor baby."

"Well, it's not Christmas *yet,*" he amended.

"Two more days."

"Hardly enough time to find someone to share it with," he commented.

"A lot can happen in two days."

"Is that an invitation?"

"You're putting words into my mouth."

He could think of other things he'd like to do with that mouth. Kiss it thoroughly, for instance. Somehow, he wasn't surprised that he and Kim could still enjoy casual banter even though she'd ended their affair so abruptly. Since then, he'd realized he hadn't really gotten to know her at all during their time together; she'd asked him to contact her at work and insisted they meet at his town house rather than her apartment. Now he was wondering about the little things he'd missed, like knowing how her place was decorated and what she kept in her refrigerator. "C'mon," he suddenly said. "Company might be nice. Dinner. A bottle of wine."

"Who said anything about company?"

"I did."

"You're not going out of town?"

"Nope."

"Why?"

Because he didn't want to go to his buddy Carey's farm in Lancaster. Or to Zach's place in Jersey. Both his foster brothers had married last year, and now both had babies. While he'd be welcomed, Timothy wanted to snuggle up with a babe of his own for the holiday. Preferably Kim. "Long story," he finally said.

"Want to tell me about it?"

"If you're good."

He crossed the room, circled the desk and paused in front of her, coming close enough that a wintery draft through a floor-to-ceiling window behind her brought a whiff of her perfume. Impulsively, before she could protest, he threaded his fingers through hers, then gently spun her to face the window. As she landed against him, with her back to his chest, he slid an arm around her waist, pulling her dangerously close. "C'mon," he murmured. "Be nice, Kim. It's Christmas."

"This is my workplace," she reminded.

He could feel the tension in her body. "The door's shut."

She sighed. "I've missed you," she admitted. "I really have…but I told you why we needed to stop seeing each other."

"You said you're still grieving."

"And we work together."

"Both things were true when we met, yet we still

ended up together." When she didn't respond, he lowered his voice to a whisper. "You said you wanted to keep it simple. I'm not asking for more."

"I know. And I also know that when we met I…I told you what I wanted."

Timothy chuckled, his body warming, heat sliding through his veins. "Hot sex. No strings attached."

"And we had that for a while."

Enough that she'd left him craving her. The first time they'd made love, they'd barely made it inside his prewar town house on Society Hill before their clothes hit the floor. Then they'd proceeded to try every surface from his white overstuffed sofa to the faux bearskin rug and hammered-copper dining table. Because he was cursed with quite an imagination, Timothy could still see Kim lying on top of the table wearing nothing but white panties and lace topped stockings.

"It's over," she murmured as his arm tightened possessively around her waist.

"I've seen your eyes," he countered. "How you look at me. You still want me, Kim."

"That's not the issue."

Then what was? He'd given up on pressuring her, so when she said nothing, he stared outside. Past their joined reflection in the darkened window, downtown Philly looked like a candy store. Glittering snowflakes spiraled onto Broad Street, and lights in the shapes of Christmas trees hung high above the ice-slicked pavement. White lights in the trees on the median sparkled like diamonds. The city of love, he thought. Too bad it was *brotherly* love.

"I can tell you miss this…." His lips grazed her neck, then trailed sensuously toward the open collar of her blouse. As if against her will, she shut her expressive dark eyes as he kissed her. Yes, she'd ended their affair. And yes, she'd been avoiding him. But she'd definitely missed him.

Suddenly, the phone rang. "Bad timing," he whispered.

"That's a matter of opinion," she whispered back, blinking as if relieved that something had brought her to her senses. She edged away, and he was surprised to see her fingers tremble as she hit the speaker-phone button. It was nice to know his kisses had affected her that much. Even nicer to hear her voice shake. "Kim Winkler speaking."

"It's Wendy," said her assistant. "I just wanted you to know I'm on my way to the airport. I'll see you after the New Year."

"Have a great holiday."

"I'll get those dolls you wanted before I leave. The Pittsburgh warehouse sent down a box for the employees. I'd better grab yours before they're all gone."

He shifted uncomfortably, since he'd taken issue

with Kim's decision to drive up the demand for the dolls by withholding some in the warehouse.

"I'll just leave them on my chair, okay?" asked Wendy.

"Terrific."

As Kim finalized business matters, Timothy took in the pictures of Dr. Ooze dolls strewn across her desk. The cartoon action-adventure hero Timothy had created was tall with rock-hard pectorals and a V-shaped torso; he was the perfect replica of what Timothy had conjured with his childhood imagination during long dark nights when he'd lain awake spinning tales about the ultimate escape artist.

Strange, he thought now, that a lonely little boy's alter ego could turn into a multimillion-dollar business almost overnight. Not that his other cartoon creations hadn't done well. But Dr. Ooze was his crowning achievement. The comic book he'd begun selling in college had caught the attention of Smart Markets, and in the past year Kim had not only turned the comic strip into a prime-time Saturday-morning cartoon, but she'd made Dr. Ooze this year's most sought-after toy. He respected her head for business. She'd driven a hard bargain, demanding a percentage of the profits for her own company. His eyes scanned the office, taking in the other products Smart Markets was turning into household names, everything from vitamins to home security systems.

Then his gaze returned to the pictures of Dr Ooze. They brought a flood of memories. He'd been five when he'd first imagined the man in the silver costume who'd been gifted with special powers—after a freak accident in a hospital lab, he'd become able to heal any malady and escape any bonds.

Kim pressed the phone button, turning off the speaker. "I guess I'd better get home now."

"Bah, humbug."

She wagged a manicured finger that he could easily recall wrapped around choice parts of his anatomy. "Don't be a Scrooge."

"Are you sure you don't want to come over and model an elf outfit?"

"Not a Santa hat?"

"I'm not picky."

He could swear she was going to change her mind, but then she said, "Maybe another time."

But there wasn't going to be another time, and he could barely stand it; he was still tasting the salt from her skin. "You're going to force me to watch the evening news with only a beer for company?"

"You can learn a lot from the news."

"But the news depresses me. This time of year, it's all human interest stories. I don't even have a tree, let alone kids to get gifts for."

"That's a good thing," she pointed out. "I've made sure there aren't any Dr. Ooze dolls left in Philly, except for the three being raffled off at the Gallery tonight."

He started to say she shouldn't make light of his situation. Or hers. It sucked to be alone on Christmas. "Your loss."

"Probably," Kim agreed with an airy sigh. "But I'm going home to take a nice long bath."

He raised an eyebrow.

"Alone," she said.

But another sudden twitch of her lips gave away her desire, as did the soft chuckle that had so often warmed his blood. Over a three-month period, they'd gotten together exactly fifteen times and each time had been unforgettable. So what gave? She'd been widowed after a nine-year marriage, sure, but her husband had died almost two years ago and now she lived by herself. No doubt, she hadn't decorated any more than Timothy had. "Last call. I overheard you saying you were staying in town, instead of visiting your folks."

"Has anyone ever told you that you need to learn to take no for an answer?"

"All the time."

"Then I give up."

He laughed. "You're alone. I'm alone." And the longing in her eyes was making him believe she'd like nothing more than to spend tonight in bed with him.

Her gaze softened. "I appreciate it, but…I'm sure."

He didn't understand, but he forced himself to shrug in acquiescence. Before she could protest, he brushed a kiss across her cheek, then he headed for the door. When he reached it, he turned. His eyes met hers. "Have yourself a merry one, sweetheart."

"You, too, Timothy."

"Thanks." Turning, he headed down the hallway, forcing himself to softly whistle "Holly Jolly Christmas." His heart wasn't in it, but he definitely didn't want Kim to think her rejection could ruin his holiday.

Two hours later, Kim was standing in the Gallery, clutching her cell phone, half listening to her six-year-old daughter's complaints. She could scarcely believe that she—the person who'd created the craze for Dr. Ooze—hadn't managed to get her hands on at least one doll for her little girl. At least Wendy hadn't mentioned Kelsey in front of Timothy. During the phone conversation, Kim had been sweating bullets, since she'd never told Timothy about Kelsey. Now she glanced around. The shopping mall where they were raffling off the last three dolls was packed, and for the umpteenth time, Kim wondered what had happened to the dolls Wendy was supposed to leave on her chair. How could her assistant have forgotten?

"Step right up to the platform," called an announcer. He was bellowing into a microphone, but it was so loud in the mall that Kim had to strain to hear. "I'm standing here with Dr. Ooze, himself, who's about to draw the next winning ticket," said the announcer. "Listen up because we're drawing for the city's only remaining Dr. Ooze doll."

Under any other circumstances, Kim would be congratulating herself on the success of this promotion—turning a comic book character into a national phenomenon wasn't easy—but she felt every bit as desperate as the other parents pushing and shoving toward the stage. Guilty, too, since she shouldn't be participating in her own company's promotion.

"Mom, you forgot," her daughter was saying.

"Kind of," Kim admitted, speaking into the cell phone in a hushed tone. "It's a long story, hon. But I'm trying to get whatever Dr. Ooze dolls I can."

"The other parents already came to pick up their kids," Kelsey protested. "So I can't give the dolls away to them now."

"Well, I'm on my way to get you," promised Kim.

The announcer's voice sounded. "Dr. Ooze is stepping forward, folks, to draw the first number."

Please, let me win. "Honey, I'm really sorry, but I've got to go."

"You're at the raffle," Kelsey accused.

"Of course I am. It's my job," Kim countered, even though Kelsey had guessed the truth; she was here strictly to try to get a doll for her. After another of Kelsey's protests, Kim powered off the cell, then fixed her eyes on the stage—and the perfect physique of the actor playing Dr. Ooze. The silver costume was perfect. A cape swirled around him, revealing a to-die-for body encased in skintight silver Lycra; a silver mask obscured a face supposedly damaged during the lab accident that had given Dr. Ooze his powers. Glancing down at the ticket in her hand, Kim mouthed, *742036.*

Please call my numbers! Why had she put off getting the dolls she'd promised Kelsey? The box sent by the Pittsburgh warehouse had been right outside her office all week. Before tonight, it had been so full….

But something always required her attention, and with so much work to do, she felt scattered. Had she taken on too much putting the business she'd started with her husband back into the black? And how could she explain her distractions to a six-year-old?

Already, with her father's death, Kelsey's innocence had been stripped away....

"Seven," came the voice.

Relief washed over her. Maybe she'd win. She felt guilty for participating, but it was so important that she try to get at least one doll. Later she could get some for Kelsey's day-care friends. Kim's heart ached. Wasn't it enough that she and Kelsey had lost Larry right after Christmas, the year before last? Didn't she deserve to win this? To have something go right?

"Four," the announcer called.

Kim's heart missed a beat. Was it possible? Could she actually win? Would this redeem her in her little girl's eyes? And her own? She just wished she'd gotten the dolls herself, rather than relying on Wendy, who'd tailed her.

"Two."

"Thank you," she whispered, barely able to believe another of her numbers had been called. Maybe there was a Santa, after all. As people drifted away, another wave of guilt washed over her; there were still dolls in the Pittsburgh warehouse, after all. Not that she was wrong to hold them in reserve. Driving up the demand had increased the percentage she'd negotiated with Timothy and had saved Smart Markets from financial ruin; now she could pay debts and secure her and Kelsey's future. She'd had no choice.

"Zero."

Two more numbers to go! Her heart lurched with hope. Maybe getting Kelsey the perfect present would turn the tide. Maybe after tonight, Kim wouldn't come home to tales of Kelsey's inability to share toys or snacks with kids at day care. At home, Kim had gone full-tilt with decorations, too, hoping she and Kelsey could start creating their own traditions without Larry. It was why they weren't visiting her folks and in-laws in Florida. And why she'd ended her affair with Timothy.

At the thought, sharp visceral longing claimed her body.

But Kelsey had enough to deal with, and every time Timothy kissed Kim, he'd threatened to make things too complex. She missed him, though. He was smart. Cute. And hot as tamales, with longish blond hair, a tall, trim, broad-shouldered body, and a naughty twinkle in his blue eyes that he made good on in the bedroom. She sighed. Maybe her mother-in-law was right when she'd said Kim needed to move on with her life and that she couldn't let a six-year-old determine her dating practices. But no one understood. Kelsey was her baby girl. She came first. Always.

"Three," said the announcer.

One more! All she needed was the next—
"Six."

"That's me!" Kim waved the ticket as she began to elbow her way through the dispersing crowd. Once they'd realized they'd lost, they barely noticed her, not caring who'd won.

Suddenly, she saw a flash of red. Just as she registered the parka sleeve appearing from behind her, beefy fingers reached over her shoulder and snatched her ticket. "Give that back! It's mine! I won!"

She whirled, but he'd vanished! Eyes wide, she pivoted again. Where was he? *There*. He was moving quickly through what was left of the crowd, wending through dejected parents who were now rushing off, anxious to get home or finish shopping. The man had almost reached the stage.

That doll was for her baby girl! This was all Kim's own fault, of course. She'd created the craze that had made other parents this desperate. Her chest constricted in panic as she pushed against the wave of jostling bodies. "Wait!" she called.

But Dr. Ooze was handing the last doll to the man…the thief. Just days ago Kelsey had seen a department-store Santa remove his beard in this same mall. Only a mother could know the wrenching pain that came from seeing that small illusion stripped away. Kelsey had lost her daddy, too. Now,

Kim needed that doll! She vaulted onto the stage just as the man in the red parka began stepping down.

"Give the doll back!"

Because he showed no signs of doing so, she kept her eyes intent on the parka and lunged. But something caught her from behind. Strong arms wrapped around her midsection and a husky male voice said, "Hold it right there."

She spun wildly. Or tried. The other parents were almost gone, and whoever had grabbed her had lifted her off the floor! Her feet were pedaling in midair. As she clawed the muscular forearms squeezing the breath from her ribs, she glanced down and realized the arms were encased in silver Lycra. It was Dr. Ooze. "I hired you!" she exclaimed as her feet gained purchase. "I'm Kim! Kim Winkler! From Smart Markets! Don't you recognize me? I know I shouldn't have participated in the raffle, but I did. And I won. But that man stole my ticket! The doll's for my daughter!"

When he didn't let go, she wrenched, grunting. Why hadn't she had the foresight to hire someone smaller? Half dragging him toward the edge of the stage, she kept her eyes on the man in the parka, but he'd nearly reached the doors! "Please, let me go!"

She felt, rather than saw Dr. Ooze stumble. Good,

she thought. Taking the sudden advantage, she tried to slip from his grasp. Instead, she mistepped, and her foot dipped over the side of the stage, away from the few people still milling around it. Gasping, she swiped vainly at the air, and as she tumbled over the edge, her hand grasped around the silver sleeve of the action-adventure hero's costume.

To his credit, he didn't let go but twisted his body to protect hers. Landing on his feet, he staggered backward a pace before his knees buckled. Rolling as he fell to the tile floor, he pulled her protectively on top of him.

"Some superhero!" Kim muttered, trying not to notice the hard, enticing muscles rippling beneath the revealing Lycra. "You're supposed to chase the bad guy!"

"I saved you from cracking your skull."

"He took my ticket!"

"So much for this being the city of love."

Because his voice was muffled by the mask, she hadn't recognized it before. "You," she whispered simply.

Timothy Toye had yanked her so close that their lips nearly brushed. "Mind telling me why you—of all people—can't get your hands on a doll?" he began. Before she could answer, he added, "And did I just hear you say *daughter.*"

No doubt he'd been watching her in the crowd,

noting how her eyes had lit up with parental hope. He'd heard her mention her daughter, too. Lying would be futile. Heat flooded her cheeks. Maybe she should have told him. But he'd only seemed interested in a fling. Besides, Kelsey wasn't ready for her mom to bring men home. "I know I gave the impression that I lived alone," she managed.

"You lied," he corrected.

"Not really."

"By omission."

And it was a big omission. She could see that now. Swallowing hard, she wished the contact of his body wasn't making her pulse leap. "I should have told you," she admitted. "But it just never came up...."

"It never came up because I didn't know it was a possibility."

Heaving a sigh, she decided it might be best to shift to the offensive. "What are you doing here, anyway? You shouldn't be doing something like this. We hired an actor."

"He called in sick."

"Is he okay?"

"You're changing the subject."

She'd definitely been trying to. Abruptly, he shifted his legs and sweet maddening sensations rushed through her extremities, making her wonder if nerve endings could really shiver. She'd been watching his lips move under the mask's mouth hole, and suddenly she wanted to feel the touch of his lips on her neck again as she had only hours ago in her office.

As a traitorous shudder wracked her body, he said, ''You should have told me you had a kid.''

An idea flashed through Kim's mind—as a marketing executive, she was prone to getting a great many ideas—and she found herself saying, ''You're absolutely right. And I can explain everything. I should have told you about Kelsey. How would you like to meet her?''

His voice was tinged with disbelief. ''Meet her? After you lied to me?''

''Omitted the truth.''

Now he sounded suspicious. ''When?''

Kim mustered her brightest voice. ''What about right now?''

''Right now?''

''Yes.'' She nodded. ''Why don't you come over for dinner?'' Despite his good looks—the ice-blue eyes, high forehead and chiseled jaw—she was suddenly very glad she couldn't see his face. She could only imagine his stunned expression when she added, ''There is, however, one condition.''

''What?''

She took a deep breath, then firmly said, ''You'll have to wear this costume.''

CHAPTER TWO

"KIM, I'm so sorry, but Kelsey's gone," said Anna Carver breathlessly a half hour later. The worried, heavyset, black-haired woman who met them at the door of the day care in Society Hill didn't even cast a glance at Timothy's absurd costume. She pressed a hand to her heart. "Kelsey told me you were here to pick her up, then she ran out the door. I followed, to wave at you, the way I always do, but Kelsey was hopping into a cab. She's only been gone a minute. I don't know what on earth gets into that child!"

Kim scanned the traffic, her eyes searching for the cab.

"She told some of the kids you were bringing dolls to give to them, and when you weren't here—" Anna cut herself off. "I'm sure she went home."

Kim, who'd already started back down the stairs to the sidewalk, was punching in numbers on her cell phone. She seemed barely aware that Timothy was following her. "If she's not home," she called over her shoulder, "I know where she is."

"She won't be home yet, Kim."

"I'll try calling anyway."

"Is there anything I can do?" Anna called.

"No." Kim shook her head. "But thanks. Like I said, I'm sure I know where she's going. I just wish she wouldn't do things like this." Drawing a deep breath, she spoke into the phone. "Honey, it's Mom. Are you home yet? If you are, please pick up."

Just as Kim turned off the phone, Timothy got into the passenger seat of her Jeep Cherokee and slammed the door, wondering what he'd gotten himself into.

"She's not home," Kim reported, replacing the phone into her shoulder bag.

"How old is she?" he asked as a nearby car's horn tooted the opening bars of "Jingle Bells." He couldn't help but add, "If you don't mind me asking?" After all, Kim hadn't even wanted him to know Kelsey existed.

"Six." Kim drew a sharp breath. "Going on thirty-five."

Squinting in the Jeep's interior, Timothy surveyed Kim's tense expression as she pulled from the curb, and he felt torn. It was one thing that she'd never invited him over, another that she'd never mentioned Kelsey. His mind was still reeling. In the three months he'd slept with Kim, shouldn't he have guessed? Shouldn't he have noticed some sign that she was a mother?

He tried to tamp down the feelings, but his worst fears seemed realized. Since he hadn't grown up with his parents, maybe women sensed he wouldn't make a good parent himself. Distractedly, he chewed the inside of his cheek, hardly wanting to think about never having a family of his own, not that he'd ever come close to getting married, of course. "Six," he finally echoed, then after a moment added, "You look worried."

"I am."

"Your neighborhood's safe." He'd never been to her apartment, but he knew she lived across from Rittenhouse Square.

"We'll stop in the park, if you don't mind."

"The park?"

"She used to go there with her dad all the time."

Her dad. A man Kim was still grieving, though he'd been gone nearly two years. Or was she? Maybe she was ready to move on, just not with Timothy. Maybe she'd just wanted to keep *him* from meeting her daughter and becoming a more significant part of her life. Hours ago, the fact that Kim had previously wanted sex with no strings attached hadn't bothered Timothy in the least. In fact, he'd been wowed by how in touch she was with her sexuality. But now, there was obviously much more involved in her rejection.

Kim was clutching the steering wheel. "Christmas is the anniversary of Larry's…"

Death. Softly, Timothy said, "I know. You told me."

Kim used an ungloved hand to rub clear a patch on the windshield as she made her way through the heavy city traffic. "Do you see any cabs?"

"No. I'm keeping my eyes peeled."

"Two weeks ago she cut off all her hair," Kim murmured anxiously. "She had the most gorgeous golden-blond hair that fell past her shoulders."

Timothy couldn't help but reach to lightly grasp a lock of Kim's own. "I bet it was pretty."

"She used to love having me fix it," Kim continued, seemingly not noticing the touch of his fingers. "I put bows in it and barrettes. Now it's only an inch long. It was shaggy—she used my pinking shears—and after I took her to a salon, so they could fix it, she looked nearly bald."

Timothy wasn't sure how bad such an incident really was. He had only his own childhood to compare with, and he and his foster brothers had raised holy hell. Just squabbling over who made the best Philly cheese steaks—Pat or Geno—had landed them in full-scale rumbles. "What else has she done?"

"She begged me to let her hang Christmas lights," Kim continued, "and when I finally said yes, she pretended she'd been electrocuted. When I went into the living room, she was holding the light cord and writhing on the floor—"

He couldn't help but chuckle, though he stopped when Kim took her eyes from the windshield long enough to send him a mortified glance. "Sorry," he said quickly, noting the tension in her body as his gaze flickered over her. "But that's the kind of thing I used to do as a kid."

"Really?"

He nodded. "Yeah. I have a feeling I just might like your little girl."

Unfortunately, the comment only exacerbated Kim's nervousness, and when he registered that, Timothy felt another wave of discomfort. And anger. He'd only been invited to meet Kelsey because he was wearing this ridiculous costume. He pushed away the thought. Maybe Kim had been right not to involve her in her life. He didn't know anything about kids, anyway. For all he knew, he wouldn't even like being around one. Carey's and Zach's were still babies, so Timothy had no idea what to expect from a six-year-old.

"Some of the behavior's amusing, I guess," Kim suddenly conceded nervously. "Inventive, anyway. But Kelsey's in first grade now. She's not paying attention at school, and Anna's having trouble with her at day care. Kelsey won't share with the other kids.''

Won't share… Timothy pushed aside a vision of the Dr. Ooze dolls that Kim had stored in the Pittsburgh warehouse. Then he thought about Kim not sharing Kelsey with him. He'd watched Kim negotiate with the television network that had bought the rights to use the Dr. Ooze character, so he knew firsthand the woman drove a hard bargain. Businesswise, she was sharp, no-nonsense and professional. In bed, she was a wildcat. But now, it turned out she had a whole other role he hadn't been at all privy to: mother.

''She can be bullying,'' Kim was saying, ''and I know it's my fault—'' She emitted a sigh, then changed the subject saying, ''She'd better be in the park.''

''She is.''

''What are you? Psychic?''

''No.'' He flashed an encouraging grin. ''I'm Dr. Ooze.''

''I can definitely use a superhero.''

He shrugged. ''You said she always goes to the park when she's hurting. About the toys,'' he added, ''Kelsey will forgive you.''

She chewed her lower lip. ''I hope. I just hate to disappoint her. I don't think they like her much. The other kids," she clarified. "She's a sweet little girl, she means everything to me, but she's been through a tough time. My getting those dolls was supposed to help her win their approval, but Wendy didn't leave them for me."

"Wouldn't it be better if Kelsey wowed the other kids without offering gifts?"

"Of course, but when your child pressures you…"

"Just explain that your assistant forgot."

"I hope she accepts that." Kim's eyes were scanning the traffic again, looking for the cab. "At least this part of town's well populated, and the streets are crowded. Everyone's out doing last-minute Christmas shopping."

"Lots of kids hang out in the park," he added. "And it's well policed."

"The first six months after Larry died," Kim suddenly said on a sigh, "I was so hurt. I honestly don't know how I got through the days. Everything was a fog."

Loss was something he could definitely relate to. He'd been a year younger than Kelsey when his parents had been killed in a car wreck. It was the fantasy about saving them that had caused him to create Dr. Ooze. "But you moved on?" The words cost him, since she'd ended their affair by saying she was still grieving.

"Not really. Even after I did emotionally, I realized Larry had left a lot of debt. He handled the financial side of our business. Or at least I thought so until I saw the books. I was always the creative part of the partnership."

"What you've done with Dr. Ooze is amazing."

"I've tried. The deal you and I negotiated was important for us. Larry made some bad investments."

No wonder she'd kept those toys in storage. "Is the business stable?"

"Now it is."

She fell silent, concentrating on driving. He could see her throat working as she swallowed, and the sight made his heart constrict. She had a beautiful neck. The rest of her was just as gorgeous. In the dark car, with hints of illumination from the Christmas lights along the avenue brightening her features, her winter-pale skin looked ethereal. Suddenly he wanted—no, needed—to touch her.

Given her circumstances, he wondered what their affair had meant to her. He imagined it had been a strong release. It sure had been for him. Previously, he'd imagined her going home to an empty apartment. Maybe watching videos. Or talking with girlfriends on the phone. Instead, she'd been cooking dinners, laying out school clothes and helping her daughter with homework. It put a whole new spin on the urgency of their lovemaking. "Why didn't you tell me about her?" he suddenly asked.

"I…I don't know. I wanted you, Timothy."

The admission should have felt good; it warmed his body, just not his soul. "But you never brought me home."

"I couldn't. Not now. Not when I'm so worried about Kelsey. She blames me for her father's death."

That took him aback. "I thought you said he had pancreatic cancer."

"He did!" she exclaimed. "But she's only six. He was gone in a month. And she'd heard us fight about the business. I'm sure of it. I took her to a child psychologist, but that only made things worse." Blowing out a sigh, she added, "We're here. Thank God."

After parking at the curb, she quickly turned off the ignition. He swung open his car door just as she did. As they jogged into Rittenhouse Square, he could feel her body jostling his, sending warmth down his side. When he spoke, his breath fogged the air. "Which way?"

She pointed.

He nodded. The park was huge. Nine separate tree-lined avenues led from the street into a circular lane in the park's center.

"Dr. Ooze!" a child shouted.

Turning his head as he continued jogging along-side Kim, Timothy glimpsed a boy in a blue pea coat waving from a sled. Timothy waved back. "Merry Christmas," he called. For good measure, he added the phrase that Dr. Ooze was best known for, "It's been a good day for justice!" Lowering his voice as he and Kim turned into a tree-lined lane, he said, "What's she look like?"

Kim sounded winded. "Like me. Gold hair. A white parka. A baseball cap." She pointed. "She's up in that tree." Beneath a hardwood, a German shepherd was hunkered down, his head raised.

"A dog's treed her," Timothy muttered as they approached. The dog didn't look dangerous, but it was big and should have been on a leash.

While Timothy glanced around for its owner, Kim shouted, "Honey, can you climb down?"

"Did you get my dolls at the Gallery to give to the kids?"

"No. I tried. And we'll work it out. I'll get them after Christmas. Meantime, do you think you can climb down?"

"Not with that dog down there. Mrs. Carter made me take a cab home, but I didn't want to go…"

"Now, Kelsey," warned Kim. "Mrs. Carter said you told her I was outside."

"I'm sorry!"

The kid sounded genuinely frightened.

Timothy eyed the branches until he found her perch. She'd climbed nearly to the top. How had a kid that small gotten all the way up there? "I'll hold the dog, honey," Kim called, grabbing the shepherd's collar. "See? I've got him."

"But I can't…"

Timothy glanced away from the twisting, snow-laden branches toward Kim. When his gaze landed on her, his chest felt strangely tight. Those huge dark eyes were more vulnerable than they'd ever looked in the heat of passion, and he realized he'd felt closer to her in the past twenty minutes than he had when they'd shared a bed. He was seeing her as he never had before, and he liked what he saw. She was real now. Not some fantasy sex kitten who'd always vanished by the stroke of midnight.

"I'm stuck up here!" Kelsey cried.

"Don't panic," Timothy found himself saying. As he stepped toward the tree, light from one of the wrought-iron lamps illuminating the park made his silver cape glimmer. He turned toward Kim. "I'll climb up and get her."

As he moved toward the tree trunk, Kelsey's soft, astonished gasp sounded, further melting his heart. "It's Dr. Ooze!"

HOURS LATER, as Kelsey skipped toward the dining table, wearing red flannel pajamas printed with tiny green Christmas trees, Kim smiled. It startled her how relieved she felt at the way the evening had progressed. "C'mon," she murmured, "sit back down and eat your ice cream before it melts."

"I am," promised Kelsey, dragging a hand through what was left of her short, golden curls. She glanced toward Kim with bright green eyes, her father's eyes. "But I got a present!" she exclaimed.

"Is that so?" Timothy laughed.

She nodded sagely. "Yep. It's for you, Dr. Ooze, because you got me outta the tree."

"He was quite the hero," agreed Kim, glancing from the table through open louvered doors that led to the living room—and the lighted tree she and Kelsey had decorated earlier in the week.

"Ah." Timothy was maneuvering a bite of fruitcake through the mouth hole of his mask. "I assure you that Dr. Ooze never turns down a gift from a pretty girl."

"Nobody turns them down at Christmas," remarked Kelsey with finality, "not unless you're a big ol' Scrooge." Her green eyes sparkled flirtatiously. "You're not one of those big ol' Ebenezer Scrooges, are you, Dr. Ooze?"

"Nope." Timothy dutifully shook his head as Kelsey set a small, oval purple stone in front of him.

"It's a power stone," Kelsey explained, sliding into her seat and starting in on ice cream flecked with bits of candy cane. "It's for when you're lonely. You're supposed to rub it and it makes you warm all over."

Timothy nodded. "Is that right?"

"Uh-huh." Kelsey bobbed her head. "You could use it when Trapper traps you."

Trapper was Dr. Ooze's archenemy. "Good thinking."

"I am a good thinker." Kelsey shot him a guilty glance. "But right now, I'm an under-chiever."

Timothy smiled. "I think that's under-*a*-chiever."

"See," said Kelsey with mock solemnity as if the mispronunciation proved her point.

Timothy laughed, and the sound warmed Kim's heart. As she continued listening to him talk to her daughter, Kim simply couldn't believe it. How could she have so misjudged a man? Or Kelsey? Kim had been terrified to bring him home, so much so that she had ended their affair, but Kelsey was charming the pants off the man. Or, Kim amended with a smile, the silver Lycra tights.

She sighed wistfully. She'd always remember him in Rittenhouse Square, stepping from the darkness of the avenue into the light, his cape shimmering as he'd approached the tree and begun to climb. The look on Kelsey's face had been pure Christmas magic. Being rescued by Dr. Ooze couldn't compensate for Kim's not getting the Dr. Ooze dolls for the day-care kids, but it had helped.

Tomorrow was Christmas Eve, and with Timothy's presence tonight, it was starting to seem as if Christmas might turn out right, after all. It was so important to create a new holiday tradition without Larry. Releasing another surreptitious sigh, Kim glanced toward Timothy. Why hadn't she guessed he'd be good with kids? After all, he had created their favorite action-adventure hero.

As her eyes drifted slowly over him, she thought of the articles she'd seen about him in the paper. As a well-known cartoonist, he was affiliated with the Philly arts scene, and she'd seen him featured on the society page with more than one willing-looking female.

No wonder. As she continued staring, Kim wasn't the least bit surprised to feel her heartbeat kicking up. He was definitely mouthwatering. And the Lycra left nothing to her imagination. Not that she hadn't seen everything before. But now that she realized how much fun he was having with Kelsey...

She could merely shake her head. Wistful longing twisted inside her as she recalled the first time she'd seen Timothy. She'd gone on a cold call, to pitch the idea of Smart Markets handling his comic-book creations, an idea she'd gotten when she'd seen an article about him in the paper. He'd been inside his glassed-in office, talking on the phone with his back turned. Every inch of him had made her shudder. Since her husband's passing, she hadn't even noticed men, but suddenly, in a heartbeat, everything had changed. She'd been entranced. Captivated. Curious.

The black-and-white photo accompanying the article hadn't done him justice. He had fine straight light-blond hair that he wore bluntly cut and tucked behind his ears, and that had turned out to have the powdery texture of silk. A perfectly cut chocolate suit had molded shoulders so powerful that she'd immediately imagined him lifting her into his arms.

And then he'd turned around and noticed her. Yes, it was no wonder he'd become a media darling. Penetrating blue eyes had locked onto her, making her feel as if she was the only person in the whole world. A second later, he was off the phone, and when he'd come out to greet her and she'd heard his voice, she'd been utterly lost.

"Are you Kim Winkler?" he'd asked.

She'd barely registered the words. Instantly, she'd wanted to hear that voice say so many other more intimate things, such as *touch me here.* Or *there.* Or *lower.* That voice was definitely star quality. Rough, sexy and pleasantly hoarse, it rumbled from an incredibly inviting chest and made her insides shake.

Less than two hours later, she'd propositioned him, saying, "Would you like to go somewhere?"

"Like where?"

"Like your apartment."

With his throaty laughter, a devilish gleam had come into his eyes. "Do you proposition men often?"

"Never."

"Better late than never," he'd said agreeably.

She'd grinned. "Is that a yes?"

He'd nodded. "Nothing's going to stop us now."

It was the only time Kim had ever propositioned a man. She'd begun dating Larry in high school, and he'd been her only lover, but Timothy had sex written all over him. Not marriage. Not fatherhood. Not commitment. Not a cute little bungalow for three at the end of the rainbow.

Just simple, uncomplicated sex. The pictures she'd seen of him squiring women around town had seemed to substantiate that view, too. Now, watching him with Kelsey, she wondered why she'd been so sure he wouldn't want a deeper relationship.

Kelsey's voice pulled Kim from her reverie. "Want to put me to bed, Dr. Ooze?"

"Dr. Ooze has had quite an evening. It was nice of him to rescue you. But we don't want to wear him out, do we?"

"I don't mind," he assured.

Slits of ice-blue eyes twinkled from inside the mask, but she hesitated. After all, she'd broken off their affair, then practically forced him to come to dinner wearing a costume. And while he'd seemed to enjoy himself, he'd already done more for Kelsey than Kim had hoped possible. "Are you sure?"

"Dr. Ooze said he wanted to," huffed Kelsey as if her mother was taking away a prized toy.

"Not a problem," assured Timothy.

"All right," she agreed. A second later, she realized he must have been sincere because he rose, circled the table and caught Kelsey's hand in his as if he'd been tucking in little girls for years.

CHAPTER THREE

WHAT A CUTE KID, Timothy mused, his heart still singing as he returned to the living room and stood near a lighted Christmas tree under which were countless presents. He smiled to himself as he listened to the carols playing on a radio. Carey and Zach would have been stunned if they'd seen him just now, playing Dr. Ooze and tucking in an excited six-year-old. For a few precious moments, Timothy had felt just like his buddies, like a proud papa. He wondered vaguely if he'd ever really be ready to take on such a role.

Sobering, he stared into a crackling fire he'd helped Kim build in the hearth. As the sight of the tiny tongues of flame and the sound of the snapping kindling mesmerized him, he thought of how mesmerized he was by Kim. All during dinner, his eyes had been riveted on her. He couldn't tear them away. But what the hell did he want? None of the many women he'd dated had had kids. Not that Kim was asking to rekindle their affair.

He glanced around. It had been a long time—too

long—since he'd been in a home this warm and cozy. Homemade stockings hung from the mantel, and above them was a nativity scene around which Kim had arranged fragrant pine rope. The whole apartment smelled like a lush, dark, wintery forest.

Except, of course, for Kim, who brought the soft, enticing scent of spring flowers when she appeared, coming from the kitchen. She was carrying two glasses of wine, but she stopped in midstep, leaving him to wonder whether it was an accident, or for his benefit because she wound up standing beneath an arching doorway hung with mistletoe. All night, he'd wondered where this was heading. She'd asked him here solely for Kelsey, but he knew Kim still wanted him.

"What's wrong, Timothy?"

"Nothing," he managed.

But it was a lie. Plenty was wrong. Starting with how irresistibly sexy she looked. Her golden hair was pushed carelessly away from a face warmed by heat from the kitchen, and she was still wearing a white ruffly apron, embroidered with holly leaves. Gingerly, she came a step closer and set the wine glasses on an end table, close enough to the fire that sparkles of light swirled in the dark burgundy.

Lifting her gaze, she hit him with the soft, sexy voice that had driven him so crazy in bed. "Why don't I believe you?"

"Why don't you tell me?"

"Female instinct," she said with a smile. "You had that brooding male thing going on, where your lips curl and your brows get hooded."

He chuckled, wishing he wasn't wearing the costume. "You mean you could take a man seriously when he's covered in skintight silver Lycra?"

She surveyed him a long moment. "It *is* a little like a body condom."

He laughed. God, he'd missed her sense of humor. He considered taking off the mask since Kelsey was already asleep, but he decided to leave it on, just in case she awakened. Leaning over, he reached for the glass of wine she offered. "Thanks."

"No. Thank you." She was still watching him with curiosity. Instead of making a move to sit, she edged toward her previous position under the arched doorway.

"Watch out for that mistletoe," he warned.

Making a point of sidestepping, she leaned against the wall, then crossed her arms in a way that lifted her breasts and sent heat coursing through his veins. Licking his lips against their sudden dryness, he said, "What for?"

She didn't speak for a moment, and as she studied him, he eyed her cheeks. Soft, feathery, lacelike shadows from the tree were dancing on her skin and flames from the fire flickered in her eyes, made even darker by the room's dim light. He picked up a wineglass and sipped, enjoying the heady dampness it brought to his lips before its heat slid down his throat.

"For tonight." She tilted back her own glass, and the wine left her lips looking wet and kissable. "For wearing the costume. For putting Kelsey to bed." Swirling the goblet, she looked thoughtfully into it before she lifted her gaze once more. "For everything, Timothy."

"No problem."

As soon as the words were out, he realized they'd come with an unexpected rush of annoyance. She must have noticed because she said, "Are you sure?"

"I'm sure."

"You didn't mind putting her to bed?" she asked, now nervously toying with a lock of hair that looked like burnished gold. "You didn't have to do that or…"

Be so nice to her kid? He came closer, stopping directly in front of her. "I know I didn't. Your daughter's…"

Kim quickly said, "She was a little tough in the car."

True. Being rescued by Dr. Ooze had made her day, but she'd also been angry about not getting the dolls. "She was fine."

Kim suddenly smiled. When she did, her face lit up. It was radiant. "She's pretty adorable, huh?"

Yes, she was. And the most unexpected emotions were coming over Timothy. Everything about little Kelsey Winkler had squeezed his heart, and every time he'd felt there wasn't a drop left, she'd squeeze just a little more. "Seriously cute," he agreed.

He loved how Kim's voice hitched as she sought affirmation. "You really think so?"

He'd loved those little flannel pajamas, and the red-and-white-striped candy-cane toe socks she was so proud of, and how she'd given him her special power stone so he wouldn't be lonely. Every time he'd looked at the awful haircut she'd given herself with Kim's pinking shears, he'd had to fight not to burst out laughing. As soon as they'd gotten inside the apartment, he'd remarked on the red dots on her earlobes.

"Earrings," she'd informed him, not the least bit bothered that she'd drawn them on with a Sharpie pen.

"Timothy?" Kim suddenly said. "Are you sure you're all right? You've got that brooding male lip curl again."

He sighed, realizing he wasn't going to be able to hide his darker emotions. "Of course I'm not all right," he finally muttered. Out of habit, he tried to drag a hand through his hair, realized he was still wearing the mask and tugged it off in frustration. Tossing it aside, he raised an arm, so that he could rest his palm against the wall, beside her head. When heat surged into her eyes, he angled his head down to kiss her.

"Whoa." A warm hand splayed on his chest. "Not now," she said. "Not here."

"But maybe later?" he murmured, not bothering to keep his mood from affecting his tone. "Maybe somewhere else?" *At my place, where I won't get to know Kelsey or become a part of your life?*

"Yes," she agreed quickly. "Maybe your town house."

"After Christmas?" he guessed.

The fingers on his chest tightened. The Lycra was so tight that his coiled chest hairs were visible beneath, but Kim actually managed to gather the fabric in a fist. It was as if she didn't mean to let him get away. The gesture was, quite simply, sexy as hell. Lower, he felt a sharp pang of arousal, something he'd prefer not to feel when he was wearing Lycra.

"Yes," she whispered, taken with the idea. "Maybe we could spend New Year's together."

He wanted nothing more, but every fiber in him was resisting. Not that he could deny her anything when her inky liquid eyes, fringed with jet lashes, were gazing up at him so imploringly. Her chin raised a notch, bringing her lips a crucial inch nearer. He was suddenly sure she was going to change her mind and claim the very kiss she'd just stopped him from taking.

"Whoa, yourself," he teased softly, lifting a finger to lightly trace her collarbone.

"I realized it tonight," she began, her husky voice making clear she'd registered his touch. "I've missed you." Her breath caught audibly. She glanced around, suddenly smiling. "I admit, it would be fun to have sex in front of the tree and the fire…"

Fun? The sheer domesticity of it hurt. Still, he was tempted to simply grab her around the waist and pull her down to the soft rug and twine his limbs around hers. "I could lick wine from your navel," he suggested.

"Paint me in icing."

"Cover you in cookie sprinkles."

"But we can't right now," she said.

He said nothing.

Her voice held a tremor. "You've missed me, too?"

More than he wanted to admit. "That's not the problem."

Her voice hitched. "The problem?"

Until this moment, he hadn't realized they had one, either. He edged closer. Maybe too close, he thought, when his lower body brushed hers. As fire scorched down the length of him, he bit back a curse. She was just as affected. Breathlessly, he watched as her nipples tightened beneath a soft cashmere sweater she'd worn under her suit. The only thing that could have tempted his fingers more would have been her bare skin. Somehow, he beat back every impulse commanding him to cup the sloping curves of her breasts. "Kim," he managed, trying not to notice the breath teasing his lips, "we have all kinds of problems."

"Such as?"

Such as their lips were an inch apart. Their hips were tilted together. His eyes were fixed on her ready mouth. Staring at her parted lips, it was suddenly impossible to imagine any problem in the world, but then he felt another jolt of frustration, and he didn't know where to start. "Such as…" Gesturing distractedly, he glanced toward the tree. "The tree."

She arched a brow. "My tree?"

Garlands of cranberries and popcorn she'd probably strung herself looped over branches, offset by paper chains made of construction paper, probably Kelsey's contribution. Dried autumnal leaves were nestled in the branches, as well as pampas grass, pinecones and artificial birds.

He realized she looked vaguely hurt. "You don't like it?"

His jaw slackened. "Like it? It's…" He searched for a word. "Beautiful, Kim. I can't believe you've done all this. And dinner was great." She'd served a ham that was cooked to perfection, along with homemade rolls and yams smothered in marshmallow. "How did you do all that cooking when you're so busy at work?"

"I cooked most of the meal ahead of time and reheated." She was eyeing him as if she was beginning to wonder what his point was.

"It's all so…perfect."

Her lips twitched, making him feel even more tempted to kiss her. "And perfection is a problem for you, Timothy?"

As crazy as that sounded, he wound up nodding. "Uh-huh. Even the tablecloth was…" He paused, trying to describe it. "Something you did."

"Kelsey and I made it."

Regular brown paper bags had been crinkled, torn and sewn together with red and green yarn, then stamped with holiday icons—such as Christmas trees, candy canes and stockings. "And there's a fire in the hearth," he continued. "Poinsettias…"

She was starting to look pleased. "It *is* Christmas, Timothy."

He turned back to her too abruptly, and their lips nearly collided. Maybe he'd meant that to happen. It had been a while since he'd been this close to her, or to any woman. That was something else Timothy had wanted to forget. While he'd sworn their affair was casual, he hadn't seriously dated another woman since. Now that he'd seen Kim's apartment, she was going to be even harder to forget. The passionate heat stirring between them didn't help. He blew out a frustrated sigh. "I thought…"

"What?"

"That you were grieving."

"Meaning?"

"I guess I imagined your place would look like mine. No tree. No stockings." He paused, unable to put into words the strange betrayal he felt. "I thought you lived alone…" *And that you were every bit as lonely as me.* Instead, her life was brimming with love.

Her voice was a near whisper as she set aside the wineglass. "I didn't deceive you. I really was grieving."

"You have a daughter."

"Would you have wanted to know about her?"

He bit back a hoarse sound of surprise. Instinctively, he leaned nearer, the strength in the body that touched hers punctuating his words. "Yes," he muttered. "Hell, yes, Kim."

Her eyes widened. "Why?"

He wasn't quite sure, and before he could continue, she spoke again. "Be honest. Would you have wanted to get yourself involved with a family?"

Maybe not at first. "I like good, uncomplicated sex," he said honestly. "You know that."

She took a deep breath and said, "We both do."

Trying to ignore the tightening of his body, he added, "I missed you in bed." But why was that all she thought he was good for?

"Me, too."

"But you didn't want me to know Kelsey?"

"It was too soon to bring someone new into her life."

It had been two years. "What about into yours?"

"What's happened between us is the answer to that."

Lifting a finger, he trailed it down her cheek, his emotions going into a full tumble. "*Happened* is past tense."

"I want to be with you again."

There was no denying his frustration. Why couldn't he leave well enough alone? Kim was beautiful. She was an exquisite lover. What was wrong with him? Any man in his right mind would settle for some private time with her. "But only later? At my place?"

"That's not okay with you?"

He was torn. Dammit, he wasn't sure what he wanted anymore.

When she parted her lips to speak, it was too much for him. He cared about whatever she'd intended to say next, he really did, but physical hunger took over, and he brought his mouth to hers. Even he was shocked at the fierce kiss. It was urgent, full of fire. As he further parted her lips, then teased them open with his tongue, he stifled the moan in his throat. Heat flooded him like an antidote to winter. "It's been too long," he said, his mouth slackening as it shifted directions, slanting over hers.

"I knew you'd missed me," she whispered.

"Lots," he agreed hoarsely.

He'd missed everything about her: her taste, her scent, the way she parted her long willowy legs slightly, probably not even conscious that her body was saying she wanted more. He tried to hold back, knowing this wasn't the time or place, but her mouth tasted like wine-drenched honey, and her cheek against his felt like silk. Just as he brought a hand up to cup her chin and tilt it to better take her mouth, he heard a rustle. Breaking the kiss, he glanced toward the hallway and winced.

"Who are you?" Kelsey demanded, staring at his face. Her sleepy eyes were angry slits of green. "You're not Dr. Ooze."

"Oh, no," whispered Kim under her breath. Raising her voice, she said, "Honey, why don't you go back to bed? I'll be right behind you."

"We can explain," Timothy offered.

"You're here because of my mom, not me. You're just like Santa Claus. You're not real," Kelsey accused. Fat tears gathered in her eyes and clung to her lashes, ready to tumble down her cheeks. Inwardly, Timothy cursed. Why had he taken off the mask?

"She told you to dress up," Kelsey continued.

"There's some truth in that," Kim said.

"Only because she wanted to please you," said Timothy.

"I wish you hadn't come here," Kelsey whined. "You just came because my mom forgot to get those dolls for me."

Staring at Kelsey, wondering what to say, he realized that his heart was hammering too hard. It wasn't because of the kiss, either, or because Kelsey had just caught him kissing her mother under the mistletoe, but because he was in this warm, cozy house. He'd lived in one like it once, years ago, when his parents were still alive. He could barely remember it, but tonight had brought back the feelings he associated with it, and how angry he'd felt after the wreck had taken their lives. He'd been just about as angry as Kelsey looked, and, remembering that, he felt like an intruder on their grief, as if he didn't belong here. Kim had never really wanted him involved in her personal life, had she? Judging from their conversation just now, nothing had really changed.

"I'd better take off," he said gruffly, having no idea what to do next. When his eyes met Kim's again, he tried not to notice how damp and swollen her mouth looked, or the disappointment he saw in her gaze. Dammit, what did she want from him? What did she expect him to do?

"Maybe you'd better," she said quietly.

It was as if, by leaving now, he was living up to her secret bad opinion of him as some useless play-boy, or an otherwise potentially bad mate. Hell, maybe this was just as well. He was never going to fit into their lives, anyway. She didn't even want that. Turning away, he headed for the door, only realizing she'd followed him when he reached it. Impulsively, he curled his fingers over her upper arm, and his voice, when he spoke, sounded rougher than he'd meant it to. "Don't look at me like that," he murmured. "You didn't want me here, anyway."

"That's not true. I...misjudged you. You just didn't seem like the type of man who'd be interested in our lives."

"Just the type for sex?" Abruptly, he dropped her arm. "Yeah. I get it. An uncomplicated good time. No strings attached."

She looked positively stunned. "I didn't know

you'd be interested," she repeated. "You seemed…"

Suddenly, he couldn't listen anymore. "Good night," he said.

And then Timothy walked into the cold December night.

VERY EARLY the next morning, Timothy stared at the wreath on the front door of Kim's building. He had absolutely no idea what he was really doing, returning like this. All he knew was that he hated how Kim had looked at him last night when he'd left. His last glance at her face had made him feel as if he was really like the character he'd created. Dr. Ooze. The ultimate escape artist. No, it didn't take a wizard to put two and two together. Kim had seen the pictures of him in the society pages and figured him for a womanizer.

But she'd said she'd misjudged him.

Timothy didn't know what to make of it. Did that mean Kim might want more of a relationship now? And what had she expected him to say to Kelsey? Hell, he didn't know anything about kids!

"I'm only good for sex, huh?" he muttered, heading for the door, his breath fogging in the frigid air as he raised his eyes to the wreaths Kim had hung in her third-floor windows. Oh, he could see how she'd gotten the impression he was a man about town. And there was a lot of truth in it. He'd never become particularly close to women he'd dated. Deep down, he'd craved a home, and yet the upsets in his early life had left him leery.

He glanced around. Outside, flower boxes were visible, filled with pinecones and greenery, and red ribbons wound around a fire escape from which an inflatable Santa waved. He couldn't help but smile. Kim was just as inventive a decorator as she was a lover.

But he was stumped. "Now what?" he said.

Hesitating in front of the door, he got that edgy feeling that often plagued him when people got too close. He'd never shaken the feeling that they might vanish overnight, the way his folks had. As a matter of fact, abandonment of any kind drove him nuts. He hated change. Despite his warmer feelings, Kelsey's anger had been hard to take last night, especially after she'd bestowed all that childish delight on him during dinner when she'd thought he was Dr. Ooze.

"I can't believe I'm letting a six-year-old get to me," he whispered. But then, she wasn't just any six-year-old, she was Kim's daughter, and so cute that he couldn't get her out of his mind any more than he could her mother.

Stamping his feet on the stoop to remove the snow, he shuddered as he went inside, glad for the rush of heat that hit him. His coat was in the car, since he hadn't wanted to hide the Dr. Ooze outfit he'd worn again today.

He stopped in his tracks a final time, wondering if it wasn't better to let sleeping dogs lie. He could still turn around, head home, kick back with a beer and watch ball games on TV. Undoubtedly, he'd feel restless, though. He'd tossed and turned all night. Every time he'd drifted, he'd reawakened only to realize he was fantasizing about spending Christmas with the Winklers.

Just because he liked his sex sweet and to the point didn't mean he was capable of nothing more, right? He started walking again, heading through the lobby to the elevators. Carey and Zach had settled down and were having kids, and if those two hellions could wind up with wives, Timothy guessed he could, too. Not that he had those intentions toward Kim, necessarily. He winced. He just wished he knew if he was even capable of that level of intimacy.

Whatever the case, he did want to make up for last night. He never should have left in such a hurry. Surely he should have said something comforting to Kelsey. When he reached the door, he paused. Maybe Kim and Kelsey weren't even home. Or, given how early it was, maybe they were still asleep. He hoped he didn't wake them.

Taking a deep breath, he lifted his hand—only to have "Holly Jolly Christmas" begin to play. He should have known. The wreath on her door had a built-in motion sensor and played carols when anyone knocked. Just as the opening bars finished, the door opened. He glanced down to see a dark scowl crossing Kelsey's features. "You're not Dr. Ooze," she accused.

"No, I'm not," he returned bluntly, deciding to handle her head-on. "I'm a man in a costume." When she didn't giggle, he continued, "and my name's Timothy Toye. I may not be Dr. Ooze, but I'm the guy who created him."

"If you're not Dr. Ooze," she said pragmatically, not looking the least impressed, "then I want my power stone back. That was a present for Dr. Ooze, not you."

"Done."

It was in the car, in his coat pocket. He didn't particularly want to return it. If the truth be told, last night, while he'd been thinking about Kelsey and her mother, he'd actually rubbed it, just as Kelsey had shown him. The smooth little rock hadn't warded off his loneliness, of course, but it had reminded him of Kelsey and made him grin.

"Could you send it Federal Express?"

"Postal service," he countered. "Three-day delivery."

She still looked angry. "Did you come here to kiss my mom again?"

Before he could answer, Kim's voice sounded from down the hallway, nearing as she came toward the door, "Honey, who is it?"

Kelsey called, "That man."

"And in the same clothes he wore last night," Kim observed as she approached.

"I was just explaining to Kelsey that while Dr. Ooze might not be real, he is like Santa Claus in the sense that the people beneath the costumes carry the spirit of Christmas in their hearts." Granted, it sounded like a canned speech, but Timothy thought it went well.

Now Kelsey looked mildly amused. "You were not explaining that to me," she countered. "Why are you here?"

Kim looked just as curious.

"I thought if your mother agreed, we might take a little trip to a warehouse in Pittsburgh…"

Kim's eyes widened. "The warehouse?"

He shrugged. "It's Christmas Eve. The promotion's over. I thought it might not hurt to liberate a few of the…uh…" He didn't want to spell it out in front of Kelsey, in case Kim didn't think it was a good idea.

When he saw Kim's touched expression, he realized he'd been holding his breath. He'd had no idea if this was the right thing to do. "For Kelsey's friends?" she guessed.

He nodded.

"I didn't think of going there." She considered. "I mean, it's a five-hour drive."

Tim shrugged. "I don't mind driving long distances. And after that ham last night, I figured I owed you two a meal, so I brought lunch. It's in a cooler and thermos in the car. Plus, this close to Christmas, it won't hurt sales."

"What won't hurt sales?" asked Kelsey, her eyes wide and her voice full of hope.

Kim nodded, her gaze not leaving Timothy's. "Why not?"

"We're getting the dolls from the warehouse?" asked Kelsey, hopping from one foot to the other.

"It sure looks like it," said Timothy.

Then he was taken completely by surprise when Kelsey lunged right into his arms.

CHAPTER FOUR

"C'MON, you gotta sing," Kelsey urged. "It's Christmas."

Shooting a helpless glance at Kim through the darkened interior of his Oldsmobile, Timothy said, "Not in this lifetime."

"Why not?" Kelsey giggled. "See, I told you, you're a Scrooge!"

"I'm Dr. Ooze, remember? And while I have many talents, I'm definitely not musical." He smiled as she gave up, jostled against him and began crooning with the radio. Wanting to please her, he changed his mind and rustily uttered the words to "Rudolph the Red-Nosed Reindeer."

"You can't sing very good," Kelsey agreed.

"Very *well*," Kim corrected.

He shrugged. "Told you so."

"Oh, I don't know," Kim said, chuckling. "You weren't exactly Bing Crosby, but you sounded all right." A heartbeat passed, then she added, "You have a great voice when you talk."

"Better when I whisper."

"Why?" interjected Kelsey. "When you talk it's the same voice as when you whisper."

"Good point," returned Timothy. But given the sparkle in Kim's eyes, he figured she was remembering the words he'd murmured against her neck when they were having sex. He had a sudden vision of her tilting back her head, surrendering her bare skin to his greedy mouth, and couldn't stop the audible edge of need when he spoke. "Maybe later, we should experiment."

"Compare your regular voice with your whisper voice?" guessed Kim.

"Just to be scientific."

"You *are* Dr. Ooze," she agreed.

"I have a science kit you can use for the experiment," offered Kelsey. "It has a microscope and a rock tumbler."

"That might be useful," assured Timothy.

"I can't wait," said Kim.

Me, neither. All day, he felt he'd go crazy if he couldn't mold his palms over every inch of her and kiss all the spots that never saw the light of day. Maybe later he'd get to. Meantime, he hoped the cops didn't stop them. Because the back seat had been packed with Dr. Ooze dolls, Kelsey was in front, snuggled between him and Kim. She had on a seat belt, but for all Timothy knew, having kids in front might be illegal nowadays. Many of the kids he saw in cars were strapped in so tightly that they looked as if they were wearing straitjackets.

His smile broadened as he wondered how he and his foster brothers had survived their childhoods, not to mention thrived. Zach had his own home security business now, and Carey worked with computers. Growing up, they'd skated without helmets. Rumbled like gangsters. And ridden triple on the ancient red Roadster bicycle Zach had found in a junk shop. For years, they'd shared the bike, right up until they'd each paid a third and bought an old Chevy.

"You look happy," said Kim.

He felt it, too, but the statement threw him off kilter, and catching that, she squinted and added, "What?"

"I'm not used to having people comment on my emotional state," he admitted.

"That's too bad."

It was. Taking a deep breath, he thought of the warmth in Zach's and Carey's voices nowadays. Having a woman around who cared about your feelings made a difference. Not that married life was perfect, Timothy reminded himself, but he still wondered what it would be like to share that level of closeness. To live in the same house and get to know the other person's private habits and quirks. Too bad his craving for love always came in tandem with an internal tug-of-war. Feeling conflicted, he'd always wound up keeping things simple. Sexual and casual. Usually without an exchange of house keys.

When his eyes met Kim's, she said, "What are you thinking?"

He smiled. "Why do women always ask that?"

"Because men are the center of our universe."

He grinned. "I was thinking about an old Chevy I bought with my buddies, back in high school."

"Carey and Zach?"

He was surprised she remembered. "Yeah."

"You grew up with them, right?"

"Since I was five."

Her gaze said it was good to have such deep bonds. "Nice car?"

He laughed. "Nightmare. It was silver. At least the parts that weren't rusted. And it never did seem to have a decent muffler."

Kelsey crinkled her nose. "You drove a car like that?"

"Nope." Timothy glanced at Kim, his lips twitching, then he turned his attention to Kelsey again. "I didn't drive it, I just kissed girls in the back seat."

Kelsey screamed with laughter. "Yuck!" she exclaimed in delight.

Kids, he mused, flexing his hands on the steering wheel. Before he'd removed the Dr. Ooze mask, he'd let Kelsey talk him into stopping to entertain every kid they saw. He'd signed autographs as Dr. Ooze at truck stops, gas stations and rest areas while Kim had helped Kelsey hand out free dolls. Kids had been ecstatic, and parents who hadn't been able to get the dolls had wrung Timothy's hand in gratitude. Once it had grown dark, he'd finally hung up his mask for the night.

Suddenly, he said, "Oh. Here." He dug into the pocket of his overcoat and handed Kelsey her power stone. "I forgot to give it back."

Gazing up, she considered him a moment, and Timothy felt a surge of pleasure at the fleeting thought that she was going to insist he keep it. Instead, she dropped it into the pocket of her parka, then whirled the dial on the radio, raising the sound. As "Santa Claus is Coming to Town" shifted into Bing Crosby's "White Christmas," Timothy's eyes met Kim's again and he grew more solemn.

He'd met a lot of smart, gorgeous women, but more than the others, this one made his blood race and his fingers itch to touch. Tilting his head, he listened to her voice blend with Kelsey's. "I'm dreaming of a White Christmas… Just like the ones I used to know…."

Some vague association with the past—something he couldn't quite remember—teased his memory and touched his emotions. As he inhaled, he drew in little-kid smells, then Kim's floral perfume, something that evoked fresh spring rain, not winter. Suddenly, he couldn't bear the thought of going home to his sparsely furnished modern apartment. Every time he thought about it, he saw Kim's living room—the nativity scene and stockings, the lighted tree and mistletoe. He didn't even have a wreath on his door, much less a decorated tree and a fridge full of eggnog and cider.

Maybe he should slow down his emotions, but there was no use denying that being around Kim and Kelsey made him wonder about family life. He couldn't wait to get back to Philly, so he and Kim could watch Kelsey deliver the remaining dolls to the kids from her day care. Before they'd left, Kim had located the addresses in the phone book.

Early this morning, as he'd stood outside their building stamping his snow-encrusted feet on the pavement, he'd been so uncertain about whether he was doing the right thing by asking them to take this drive. Now, he knew he had. He hadn't felt this good in years. Maybe ever.

Yes, everything from a snowball fight at a rest area to simply watching snowflakes melt in Kim's eyelashes had made him long for this kind of life. And he'd slept with Kim for months, right? He'd known her for a year. When he hazarded another glance in her direction, she smiled back, her eyes locking with his, her voice lifting, still singing the words to "White Christmas," "Where treetops glisten and children listen to hear sleigh bells in the snow…"

As if the cosmos heard the words, airy white flakes began to swirl down, not so many that the roads would become slick or dangerous, not even enough to warrant turning on the windshield wipers, but just enough to make Timothy lift his gaze to the land beside the highway. Powder covered the sloping terrain of the dark Pennsylvania countryside, and the hills glittered under a full white moon in a liquid velvet sky. Stars pierced velvet, as hard and bright as gemstones.

"Why're you so sad?"

Kelsey's voice drew him from his reverie. Considering, he shrugged. "I don't know," he said, not denying he'd felt the emotion.

"You do, too," she countered.

What was he supposed to say? That in a mere day he'd started secretly wondering what it might be like to spend his life with her and her mother? The solitary holidays of his past had provided a safety zone, he realized. They'd always been fun enough, and whenever the whirlwind of Christmas parties and New Year's engagements hadn't completely cured his loneliness, he'd always found work to do. Or he'd kick back with a glass of good, strong whiskey. Now he forced a smile. "No, I really don't."

Kelsey didn't look convinced, nor did Kim, who was squinting, surveying him as she had much of the day as if she'd never seen him before, as if the Timothy Toye she thought she'd known had transformed before her eyes.

"I get sad sometimes, too," Kelsey shared matter-of-factly as "White Christmas" ended and the *Nutcracker Suite* began. "My daddy died."

So, the little girl was still mourning her father. Of course she was. Larry Winkler must have been the center of her world. Vaguely, Timothy wondered how many memories Kelsey would retain over the years. He had only a scant few left of his own folks. He didn't know what to say, but the words seemed to find him. "Mine, too."

Abruptly lifting her chin, Kelsey stared at him in awe. "Your daddy died?"

She was so young that he was probably the first person she'd met who'd shared that horrible experience. He nodded. "When I was a year younger than you. My mom, too. They were in a car wreck."

Kelsey's eyes widened until they looked like bright green saucers. "Both of them?"

He felt, rather than saw, Kim's gaze scrutinizing his face, and he hardly wanted to examine why he didn't look at her, any more than he wanted to examine the uncharacteristic feeling of vulnerability

that came over him. "Yep," he said to Kelsey.
"That's why I made up Dr. Ooze."

Looking thoroughly intrigued, Kelsey leaned forward, straining her seat belt. "You made up Dr.
Ooze when you were a little kid?"

He nodded. "Just about your age. I figured that
if I were a doctor with superpowers I could have
saved my folks."

She considered. "When you were a kid, were you
really bad, too?"

"Bad?"

"Did you cut your hair and stuff?"

He chuckled softly, shaking off his mood. "And
pretend to electrocute myself while hanging Christmas lights?" Before she could answer, he continued,
"Sure. My two foster brothers, Carey and Zach, got
into all kinds of scrapes, too."

"Like what?"

"Like cracking eggs in the toes of girls' shoes
while they were in gym class." When Kelsey giggled, he continued, "But as time went on…" Inching down some in the seat, he elbowed her. "I
changed my ways and became the superhero I am
today."

Chortling, Kelsey reached up and squeezed his
biceps. "You *are* a superhero," she agreed coyly.

His shoulders shook in merriment, and when he
glanced from the windshield to Kim again, he was

glad she was laughing. She looked so pretty when she laughed. Even in the dark, he could see the bright glint of warmth in her dark eyes, and the rosy pink in her cheeks from the winter night. "What?" he couldn't help but tease. "You don't agree that I'm a superhero?"

Kim raised a staying palm. "Far be it from me to lock horns with someone who can dematerialize and escape any bonds known to man."

"And fly," Timothy reminded practically.

"Don't forget you've got that demat—that demat—" struggled Kelsey. "That foam."

"Dematerializing foam," Timothy confirmed.

Kim had stretched her arm loosely across the back of the seat, and now her hand dropped to his shoulder, sending prickles dancing across his skin. It was so easy to remember those fingers smoothing his chest hairs and slowly traveling lower, until they felt less like fingers and more like prickles of pure heat.

Grinning, she said, "But no X-ray vision, huh?"

His eyes flickered over the top of Kelsey's head to the body-hugging red-and-green knit dress clinging to Kim's curves. "Maybe not, but I've got a good memory."

Kim's cheeks turned rosier. "So do I."

He smiled as Kelsey, who'd been making a point of pivoting her head between the two of them, said, "I hope you *don't* have X-ray vision."

"Why not?"

She shook her head fervently. "You're a man, and you could see through our clothes."

He laughed.

Feigning more embarrassment than she probably really felt, Kelsey sent her mother a long stare, then rolled her eyes as if to say he was hopeless.

As he listened to their combined laughter, his awareness heightened. Everything seemed brighter—the lights in houses that dotted the hillsides and the white center line on the road that was gleaming in the headlights. The sound of the radio seemed a fraction louder. Kelsey sounded so unfettered now, as if she'd forgotten about her father. It was because of her little girl that Kim hadn't wanted to date, but maybe Kelsey's acceptance of Timothy would change things.

Maybe Kim Winkler would become ready to give her heart to another. Now, would he?

"I HOPE this visit goes okay," Kim said nervously an hour later as she placed the list of the kids' addresses on the dashboard and watched Kelsey approach a town house in the Museum District. It was where Brittany Barry, one of the kids from the day care, lived. The brick walkway was lined with lit candles, and through a bay window, the family was visible, decorating their tree. Mr. Barry was on a ladder, and as his wife handed up ornaments so he could hang them on the highest branches, Brittany and her two brothers concentrated on lower ones. They were dressed to the nines, Brittany and her mother in velvet, the boys in suits. Probably they'd been to church or to a family dinner and, even from here, Kim could feel all the warmth they generated. It seemed to rush out through the window into the dark snowy night. With a surge of gratitude, she realized she'd had that same feeling this year, and that it was due to Timothy's being there. She'd been intent on spending time alone with Kelsey, so they could start new traditions without Larry, but somehow Timothy just seemed to fit.

His fingers curled around her shoulder and squeezed. "Don't worry," he said. "This'll go fine."

She wasn't so sure. As she stared through the passenger window, watching her daughter, her heart stretched to breaking. The last kid they'd visited, Johnny Sinclair, hadn't taken the Dr. Ooze doll, saying Kelsey had been so mean to him that he didn't want any presents from her. Kelsey hadn't even cried. That was the worst thing as far as Kim was concerned. She'd returned to the car stoically, and although tears gleamed in her eyes, she hadn't been about to let them fall in front of Timothy.

Now, her baby girl looked so tiny in the dark

winter night that Kim had to fight not to get out of the car and follow her. They grew up so fast. As her heart squeezed tighter, she suddenly wondered if Kelsey would be her only child, and she couldn't help but slide her gaze to Timothy. Would she start a new relationship? Marry again? Start another family?

Pushing aside the thoughts, she continued watching Kelsey make her way up the walk. Against the snow, her daughter's white parka made her seem to fade away, making Kim somehow glad for the bright red flashes of her snow boots and knit cap. "She looks so little," she couldn't help but whisper.

"She *is* little," Timothy whispered back.

"Every time I blink, she's another year older."

His voice was invitingly husky. "She's growing up."

Her throat tightened. "I know."

"She's a kid," he said softly. "They're supposed to grow up."

Feeling glad for the warmth in the strong male hand rubbing slow circles on her shoulder, Kim sent him a long, appreciative glance before returning her gaze to the town house. She watched as Brittany hung a silver star on a branch. "I guess they wait until Christmas Eve to decorate," she murmured.

"We did in the foster home where I grew up," offered Timothy.

Tearing her eyes from Kelsey, she surveyed him, feeling her heart warm, as well as the rest of her. Although their previous relationship had been un-complicated, she'd found out some things about Timothy, such as that he'd grown up without his parents. Still, she'd been surprised and touched to find he'd created the Dr. Ooze character when he was a child. She hadn't known that. And, given to-day, she'd realized there was a great deal about Tim-othy Toye that she had yet to discover.

If he let her. Oh, on the surface, he seemed to be interested in sharing more with her, but she could tell other feelings plagued him, too. Deep down, he had scar tissue from his past. Probably, that was why he'd been seen around Philly with so many women, and why it had been so easy for him to maintain just a casual affair with her.

She hoped she'd been wrong and that Kelsey might be amenable to him coming into their lives. Which she would be, Kim imagined, given how she was acting today. Still, Kim would have to wait and see, and getting Kelsey back on track had to remain her top priority. The solid foundation of her child-hood, especially the understanding of how important her feelings were, would carry Kelsey through the rest of her life.

Not that kids with less didn't pull through. When Timothy had told them about the loss of his parents,

Kim had gotten the message, too: kids acted out but they could change. Blowing out a sigh, Kim murmured, "They're coming to the door. I just wish she'd let us go with her. I hope Brittany takes the doll."

"She will."

"Johnny Sinclair didn't."

"Maybe that's good, too."

"How so?"

"She'll understand that when you hurt people they aren't obligated to accept it when you have a sudden change of heart."

His fingers curled, cupping her shoulder, and drawn by the enticing feel of his hand, she leaned closer, her back to his chest. She cocked her head, so she could better feel his hand near her neck. He seemed to read her mind, and the next thing she knew, the hand was in her hair. Her breath caught with the touch. It was as if the hand had put fire to kindling. The car's temperature seemed to climb. Briefly, she shut her eyes.

"That feels so good," she whispered.

"Then I won't stop."

"Good." She'd wanted him to touch her all day. Opening her eyes, she watched as Brittany's mother waved from the doorway before beckoning Kelsey inside.

"See. She's fine." Timothy's voice lowered another seductive notch as those long, strong fingers stroked her scalp, massaging pure magic deep into her skin until simple pleasure became something more urgent.

"She's fine," he said again.

And Kelsey was. From the living room, Kelsey looked toward the car and offered a thumbs-up.

Kim was surprised to feel tears sting at her eyes. "Thank you," she said as Timothy continued his ministrations, gliding his fingers through the short strands of her hair. He lifted them, let them fall, only to lift them once more, seemingly studying each strand in the darkness.

"For what?"

"I haven't seen her this happy for a long time." Timothy chuckled. "She wanted those dolls."

But it was more than that. Timothy was a good influence. "I just hope the rest of the kids take the dolls as a peace offering," Kim managed. "Maybe that will encourage her to straighten out some of her behavior after the New Year."

"It will." Lowering his hand, he gently dragged his fingers along the sensitized skin of her neck before gliding his palm around to cup the nape.

Inside, Kelsey was obviously having fun with Brittany, so Kim turned her attention to Timothy again. Her breath stilled. He'd been watching her, his piercing blue eyes intent in the dark. Shadows were moving across his face, so she saw his features as if through a veil of lace. She squinted. "How do you know? You sound very sure."

Leaning, he brushed his lips across hers, and she could barely believe the rush of need it sent through her. "Because she's such a good kid," he said huskily. "There's no real meanness in her."

"Ah. Dr. Ooze not only dematerializes and flies, he sees into the human heart?"

His eyes didn't leave hers and when he spoke, his voice was lower still, almost lost in the steady hum of the car's engine. "Sometimes."

She was fighting that lump in her throat again. "She likes you, Timothy."

Angling his head downward, he kissed her again, his lips firmer, dryer and sweeter than she'd expected. Despite their intimacy, he'd never kissed her with so much tenderness. He said, "So do you, Kim."

"Yeah," she agreed. "I do."

Their eyes held. Everything in the car, like her breath, stilled. In the periphery of her vision, she was aware that Kelsey was hanging ornaments on the Barrys' tree, and that, outside, snow had thickened in the darkness, so that big, wet flakes kissed the windshield, melting onto the glass. Inside the car, the radio was still playing. Vaguely, she was aware of the things happening around her, and yet everything seemed to have been reduced to mere inches of space, to the scant fraction where air circulated between his lips and hers. Smiling, she raised a finger and pointed upward, toward the dome light. "Watch out for the mistletoe."

"In here?" He squinted. "I doubt it."

She frowned in disappointment.

"Don't worry," he murmured, coming close enough that his lips brushed hair, and she could feel his breath on her cheek. "I'll kiss you, anyway."

"You're making this Christmas so wonderful," she whispered.

Just as a female vocalist began singing, "Have yourself a merry little Christmas," Timothy's mouth descended for a deeper kiss that filled her and burned like all things Christmasy: spitting fires, hot cider and bright lights. Feeling the pressure of his parting, guiding lips, she flicked her tongue between his, eliciting a moan. A shiver snaked between her shoulder blades as she reached a hand around his neck, urging him nearer, pulling his lips closer.

Another sound came from his throat, further arousing her. She didn't know why. It was nothing more than a slight hitch of breath. A sudden intake of air. A barely audible hint of desire, but it made her arch from the seat, her mouth stretching for his, her tongue dancing. Feeling her need, he slanted his mouth over hers and went deeper still, his mouth crushing down harder. His lips cradled hers, then clung like dew on grass. When a whimper was drawn from her, she realized he was stirring responses they could never indulge here. Not in a car, not like this. She whispered, "We'd better stop."

He pulled back with a shudder, his lips still hovering, his chuckle strangely giddy and shaky. He sounded just the way she felt. "Yeah. You're right."

"For now," she managed.

"I wish we didn't have to stop, though."

"Me, too," she murmured throatily, glancing toward the town house just in time to see the door open. "I could do this all night. All day tomorrow." Kim returned Brittany's mother's wave as Kelsey pranced down the stairs, grinning. Gratitude surged through Kim, mixing with heat from the kiss. She really hadn't seen Kelsey look so happy in a long time.

"I know I already said it, but today was the greatest Christmas gift anyone could give me." Kim glanced at him over her shoulder again. The hours of pleasure with him and Kelsey were the gift of hope she'd wanted. Today made her sure that she and her little girl would be able to create a new life together, one as full of joy as the one they'd expected to share with Larry.

"I had a good time, too."

Months ago, she'd felt so alone, so desperate to

be held by a man, by him. "Would you like to stay awhile?" she suggested. "I mean, when we get to my place? It's late, and Kelsey's going to start getting cranky…" Her voice drifted off.

"Maybe I can help you put her to bed."

"She'd like that."

Would you, Kim? He didn't say it, but the question was in his eyes, and she was glad to see it. Hers answered: *yes.* And for the first time, she realized how much she wanted him to like her, maybe even love her. Heat surged inside her, and she wanted to ask all the questions that came to a woman's mind at such moments, questions that begged to be asked even though it wasn't the appropriate time to speak them. Where was this leading? Anywhere or nowhere?

A smile claimed her mouth, and right before Kelsey opened the door, she added, "After she's asleep, would you like to stick around and play Santa?"

CHAPTER FIVE

WHAT AN ADRENALINE RUSH, Timothy thought, scooting forward on his belly so that he could better nestle another wrapped present between the ones already under the tree, then muttering in soft protest when a shirt button snagged on the carpet. At least Kelsey had finally relented and let him run home long enough to change into jeans. As much as he'd loved playing the hero, twelve hours dressed in silver Lycra was about all he could take.

He just wished he'd be here in the morning to see Kelsey open all the gifts. Who would have guessed that arranging presents for a kid could be such fun? He chuckled as he glanced over his shoulder toward where Kim was busying herself near the mantel, and he saw that the fire had burned down to red glowing embers. "I haven't felt this excited since I was a kid."

Distractedly, Kim murmured, "Hmm?"

"Reminds me of how I used to feel," he added, lifting his voice to be heard over the CD, a collection of country vocalists singing carols, "when I was hanging out with Carey and Zach."

"You're comparing playing Santa to rumbling with your childhood buddies in South Philly?"

As he repositioned some presents for more dramatic effect, he returned her smile. "I just meant that I was having fun. You make us sound like gangsters."

"By your own admission you were bad boys."

As his eyes dropped over her figure, his lips curled into a barely suppressed smile that made his blue eyes dance. "I still am."

"I've noticed."

When their eyes locked, heat sizzled between them. He watched as she whisked off one of the velvet ribbons looped around her neck and began fashioning a cheerful band around a doll's head.

"Do you always hide her presents?"

"Yeah." Kim's cheeks were rosy with anticipation. "Kelsey finds them for days. I started hiding some of them the year before last." She shrugged, stepped back to admire the bow, then leaned to tweak the ends so that they hung just right. "The Easter she was three—I guess that was the first year she could hunt for eggs by herself—she had such a blast that…"

"You decided to hide her Christmas presents, too?"

"Just small ones."

He glanced toward a shiny purple mountain bike with training wheels. "There'd be no hiding that."

"That's the big event," she agreed. Crossing her arms, she blew out another long sigh. "Not that she believes in Santa anymore. I took her shopping at the Gallery and she saw the mall Santa take off his beard."

"In one of the stores?"

Kim shook her head. "Nope. In the parking lot. He was getting into his car, apparently going home."

"You'd think he'd wait until he left the mall."

"You'd think," she echoed. "Kelsey cried. I was hoping she'd believe for another year or so."

"With someone like you around," he assured, "she'll believe forever."

Her dark eyes sparkled and reflected lights from the tree. "I love being flattered."

He shrugged. "It's not flattery. Looking at all you've done makes *me* believe again." He flashed a grin. "And I'm a die-hard cynic." Some people he'd known would never spend so much time and energy on making things this perfect, not even for a child.

"Before getting to know you better, I would have said you were."

"A cynic?"

She nodded.

"But now?"

"I know better." Turning from the mantel, she headed toward him. "Your wearing a Lycra suit all day convinced me otherwise."

His eyes had fallen to the bike again. The purple paint gleamed, and the pink streamers hanging from the handlebars matched the pink tires. Touched by all Kim's attention to detail, he sighed. "She's going to love all this, Kim."

Kim's heart-stopping brown eyes were bright with hope. "I put the horn on the bike myself," she explained, "and when I saw that little bouquet…"

He admired the spray of tiny pink and purple rosebuds she'd wired to the handlebars. "It looks amazing."

Her side brushed his as she stepped back to observe their handiwork, and a jolt of awareness shot through his entire system; it moved with the speed, heat and intensity of a lightning bolt, and it took him a second to recover.

"We did good," she pronounced.

He gave the room another long look, taking in each detail: a Barbie in a Santa outfit was perched in a wreath hanging against a living-room mirror, and Ty Beanie Babies sporting tiny red velvet ribbons around their necks were hidden in the pine rope on the mantel and in the twinkling branches of the tree. A stuffed polar bear peeked from beneath the sofa while a fuzzy green frog seemed to hop toward the dining room.

Kim's eyes were roving over the tree branches as if she half expected to find something out of place. Outside, the snow had stopped falling, and when Timothy shifted his gaze to the darkened windows, he saw that the night had turned bright and clear. Stars twinkled through the glass, looking almost as if they were an extension of the twinkling white lights on the tree. Icicles hung from the railing of the fire escape, and they, too, glimmered.

Sighing, he realized he'd lost track of time. It was probably past midnight, which meant he'd better go. Just as he turned to face Kim, she pivoted toward him. When she gazed up into his face, his heart stilled.

Her voice was nearly a whisper. "Thanks, Timothy."

"Stop," he murmured.

She lifted her brows. "What?"

"Thanking me." Raising a hand, he trailed an index finger down her cheek, his breath turning shallow as he registered its soft-as-silk feel. He hooked his thumb under her chin and lifted it. "You've been thanking me all night. It's not necessary. I'm glad to help. I *want* to help."

"I know, but..."

Yes, she'd definitely stolen his breath. Just looking into her eyes was enough to make his throat tighten and, once more, he wished he'd be here in the morning—watching her sleep, maybe even capturing the exact moment her eyes opened and she realized it was Christmas. He guessed she'd look like a kid again herself, given the way she was anticipating Kelsey's excitement. "No buts," he said, his voice low as he pressed a finger to the lips he was about to kiss good-night. "I've had a good time, Kim."

He wanted more from her, too, although he wouldn't say so. He wanted to spend the night, and awaken to Kelsey hopping out of bed. He could only imagine her delight when she saw how her mother had transformed their living room into a magical toyland. "A really good time," Timothy added.

Tilting his head, he brought his lips to just above hers. They teetered a drunken second before he pressed them to a mouth as soft as water. While they'd decorated, she'd sipped spiced cider, and after he'd kissed her, he raggedly whispered, "You taste like cinnamon and apples." He paused, pressing his mouth firmly to hers once more. "Sugar, too." He applied another dose of dizzying pleasure. "You taste like you."

Reaching on her tiptoes, she tried her own kiss, then supplied, "You taste warm."

"I feel warm."

Casting another glance through the window, he surveyed the sharp brightness of the night and dreaded the cold outside. "But it's late," he forced himself to say, his eyes returning to hers. "And I bet Kelsey'll be up at the crack of dawn. If I leave now, you might actually get a few hours of shut-eye."

He didn't move, however. Neither did she. And he was suddenly, sharply conscious of her floral perfume, how it mixed with the scent of pine and a female scent he found positively maddening. Her breath hitched, the sound barely audible, and he could feel its unsteadiness where it feathered against his cheek. Glancing down, he saw that the tips of her breasts had peaked against the cashmere dress. She favored the fabric, and because of her inner softness and warmth, he thought it suited her.

He considered caressing her there, simply reaching and curving his hands over those gentle slopes. Tall and slender, she wasn't overly endowed, but perfect in his view, with breasts just large enough to fit into his palms. Even without moving, he could imagine the downy softness of the fabric as he stroked her, then tweaked the stiffened buds. Did she have any idea how much he missed their lovemaking?

She was staring at him in the exact way he was

staring at her, as if entranced. After another second's hesitation, he lifted his hands, and using each, traced her collarbone before locating the ends of a velvet ribbon looped around her neck. Lightly tugging them, he drew her closer as he swooped his head down once more so he could kiss her. Slow heat built as their lips collided and locked and as her mouth eased farther open. Her hands began caressing his shoulders while his came to settle on the inward nip of her waist. As he deepened the kiss and his tongue plundered her mouth, he realized his heart was pounding too hard. It seemed deafening in the silence. He could hear it inside his head, and in the blood racing through his veins. Judging from the rapid pulse beat he saw at Kim's throat when he leaned away, he knew she felt the same way.

"Stay just a little longer," she whispered.

He hesitated. "Are you sure?"

One of her hands reached down and found his. As she twined their fingers, she whispered, "C'mon."

"Where?"

She was leading him toward the hallway. "To bed."

It was more than he'd hoped; when they'd reached the bedroom, he whispered, "Are you sure it's all right?"

"Positive."

As Kim locked the door and flicked on a bedside lamp, he looked around and his chest squeezed. There were still hints of masculine taste in the room—heavy carved wooden furniture, an antique globe, a model of a sailing ship—all reminders that she'd shared this room with her husband. Fleetingly, he wanted to love her so deeply that she'd completely forget the father of her child. Instead, he caught her waist again and pulled her against him, telling himself that her past was behind her. Maybe the future didn't matter, either. All that mattered was right now.

Her voice was as hazy as the light filling the room. "I was so wrong about you."

He kissed her, then leaned back. "In what way?"

"Before I met you, I'd seen pictures of you in the paper at art events…"

Smiling down, he brushed hair from her temples, his groin tightening as he pressed his lips to hers once more. "And you thought I dated a lot of women?" His lips stayed so close that their breath mingled. "That I didn't get serious?"

"Yeah," she whispered.

"It's true." His voice lowered a notch in response to her proximity. He couldn't quite believe she was his now, that they were about to make love for the first time in months.

"Is it because your folks died so abruptly?"

He nodded. "That's part of it."

"And the other part?"

Often when women wanted to get closer, he'd feel hemmed in. Edgy. Even last night, as happy as Kim and Kelsey had made him, the homey atmosphere had started to turn on him. "Familiarity, I guess. I've been alone a long time."

"You deserve more. You miss out on a lot not letting anyone get close. Trust me, I know."

He shrugged, fighting the urge to cover his discomfort with a kiss. "You're not the first woman to say it."

"They're right."

Angling his head down, he drank from her mouth once more. As his tongue glided effortlessly against hers, the cinnamon-apple taste darkened, becoming more potent than cider. When he leaned away, he stared into her eyes, his finger tracing her jaw. "You're not the first woman to say it, Kim," he repeated huskily, "but you're the first I've wanted to prove wrong about my so-called cold heart."

"Is that what you're doing?"

"No." He chuckled softly. "Right now, I'm just kissing you." But as she kissed him back with increasing fervor, he realized that everything was different with Kim. Possibly his desire for her might wind up outdistancing his need to play it safe. With a kid in the mix, it was hard to hold himself back emotionally. The two together—Kim and Kelsey— promised so much more than a woman alone. There was a whole life here. Love. A home.

His jaw slackening, Timothy slanted his mouth across hers, and as he tumbled with her onto the bed, he felt his emotions translating into desire, his blood thickening with need. Her body had connected with the most intimate part of him, and the hardness of her pelvic bone against his erection sent him into overdrive.

"Kim." Turning shallow, his breath came out as a pant. "I want you."

"I want you, too."

The blood pounding in his head made him giddy; she was trembling all over. Her thighs on top of his were shaking, just like her breath. "Here," he murmured. "Let me…"

Raising, she allowed him to pull her dress over her head. In his palms, it was soft and warm, but nothing compared to the skin he touched after he tossed it away. Gliding his hands down her silken sides, he turned and brought her beneath him. Sending a hot glance downward, he traced her ribs before flicking open the front catch of her bra. A wave of fire crested inside him as her breasts spilled into his hands. They were firm and high, so creamy that he swiftly brought one inside his mouth. Suckling hard as he removed his shirt, he drew her deeper between his lips, his tongue swirling around a turgid peak until she moaned.

Fire swept over him as her fingernail scraped his belly, and then she was tugging hard at his jeans, trying to get them off. He gasped as denim tightened against his aroused flesh, his erection chafing on the fly. It was only a zipper, but it felt unforgiving as she dragged it down with an excited jerk of her hand. Shifting to her other breast, he suckled harder, swirling his tongue hungrily until she cried out. Just then, as she whimpered and arched, her hand closed around his velvet thickness. At the touch, his mind went as dark as the winter night.

Vaguely, he wanted more hands. Moaning, he wanted to touch her everywhere at once. Squeezing a breast, he used the rough pad of his thumb to circle the tip now, then suckled once more as he slid a hand over her panties.

She was damp. So damp down there. Through white silk he could feel every nuance. Slipping a hand inside, he fondled her as she pushed his jeans and briefs down on his hips, offering a soft sigh as he pushed a finger inside.

"Later," she said, with an urgent pant.

The word fueled his desire. Maybe there would be other nights. Other days where they could make love slowly. Times when they might choose to torture each other for hours, eliciting passion that verged on madness. Places that promised them long, drawn-out bliss.

But not now. Urgency filled her, reddening her skin, turning her dark eyes feverish. Rolling away, he finished pulling off his jeans, and as he knelt beside her, he dragged his eyes down the length of her. His eyes on her rosy skin, he watched her pull off her panties, then he used his knees to further part hers.

"A condom," he managed hoarsely.

Lips that his kisses had left dark and swollen suddenly parted; she looked stricken. "Oh, no…I don't…oh, wait a minute." She swallowed hard. "In the drawer. I think I might have some. I hope…if we have to run out to a store on Christmas Eve…"

He was already sifting through the articles in the drawer—a necklace, some envelopes, a pair of nail clippers. "Here." Relief coursed through him as he ripped open a foil packet, but, for a second, he was sure he couldn't sheath himself. He was too thick, almost hurting, filled with need. Sucking a breath through his teeth, he readied himself. Then his eyes locked on hers and remained there, riveted to those shiny dark eyes he thought were so magical. He lowered himself to an elbow, then furrowed a hand into her hair. When his sheathed flesh nudged her, a whimper was torn from her throat.

Her voice caught. "I'm ready."

"I know."

As he thrust inside, going deep, she senselessly whispered something he couldn't understand, then she gasped, her shivering inner thighs squeezing around his waist, her ankles locking on the small of his back.

Shuddering, he felt a tremor ripple through his whole body. His hands splayed to curl around her head, his fingers diving into the strands then using them to arch her neck back, thrusting as he did so, ripping another cry from between her lips. Shaking, he rode her as his hand glided possessively down her side, curving over her hip, the satin of her skin forcing him right to the brink.

He hung there. Suspended. Swaying in darkness. Even when he felt the maddening, shattering spasms of her release, he couldn't let go. He wanted to stay. Right here. Like this. "I just want you to know that—" Gasping, he went over the edge, his mind emptying in tandem with his body.

Then slowly, reality returned and he became aware of her hitching breath, the dampness of their skin, the fiery heat left by the joyous friction.

Her voice caught, so gravelly he barely heard it, although her lips were only inches from his ear. "What do you want me to know?"

I love you.

"Nothing," Timothy managed. He could barely believe what he'd almost said in the heat of the moment. Gently, he stroked her hair, his hand still trembling. He was still stroking it when her breath turned steady and he realized his Christmas angel had fallen asleep.

"WHAT'S HE doing here?" Kelsey demanded angrily the next morning. She was standing in the hallway, clutching her hand around a towel so tightly that her knuckles had turned white.

Kim glanced toward the bedroom. The door was open, just enough that Timothy's shoes could be seen. Deciding honesty was the best policy, Kim said, "He stayed the night, Kelsey."

Kelsey's lips parted in stupefied shock, and the pulse was ticking wildly in her throat. "Overnight?"

Kim could barely collect her thoughts. Hours ago, she'd gotten up to put the turkey in the oven, then she'd gone back to bed until moments ago, when she'd risen to go to the bathroom. Pulling together the sides of a robe she'd thrown over pajamas, she tied the ends, surveying her daughter and blinking sleep from her eyes. "I thought you liked Timothy." Hadn't he won her over yesterday?

"He's in our apartment!"

"I know, but you enjoyed our trip to Pittsburgh yesterday, Kelsey. I thought—"

"He doesn't belong here! Not on Christmas!"

"Shush," Kim managed, reminding herself that Kelsey had been up too late last night. "Keep your voice down. He might hear you."

"I don't care if he hears me."

"Well, I do." She'd had such high hopes when she'd slipped from bed at five to put in the turkey. She'd been so sure she'd been wrong and that Kelsey was ready to move on with their lives. "He's our guest."

"He's not my guest."

"What happened, Kelsey? What's different today?"

When Kelsey didn't answer, Kim's heart hammered. *Please,* she pleaded silently, *don't create a scene.* Right now, she felt so open, so raw. She'd just awakened and she was still reeling from Timothy's lovemaking. As passionate as before, it now held caring and closeness, too. Heat flashed through her as she recalled the beauty of how their bodies moved together. "Please," she managed. "Don't ruin this, Kelsey. You do like him."

"He's not Daddy!"

Maybe Kim should have expected it, but the comment came out of the blue. Inviting Timothy into their lives for a day of fun was one thing, but apparently having him sleep in the bed Kim had shared with Kelsey's father was another.

"Of course he's not. He's a friend of ours. Now, c'mon. Don't you want to open your gifts?" It was a bribe, but maybe it would calm her.

"No!"

Kim tried not to think of the past two years. She'd put her life on hold, hadn't she? She'd put the business back in the black after Larry had gotten them into debt, and despite all the pressures, she'd always done what was best for Kelsey. On a surge of anger, she stepped forward, slipping a hand around her daughter's upper arm. "Why is it so hard for you to share this day with someone?" she asked, leaning low, her voice an angry, exasperated whisper. "With someone who doesn't have a family? Why are you always so selfish?"

The second the words were out, she hated herself. Kelsey was just a kid. And she was scared. She couldn't let go of the past they'd shared with Larry.

"I don't want him here," Kelsey insisted.

"I understand." Just as Kim had been about to respond, Timothy's voice had sounded. When she turned in surprise, Kim realized he'd heard everything. Her heart sank. He'd dressed hurriedly, and his hair and clothes were rumpled. "She's right," he said. "It's Christmas. It's a family holiday." His eyes swept over them both. "I'd really better go."

CHAPTER SIX

"C'MON," Kim managed to say moments later, smiling through tears she could scarcely hold back. "You want breakfast, don't you, hon?"

Kelsey, who'd kept her eyes on Timothy as he let himself out of the apartment, was still standing in the hallway. "I want to open my presents."

As Kim heard the door click shut behind Timothy, she felt as if her heart was being wrenched from her chest. Should she follow him? she wondered, glancing away from Kelsey, feeling torn between him and her daughter. He'd been so excited about spending the morning here. Seeing his pleasure in watching Kelsey open gifts would have meant so much. Why couldn't Kelsey have been more generous?

Sighing, Kim tried to remind herself that her little girl had been through a rough time after Larry died. Her father was gone, and Kim had had to work longer hours. Kelsey also hadn't slept enough last night. Besides, Christmas wound kids up like toy tops, and while Kim knew Kelsey needed to be reprimanded, she was also determined not to further ruin this holiday. Still, she had to say something. "Timothy was hoping to watch you open your gifts."

Guilt crossed Kelsey's features. "Sorry," she murmured, and even though she said nothing more, Kim was pretty sure Kelsey was thinking of Johnny Sinclair, the boy who'd rejected the Dr. Ooze doll the night before. "You may be a little girl," Kim forced herself to add wisely. "But that doesn't mean you don't have the power to hurt other people. Now go on. I'm behind you."

Whirling, Kelsey took off like a flash, running down the hallway. Despite her excited skip, and the fact that Kim hadn't gotten overtly angry, the morning had soured and they both knew it. Tension was in the air now. And it was all because Timothy Toye was gone.

Oh, he was a big man, broad-shouldered and with a masculine roughness to his features. And, yes, he'd had a rough-and-tumble childhood in South Philly, but at Kelsey's rejection, he'd looked positively crushed. He'd really wanted to stay for breakfast and be a part of their family. He'd never gotten a chance to play parent before.

Everything in his eyes had said this goodbye was final, too. Worse than that was the realization that something so simple as a child's rejection could send him packing. But then, Kim, too, was guilty of letting Kelsey run roughshod over her. Damn, she thought. Timothy had slipped away like a Christmas ribbon caught by the wind and she couldn't stand the thought. She'd never find a man so passionate. Nor one who'd dress up in a silver suit like a damn fool—just to please a child.

Realizing she'd paused, Kim forced herself to keep moving. She just wished the doorbell would ring. She could almost see herself opening the door to find him there. He'd shoot her a sexy grin and say, ''I changed my mind. I know Kelsey's in a snit, but maybe if I just talked to her…''

But he was gone. He'd even admitted a number of women had judged him to be noncommittal. And while he'd said Kim was the first he'd wanted to prove wrong, he'd taken off at the first sign of trouble—not just this morning, but two nights ago, also. Maybe he was like the character he'd created, after all, the ultimate escape artist.

Still, she'd fallen for him, hadn't she? There was no denying he'd left her aching for a deeper relationship. Not that she could make him come back. You couldn't bend others to your will. Nine years of marriage had taught Kim that.

She swallowed around a lump in her throat. Yes, she'd fallen for him, probably from the first moment she'd seen him in his office. Just now, as he'd left, the same arresting blue eyes that had first captured her attention had locked with hers. Sparks had flown between them. *She's just a child,* her eyes had said to him. *Don't let her dictate your actions.*

His eyes had said, *Why not? You are, Kim.*

But then, she could swear he'd looked relieved, as if he was glad to have a way out, and that meant it was over, didn't it? After the past two days, they could never resume their affair, not unless they were willing to let it become something more.

"A BIKE!" Kelsey squealed.

Stepping into the living room, Kim watched her daughter dive through packages, tear off paper and toss bows. Easing into an armchair, Kim couldn't take her eyes from her little girl. She watched as she unwrapped the sled, the tennis racket, the roller skates....

And then Kelsey glanced up. Seeing her injured expression, Kim felt her heart lurch. "What's wrong?"

Kelsey merely shook her head, looking adorable and oddly orphaned, sitting waist high in crinkled, discarded wrapping paper and curled ribbon. "Keep opening," Kim urged. "You're nowhere near done. There's plenty to go."

But Kelsey's downturned lips had started to quiver, and a tear glittering in the corner of her eye spilled into her eyelashes and rolled down a powdery china cheek.

"I shouldn't have made him go," she whispered. "And I didn't even get you anything. You're right. I'm selfish."

Guilt twisted inside Kim. She loved her little girl too much to fault her selfishness. Besides, she was just a little girl. She didn't know any better. "It was wrong of me to say that, Kelsey. You made me the ornament at day care, remember?"

"Everybody at day care hates me."

Kim couldn't exactly deny it. "You're going to be better after the New Year."

Tears made Kelsey's eyes as shiny as Christmas lights. She was probably still remembering the boy who'd rejected the Dr. Ooze doll. "Hon," Kim said gently, "everything's going to be all right. I just want to see you enjoy your gifts."

Kelsey shook her head. "No," she said throatily, her voice thick with tears. As she swiped the back of her hand across a stained cheek, she said, "I can't open any more until I make things up with Timothy."

THE SECOND he opened the door, Kim wondered why she'd let Kelsey talk her into this. *Because I spoil her rotten and don't deny her anything,* Kim admitted. "Hi," she managed.

Whatever his surprise, he quickly masked it. Not that his clearly frosty attitude undermined the rush of pleasure Kim felt at seeing him. He was gorgeous. Fresh from the shower, he held a glass outer door open with his knee and continued buttoning a fresh white shirt over a chest tangled with thick blond curls. It was frigid outside—his breath was fogging the air—but otherwise he didn't look the least bit affected by the cold.

"Sorry," she murmured. Planting a hand on Kelsey's white knit hat, she glanced over her shoulder at the Jeep, wondering if she could find a graceful way to simply turn around and get back into it. "I tried to call, but the line was busy…."

"I took it off the hook in case Zach or Carey called when I was in the shower."

"Sorry," she said again.

"No, no," he murmured, raking a hand through the still-wet strands of his hair. Water had turned it dark blond, almost brown, and as he slicked it back, his blue eyes looked even darker and more penetrating. "Uh…come in."

"Are you sure?"

He looked undecided. "Yeah."

Kelsey bounded inside. They hadn't showered, just thrown on clothes, but obviously it had been the wrong thing to do. Realizing the damage was done, Kim followed Kelsey, letting Timothy shut the door behind her. "We can only stay a minute," Kim assured. She extinguished any hope she'd had of winding up in an embrace with her arms wreathed around his neck while he kissed her senseless. "She wanted to apologize," Kim explained quickly. "She felt bad…"

He looked vaguely embarrassed. "You didn't have to bring her over."

Her lips parted. Clearly, Timothy thought this was her idea. Before she could respond, he continued, "Would you like some coffee? I just made it."

"Sure."

As he headed for the kitchen, she made the mistake of looking around, realizing as she did that she was standing awkwardly in the foyer, leaning against the very door where they'd first made love. When her gaze strayed to the dining table, a new set of erotic memories arose.

"Sugar?" he called from the kitchen.

As if he didn't know. "Black." She couldn't help but add, "I usually take it that way." He knew that, but he was choosing to act like a stranger. Not a good sign.

"Black," he returned distractedly, as if his forgetting wasn't an intentional oversight meant to create distance between them. "Coming up."

"Thanks."

Somehow, she had a sneaking suspicion she

wouldn't be staying for the whole cup. He hadn't even taken their coats, something Timothy—ever the gentleman—never overlooked. Now she heard the sound of the toaster, and her heart sank. *Great.* He'd been making toast when only an hour before he'd been looking forward to sharing the breakfast spread fit for royalty she'd had planned. She'd been hoping he'd stay for turkey, too.

As she headed toward the living room, she decided the place looked more modern than she recalled. Emptier. Overstuffed white armchairs surrounded a fireplace bracketed by onyx end tables. On a glass center table, silk orchids shot from a steel vase. After the homey, lush greenery in her apartment, Timothy's town house seemed impersonal and beautiful, like a picture on the cover of a magazine.

"Look," said Kelsey, "he's drawing Dr. Ooze."

"I can see." That was even worse. He'd come home and started working. As she seated herself, Kim's eyes settled on a drafting table set up near a living-room window. Pens were tossed haphazardly over the cartoon he'd been working on.

As he entered with the coffee and toast, he said, "Hope you don't mind if I eat. The toast was already in the toaster."

"Not at all."

"You were working?" Kelsey chirped, skipping toward him in her jeans, parka and snow boots as he seated himself in an armchair opposite Kim. "On Christmas?"

"Yeah. I was."

As if realizing he'd done so because of her, she kept a smile plastered on her face, determined to make things right. "Hmm. You have a Christmas tree!"

Kim tried not to cringe. The foot-high, predecorated, fiber-optic tree was near the fireplace, probably a gift from a business associate. "We came to watch *you* open *your* presents," Kelsey continued.

"Kelsey," Kim murmured in warning.

Looking uncomfortable, Timothy said, "I don't have any."

"Sure you do!" Looking confused, Kelsey headed for the tree and returned with two wrapped presents from beneath. "Here's some. Did you forget?"

Setting them down, she went back for the rest. They were token gifts, probably from people with whom Timothy did business, and under other circumstances, Kim would have laughed at Kelsey's childish mistake. Now, she wished the floor would open and swallow them.

Lifting a package in blue foil, Kelsey demanded, "This one first."

"Really," Kim ventured again. "Timothy might be saving his presents for later...."

"Please," crooned Kelsey.

"That's okay," he said.

To his credit, he forced a game grin and made a show of slowly pulling off a bow for Kelsey's benefit. Blue foil paper followed. "Chocolates," he pronounced, displaying a few red-and-green wrapped Hershey's Kisses.

"Now this!" squealed Kelsey.

When he had trouble unknotting the bow, Kim reached into the drawer of the end table beside her, pulled out a pair of scissors and handed them to him. "Here."

When their fingers brushed, she couldn't help but wonder if it would be the last time, and a memory shook her—fast, hot and visceral—of his hard muscular body gliding along the silk of hers. Kelsey's voice brought her back to reality. "How did you know the scissors were there?"

"Mommies know everything," Kim quipped, avoiding Timothy's eyes. At the moment, she hardly wanted any shared acknowledgment of their time together. She'd forgotten that her daughter would have no idea that she'd been here before. She'd gotten to know a lot about Timothy, too, Kim realized now. In the shower, he scrubbed his chest before any other part of his body, for instance. And he always put his pants on left leg first. When it came to his male equipment, he liked it to the right side of his pants zipper—all just small details that only a lover would know.

"Ah." At his voice, Kim lifted her gaze. "A corkscrew!"

A holiday cocoa mug followed. Then a set of dish towels printed with holly leaves and a box from Harry and David's with two golden pears inside.

As he neared the end of the meager stack of gifts, the room grew unnaturally quiet. Suddenly, Kim wished he'd turned on some music, or that somebody—maybe a neighbor—would happen by with a basket of fruit or something. As she imagined the phone ringing with the calls he was expecting from Zach and Carey, she felt her heart miss a beat. Timothy had taken the phone off the hook while he showered just so he wouldn't miss his friends' calls; that's how important those calls were to him. Possibly, they were the only ones he'd get all day. She thought of her own phone. With her gone only an hour, the machine would be filled with family messages.

"Well, that's about it," he said, trying to sound bright. "That's Christmas."

Kelsey's eyes flickered over the gifts, and while she'd been initially impressed, she now forced a smile. "Well," she conceded, "you can come to our apartment now." She slid her eyes to the toast and added, "We have a turkey."

"I appreciate the offer, but I can't."

"Honey," Kim interjected, realizing she'd been holding her breath, hoping he'd come spend the day with them, "why don't you go wait in the car? I'll watch you from the door, okay?"

Kelsey glanced guiltily between them, knowing she was to blame for ruining whatever special feelings had begun to evolve between them all. "Okay."

Rising, Kim lifted her own coat as Kelsey headed out the door. "We'd better get going," she said.

"Right."

"Kelsey felt bad," she explained again when they reached the doorway. "She didn't want to open the rest of her gifts until she apologized. She wanted to invite you over." Her voice suddenly caught. "Won't you come?"

"Like I said, I appreciate the offer, but..." Glancing over his shoulder, he looked at the drafting table. "I've got things I should do."

As if anyone really wanted to work on Christmas. She managed a nod. "She really is sorry. And I am, too. If you change your mind. I mean, later. Anytime today..."

"I won't."

Her lips parted softly. Dammit, she knew she was supposed to turn around and walk away, but she just couldn't. "You don't want to work today," she found herself saying instead. "I know you don't. It's Christmas, Timothy. And you're alone here. Eat breakfast with us. Watch Kelsey open the rest of her gifts. She just ran into a rough spot. She didn't expect to see you in the apartment this morning. If you come over, you can call Carey and Zach from our place."

"Really," he said. "I..."

She knew she should stop, but she plunged on. "Last night...this morning...I could tell you wanted to be with us."

Clearly, her pushiness had touched the wrong nerve. "Well, I'm here now." His voice became almost curt. "Maybe some other time."

"You said you wanted to prove me wrong."

He parted his lips to speak, but then said nothing.

"You changed your mind," she added, "because of what Kelsey said this morning. Is that really all it takes to make you walk away?" Her eyes implored him. If he'd only try, what they shared could turn out to mean so much.

His jaw set. "Let it go, Kim."

She'd pushed too hard. She was sorry for that, too, but she still didn't want to leave. Feeling close to tears, she had to force herself to turn away. Her eyes were burning, her throat closing so tightly that she could barely breathe. She scarcely felt the cold.

Unable to stop herself, she turned around once more, just long enough to look over her shoulder.

"Maybe next time," he repeated.

Her eyes fixed on his. "You know there's not going to be a next time."

He simply nodded.

And then she turned again and headed down the walk.

"Where's Timothy?" Kelsey asked from the back seat, her eyes widening as Kim slid into the driver's seat. "I thought you were gonna make him come."

There were some things even moms couldn't do. "I can't."

"But he doesn't wanna be alone on Christmas!"

"I know."

"So, why doesn't he come with us?"

Reaching a hand between the seats, Kim rubbed her daughter's shoulder. "He has other things to do," she said, training her gaze away from the door of the town house. She managed a smile through the tears she blinked back. "But don't worry. We're going to cheer ourselves up and have a great time. Just us girls."

Kelsey didn't look so sure.

Within the hour, she'd be fine, though. That was the thing about kids, Kim thought, as she inserted the key and turned the ignition. They were so resilient. About herself, Kim wasn't so sure. Larry had been her first and only love. She'd never expected to feel this interested in someone again.

As the engine hummed to life, heat blasted from the vents, and "Holly Jolly Christmas" poured from the radio speakers. Bracing her hands on the wheel, Kim told herself to pull from the driveway without looking back.

"Wait!" Kelsey exclaimed. "I forgot!"

Before Kim could stop her, she'd flung open the back door, bolted from the Jeep and started running up the walk. Kim craned her neck toward the porch in time to see Timothy reopen the door. Standing on the front step, Kelsey handed him a wrapped present. Kim had no idea what it was.

The stinging at her eyes intensified. She fought the urge to open the door and run up the walkway, just as Kelsey had. Maybe Kelsey would do or say something to make Timothy reconsider, to make him realize he was denying himself something that just might turn out to be great for all of them. "Prove me, wrong," she whispered. *Prove there's more to you than the affair we had. Prove there's more of last night's passion and that you're willing to try to fall in love.*

But seconds later, the Jeep's door opened, and Kelsey lunged inside again. "What did you say to him?" Kim asked around the painful lump in her throat.

"It doesn't matter," Kelsey muttered, using the back of her hand to swipe at her eyes. "He's not coming. He's like everybody at day care. He doesn't like us."

TIMOTHY GLANCED from the Jeep to the badly wrapped package in his hand. It was small, fitting neatly into his palm, and tape covered the paper. A lopsided bow was tied on top.

She must have done it herself, he thought as he eased off the bow and ripped the paper. Besides Zach's homemade wine, and the season tickets Carey sent for football games, this was his only real gift. Given how stingy Timothy knew Kelsey could be, it meant more than any gift he'd ever had. Especially since he'd heard her mention her father earlier this morning. Apparently, she was trying to apologize. She'd been shocked to realize Timothy had been in bed with her mother, and she'd been unable to adapt quickly to the idea.

He lifted the lid off the box. When he saw what was inside, his throat tightened. "Dammit," he muttered, not particularly wanting to feel the tug of his heart. It was the purple power stone. Resting it in his palm, the way Kelsey had shown him, he rubbed his thumb over the slick surface.

But it didn't work.

How could it? The woman he wanted was about

to drive away with her daughter. Not that the passion was all he craved. It was more than that. These past two days had unsettled him. Kim and Kelsey had opened a door on a world he hadn't dared to dream could exist for him, not really.

"What are you doing?" he muttered to himself. "Throwing it all away?"

The Jeep was still out there. He placed his palm on the glass door and, for a moment, he wasn't sure if he meant to wave goodbye or push through it.

Earlier this morning, he'd gotten that bad feeling again, the edginess he felt whenever people got too close. And if the truth be told, he'd gotten it the night before, after Kelsey had caught him kissing her mother. Now he hedged. Kim hadn't wanted to come here. Apparently, it really had been Kelsey's idea. At the door, she'd said, "Mommy was right. We shouldn't have come."

Maybe he didn't blame Kim for wanting to stay home. Why would she trust him? He'd been a man-about-town. He'd never even exchanged house keys with a woman. Didn't he need to prove she was wrong about him?

No. He shook his head. The only person he needed to prove anything to was himself. Kim's coming here said she wanted to give him a chance. Maybe his early life hadn't worked out. But he wanted this. He deserved this. He could do it.

Slowly, he went out the door, pushed the storm door shut behind him, then jogged down the walkway. For a second, he thought Kim was going to drive away.

But she didn't. Circling the Jeep, he opened the door, taking in Kim's look of confusion. Her teary eyes were wide, and when he saw her mouth—a small red O of surprise—he couldn't help but lean over and brush it with a kiss.

"Change your mind?" she asked shakily.

A rush of joy coursed through him and, all at once, he felt positively giddy. In fact, he felt like Ebenezer Scrooge the day of his transformation, and Timothy had a wild urge to run through the streets of Philly, flailing his arms and proclaiming his love from the rooftops. Instead, he jerked his head toward the passenger side and simply said, "Scoot over, sweetheart." As Kim did, he slipped into the driver's seat and added, "You said the invitation was good all day."

"And tonight," she mouthed.

But he was starting to think in terms of a lifetime. Not that it would be easy. No doubt there'd be ups and downs, but he'd like nothing more than to start spending his evenings at her place. Maybe he'd take her and Kelsey to Lancaster and Jersey to meet Carey and Zach.

"Who knows how things will turn out?" he said.

"No guarantees," she returned, but the assured tilt of her lips held a promise.

His gaze held hers. "I came back to prove you wrong."

When she spoke, her voice was so sexy that he could have made love to her then and there, even though all she said was, "I'm glad."

He could feel it in the hand she rested on his thigh, and in the possessive curl of her fingers on the denim. No, Kim Winkler hadn't wanted him to walk out of her life. Tossing a glance over his shoulder, he said, "Thanks for the present, Kelsey." His eyes twinkled. "But I've got to tell you something."

She looked delighted. "What?"

"It didn't work."

She tried to look shocked. "No?"

He shook his head. "I opened it and rubbed it, but I was still lonely."

Kim inched closer. "No one should be lonely on Christmas."

"I'm not now."

"Then the power stone works, after all," Kelsey pointed out brightly.

"Maybe so," he murmured. "Maybe so."

Registering the warmth in the soft brush of Kim's side, he stared into the bright winter day and the snowflakes beginning to turn soft spirals in the air, then he leaned to press his lips to Kim's. As the kiss hummed through him, his body flooded with relief. He hadn't let her walk out of his life, and he sure as hell wasn't going to walk out of hers. Only Kelsey's voice stopped the kiss from burning out of control.

"Since your name's Timothy Toye," she quipped, "does that mean you're my favorite toy this year?"

"That's for you to answer," he returned.

"You are," said Kelsey, then added, "Are you going to eat breakfast at our apartment now?"

"Maybe a lot of breakfasts." At least he hoped so. Leaning back a fraction, he gazed deeply into Kim's eyes. "Is that okay with you?"

"Very," she said, her eyes shining.

"Does this mean you're going to get married?" Kelsey persisted with a sudden giggle.

"Kids say the damnedest things," Kim managed.

His voice husky, Timothy merely chuckled and countered by saying, "Out of the mouths of babes." After all, sometimes kids were right. And now that he was in the Jeep with them, it was getting easier by the minute to imagine himself marrying Kim and being a dad. After bending near for another quick kiss, Timothy put the Jeep into Drive and pulled out of the driveway, settling a hand on Kim's thigh. As he turned a corner and headed for Rittenhouse Square, his mind flashed forward to later tonight when, after the glowing embers of the fire had died down, he and Kim would make love. And how, before that, there would be more presents to open and a turkey to eat. Gliding his hand downward, he flexed his fingers, curling them tightly over Kim's knee. As he did so, he was thinking about the decorated tree and the fully stocked fridge, and the music and the toys.

But most of all, just like Kim and Kelsey, Timothy was thinking about the love.

Bestselling authors

ANNe Stuart
Cherry Addir
Muriel JeNSeN

Three women are about to experience
the date from hell—with really *hot* men
who are **w-a-a-a-y** too tempting.
One wicked, sexy grin from these guys
and, well…who can resist?

Look for it in January 2004.

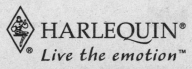

Visit us at www.eHarlequin.com

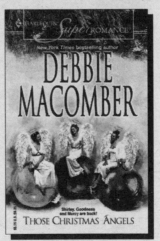

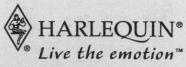